Praise for One Dog Too Many

"The author has worked carefully on the setting so that I really did feel as if I were a part of this rural town and I could picture the scenes as well as the people. Character interactions and the descriptions of daily life definitely ring true, and the characters seem to be very real. Fans of the cozy mystery will certainly enjoy adding Mae December to their list of charming detectives."

—Long and Short Reviews

"A lively tale with plenty of twists, turns, and unexpected situations to satisfy the most ardent cozy mystery lover. The story is told in several voices, including Mae, Sheriff Ben, and Detective Wayne, with Mae's best friend Tammy piping in occasionally, giving the tale several viewpoints of the mystery. Farrell's additional cast of characters are fun folks to get to know, and the setting of the Tennessee countryside is charming. Animal lovers will enjoy the interaction with Mae's kennel customers, and fans of whodunits will love figuring out the intriguing plot as the story moves along …. A fine introduction to what promises to be an exciting series to follow."

—Sharon Galligar Chance, Fresh Fiction

"The story is a combination of police procedural, rocky romance (at least two of them), and a stroll through the world of dogs. Even for readers who don't find canines especially appealing, this novel—written by a mother/daughter pair—still has its charm. The plot is fairly straightforward, the major protagonists are believable, and the perpetrator's motives are quite understandable."

—John A. Broussard, I Love a Mystery

"A tidy little mystery peppered with likeable characters, interesting back stories, and lots of canine lore. *One Dog Too Many* is an entertaining book to read on a lazy day."

—Mary Marks, *The New York Journal of Books*

5 Thumbs Up: "What a great start to a series. This debut novel contains exactly all the right ingredients needed to make a perfect cozy mystery…. Through a crisp writing style the authors bring their characters not only to life, but has them serving sweet iced tea to the reader as they progress through this book, and in this way it I found it very easy to connect with them and establish a relationship; even their gossip made me feel included in their everyday lives."

—Cate Agosta, Cate's Book Nut Hut

"With an equal mix of charm and intrigue, Lia Farrell has created a twisty tale of murder and wagging tails."

—Jane Cleland, author of The Josie Prescott Antiques Mysteries

"Dog lovers and cozy mystery fans alike will be charmed by this first book in an exciting new series featuring Tennessee dog breeder Mae December. *One Dog Too Many* gets off to a fast start as the Lia Farrell writing team pulls the reader into a dog-gone good tale of murder set in the beauty of the Middle Tennessee countryside."

—Marie Moore, author of the Sidney Marsh Mysteries

"Lia Farrell has created a strong debut mystery in *One Dog Too Many*. The plot is intricate, the characters well-developed, and the setting charming. Dog-lovers and mystery fans alike will enjoy this fast-moving tail … um, tale."

—Jennie Bentley, *USA Today* bestselling author of the Fatal Fixer Upper series

TWO DOGS
LIE SLEEPING

TWO DOGS LIE SLEEPING

A MAE DECEMBER MYSTERY

LIA FARRELL

CAMEL
PRESS

Seattle, WA

Camel Press
PO Box 70515
Seattle, WA 98127

For more information go to: www.Camelpress.com
www. liafarrell.net

Cover design by Sabrina Sun

Two Dogs Lie Sleeping
Copyright © 2014 by Lia Farrell

ISBN: 978-1-60381-969-5 (Trade Paper)
ISBN: 978-1-60381-970-1 (eBook)

Library of Congress Control Number: 2014936370

Printed in the United States of America

Acknowledgments

From Lyn:

I wish to acknowledge my family and my writing group for their support. My neighbor, Will, has helped enormously by serving as webmaster for the liafarrell.net site. I am deeply appreciative of our agent Dawn Dowdle, as well as Catherine Treadgold, Jennifer McCord and their team at Camel Press. It has been a pleasure working with you guys. But most of all, I want to acknowledge my debt to my daughter and writing partner, Lisa. Honey, I couldn't have done it without you.

From Lisa:

To Dawn Dowdle, Catherine Treadgold and Jennifer McCord; many thanks. To my mom and writing partner, Lyn; what a journey this has been. I am forever grateful to you. To everyone who read our first book; thank you so much! Thanks are also overdue to my wonderful, supportive family and friends for listening to me and keeping life interesting ... Jim, for coffee in the a.m., wine in the p.m. and everything in between, I am always thankful for you.

Prologue

—

THE TALL MAN stepped inside the tranquil nursery and looked around, swallowing the lump in his throat. The room was beautiful in the glow of a summer evening. For now, the 173-year-old Booth Mansion was quiet. All the designers and Junior League volunteers were gone for the day. Soon the historic home in the heart of Mont Blanc would be thronging with visitors, eagerly paying their twenty-five dollars to tour the house and grounds that artisans and interior and landscape designers had transformed over the past year. For tonight though, he could wander through and pretend he still belonged here.

He walked to the window and took a seat on the cushioned bench that hugged the inside of the bay. If he'd stayed, this house would have been his; this nursery would have sheltered his children just it had sheltered him. He had been loved and cherished here. He didn't know which designer had worked on this room, but it bore no traces of the years he'd spent here. Soft greens and yellows dominated the space, and tiny ducklings, amazingly lifelike, had been painted on the slanting wall above the antique cradle that stood where his bed had been.

Sighing, he looked out the window. The huge oak he had climbed so many times, sneaking out after curfew, hadn't changed. The dark green leaves of late summer were almost black, backlit by the setting sun. Leaning his forehead against the cool glass, he closed his eyes, letting the memories come.

It's so unfair to find the woman you're meant to spend your life with in high school. What a cliché. He could picture her so clearly in this room—sitting in the beanbag chair in the corner, gesturing to make a point, her dark hair falling straight and smooth over her shoulders. Somehow her perfume still floated in the air. What was it called? He couldn't remember, but he remembered the scent—like roses after rain.

He wondered if he'd made a terrible mistake, leaving fifteen years ago. Not that he'd had a choice. That decision had changed the rest of his life—and probably her life too. He hoped the letter he had just mailed would be explanation enough; he couldn't worry about it right now. He needed to search for the documents Bethany needed.

A small sound returned his mind to the present. He felt uneasy, as if he were being watched. He only had time to turn his head before he heard a muffled shot and felt a searing pain. He fell slowly, crumpling to the floor as he silently called her name.

Chapter One

—

July Powell

Turning the iron knob of the Booth Mansion door, July Powell walked in through the back entryway of the historic home. Carefully closing the heavy door so that it wouldn't slam, she kicked off her sandals. It was nearly four-thirty on August 2nd. The first day of public tours to raise money for needy families in Rose County would start tomorrow morning at ten.

She picked up the tote that held her cleaning supplies and began her final dusting and fluffing. She was glad the Junior League design committee had given her this space instead of the nursery, which was her first choice. After twelve years as a rental property, the house hadn't looked too impressive on her initial walk-through. She had re-purposed the dingy back hallway as a cubby room for the kids and the family's dogs. Now it was lively and fun. The fresh caramel wall color contrasted nicely with the gleaming ivory trim on the chair rails and crown moldings. The black lacquer paint on the baseboards enhanced the tumbled travertine floor.

Don December, her father and a professional photographer, had given her several black and white photos of family-owned dogs that he'd taken over the years. She'd created an elegant keepsake board out of ivory fabric and black ribbon, with the photos tucked in behind the ribbons. Hanging above the bench, its seat upholstered in a crisp poppy print, the keepsake board looked like a family heirloom. Working on the mansion carried a lot of prestige, but each designer paid for the transformation of their own space or did it themselves. After three months of work, she hoped the publicity would translate into new clients for Seasons Interiors, her design firm.

Two red towels hung on the hooks above the dog washing station, along with leather leashes and a black dog collar. A wall of built-in cabinets and cubbyholes stood on the opposite side, ready to hold backpacks and sports gear for the family she imagined living here. The large rug had been a lucky find. Its red, black, ivory, and caramel threads tied all the elements of the room together. If you looked closely, what appeared to be a pattern of leopard spots was actually comprised of miniature dog footprints.

She gave a satisfied sigh. *I nailed it.*

There was a sudden loud bang from upstairs and she flinched. Then she heard a faint sound from the front of the house. She waited, but heard no other noises. Thinking that a picture or mirror must have fallen, she went up the stairs to check the upper level and peek at the nursery one last time before tomorrow's crowds arrived.

Running quickly up the stairs, July remembered the night when she and Tommy were together in this house for the last time. It was after a party and they were both giggly with beer. Climbing the squeaky back stairs, they covered each other's mouths, trying not to laugh.

"Are you sure?" Tommy asked her.

July nodded. They had successfully skirted the spot on the fourth stair with its inevitable creak. Opening the door to his room that night, she saw moonlight falling on the oval braided rug. The dark heart pine floor looked almost black, and the moonlight fell in squares as it sliced through the window mullions. She remembered their closeness as they stepped into the room, hand in hand.

It was their last night together before she and Tommy went back to their respective colleges. Christmas break was almost over. Tommy smoothed the covers on the bed, gestured to her to sit down and then knelt to remove her shoes. She leaned over and pulled him to her. Slowly she began to unbutton his shirt. Running her hands up his chest, she smiled and stood up in the moonlight.

Looking down at him, she pulled her sweater up over her head and shimmied out of her jeans.

"You're so beautiful," he whispered and stood to embrace her. Pulling back, he put his finger to his lips and went to the door. He turned the lock silently and returned to hold her. They swayed together as he hummed Van Morrison's "Moondance" in her ear. It was their favorite song, and he continued to hum it as they made love that night. It was the first time for them both.

JULY TURNED THE handle on the door to Tommy's old room. It was a nursery now, decorated in soft greens and yellows. She looked across the room at the crib, standing where his bed used to be. The light was almost gone, but there was a dark spot on the floor. July stopped. It was a person—face down and very still.

Hesitantly she called out; "Are you okay?" but there was no answer. Slowly, as if she were wading through waist deep water, she moved toward the dark shape. Kneeling beside him, she touched his face. It was cool but not cold. He was barely breathing. There was blood around his body, darkening the floor. She shook all over and turned away, shuddering, but something drew her eyes back.

"Oh my God, Tommy, is it you?"

With shaking hands, she scrambled for the cellphone in her pocket and dialed 911. Picking up his hand, she held it and began to cry. Counting the minutes until she heard the ambulance siren, she whispered, "Hang in there. Don't you leave me again, Tommy. I have so many questions I need to ask." As his breathing continued to slow, she prayed, "Please God, don't let Tommy die."

His lips parted and his hand reached toward her, then fell back beside his face. Collapsing beside him, she put her ear close to his mouth to hear his whispered message.

Chapter Two

—

Mae December

USUALLY MAE ENJOYED Ben Bradley's intense gaze, but this time he didn't look as if he wanted to ravish her. Oh, no. Sheriff Ben, her very own boyfriend, was staring at her in a distinctly unfriendly way.

"Is that *another* dog?" His eyebrows went up and the corners of his mouth went down.

As she had tried to explain to Ben many times, her house tended to be a bit over-run with dogs. It was an occupational hazard; she ran a kennel out of her home. She boarded, bathed, and taught dogs to behave better—mostly for other people.

Mae also bred the "porgi," a cross between her male corgi, Titan, and her female pug, Tallulah. In addition, she still had Thoreau, a beautiful old Rottweiler. She became his owner after her former fiancé, Noah, died in a car accident.

Ben and Mae had been a couple for three months and he was generally quite tolerant of all the commotion. Her handsome, blue-eyed boyfriend served as the sheriff of Rose County. They had met during a murder investigation on Mae's street.

A three-pound puppy should not be enough to disturb his equanimity, so she was surprised to see him looking quite thoroughly peeved.

"This is not just *another* dog," Mae told him, firmly. "This is December's Sweet Potato. She is the future mother of the strawberry blond strain of porgis I intend to breed. I'm going to call her the Tater."

"But she's a corgi," Ben said.

"Yes," Mae answered, *duh.*

"That means you need a male pug," Ben's look of irritation deepened.

She laughed. "Don't worry. I have a friend who studs out her apricot male pug. I'm not getting *another* puppy. I wish my vet had told me before her fourth litter, but it's not safe for pugs to have more than three litters. We got lucky on the last one, but it's definitely time for Titan and Tallulah to retire."

"That's good for them. But where did this puppy come from?" He still sounded irked. "I was only gone a few hours. Did you tell me she was coming?"

She felt a faint twinge of guilt, which must have shown on her face.

"You didn't, did you? I knew I wouldn't forget a little detail like that."

Her guilt was evaporating, replaced by annoyance.

"I've been looking for a new female for a while, for my business."

Cradling the puppy in her arms, Mae left the kitchen. Tallulah, her black pug, was in her bed in the laundry room. She needed to meet the Tater right away. Mae put the puppy on the floor. The pug gazed up at Mae with wide eyes and then looked down at the puppy. Her lip curled, and a low growl rumbled in her chest.

Ben followed them into the laundry room.

"Tallulah doesn't look too happy about it either," he pointed out, sounding more cheerful. "Did you forget to tell *her* that the Tater was coming?"

Mae started to laugh and picked the puppy up before Tallulah became too irate.

"I guess no one else was in the loop on this one." She turned to face him. "I should have told you. I'm sorry. Here, hold her for a minute."

She put the puppy in his arms and stood back. He lifted her near his face and smelled her soft puppy fur. The Tater raised her foxy little face with oversized ears and licked Ben's nose. Looking back at Mae, he grinned and shook his head.

"You're good, December."

"Just need to get the merchandise in the customer's hand, that's all. She's a cutie, isn't she?"

"Oh, yeah, she's cute all right," he sighed. "Is she going to cry all night?"

"She's twelve weeks old, so I hope not."

"Good." He handed the puppy back. "You're going to need your rest."

He was staring at her again—the way she liked this time. He leaned over to kiss her just as the wall phone started to ring. Ben grabbed the phone and handed it to Mae.

"Mae's Place. What? Slow down."

"Who is it?" Ben asked.

"It's my sister. She wants to talk to you."

Ben took the receiver from her hand but held it between both their ears so Mae could hear the conversation.

"July, Ben here. What can I do to help? What charge?" His eyes widened, and she clearly heard her big sister say, "Murder."

"You sit tight," he told her quietly. "We'll be right there."

Mae ran to put the Tater back in her crate, grabbed her cellphone, keys, and purse and followed Ben out the door, her head in a whirl.

"Can I drive your car?" Ben asked. "I don't want to show up over there in a patrol car like I'm looking for a fight."

She nodded and tossed him her keys.

"Where is she?"

"The Mont Blanc Police Station, I guess she was working at the mansion when the police arrived. I wonder why she called you instead of her husband."

"He's at a conference in California. She probably couldn't reach him."

"I think you better call your parents, honey."

Nodding, she hit number three on her speed dial.

"Hi, baby girl!" Daddy's voice boomed.

"Oh, Daddy, I don't know what's going on, but July's at the Mont Blanc Police Station. Can you and Mama meet us there?"

"Why is she there? Has there been an accident?" her father asked, in a much quieter voice.

Mae closed her eyes for a second. "No accident. She said something about a murder."

The line went dead. Mae looked at Ben, driving so calmly. As she looked at her own shaking hands, Mae was grateful for his steady nerves.

"There must be some mix-up. July wouldn't hurt anyone, unless they threatened one of her children."

She hoped for Ben's agreement, but he just shrugged and looked away.

"Are your parents on their way?"

"They'll probably beat us there." Mae gave a nervous laugh. "You know how they are."

Ben knew from experience just how protective the Decembers could be of their girls. Meeting Mae and her family in the middle of a murder investigation the previous spring had demonstrated that pretty clearly.

"You're right," he nodded. "I better step on it."

Chapter Three

—

Mae December

IT WAS ALMOST dark outside, but still warm and muggy, when Mae and Ben walked into the Mont Blanc Police Station. July was sitting in the waiting room. Her face was blotchy, and Mae saw a dark red stain on the tail of her sleeveless shirt. July looked up at them and her face crumpled.

"I'm sorry to drag you here!" she burst out. "They said I could go home, but I'm too shaky to drive."

Ben and Mae glanced at each other. Mae reached out and took her sister's hands, pulling her to her feet. July stood there swaying and shaking her head. There was a commotion as Mama and Daddy came rushing in.

"July, sweetheart, we're here!" Mama announced, unnecessarily. Ben's cheek quivered as he turned his head away and suppressed a smile. All the Decembers were inclined to be dramatic.

Ben walked over to the desk and spoke quietly to the officer behind it. He came back to their little group and addressed Mae's father.

"Don, she's free to go. Let's get her out of here." He looked at July with a puzzled face. "Did you think you were under arrest, July? They were just questioning you." She didn't answer, so he turned back to her father.

"Do you want to take her home and we can follow you?"

"My car's still at the mansion. Can one of you get it for me?" July asked.

Ben nodded. July dug her keys out of her purse and handed them to him.

"I can't go to my house. The kids are there with a sitter. Could you bring my car to our parents' house?"

MAE AND BEN got back in her car and she drove to the Booth Mansion. Mae had helped July by providing some ideas for the design of her assigned space; a back hall mudroom July had transformed into a cozy area with hooks for coats and benches to sit on to remove your boots. It was her idea to make it pet friendly by including an area for washing dogs and one for their beds.

The opening of the mansion was tomorrow. Mae thought July's project was finished, so she wondered what July had been doing there. And why the police had been called.

"Ben, do we even know what happened? Did somebody die?"

"Yes, the duty officer said his name was Tom Ferris."

"Tommy? Oh, no!" Mae's throat tightened. She sniffed, wiping her nose.

"Do you know him?" Ben's brows drew together.

"He was July's boyfriend in high school and college. He grew up in that house. I can't believe he was even in town. It's been at least fifteen years since he's set foot around here."

"You never mentioned you knew the owner when you were helping July with ideas or when we went to the Patrons' Party."

"Tommy disappeared right after Christmas break of his sophomore year. She's never wanted to talk about him."

Mae pulled into the service drive behind the mansion. The parking area was deserted, except for one silver rental car parked next to her sister's Suburban and a dark blue sedan.

"Unmarked police car." Ben pointed at the sedan.

Mae parked and Ben got out.

"I'll see you at your folks."

In the rearview mirror, she watched him walk to the driver's side of the unmarked car. He bent down with an enquiring tilt to his head, engaging whoever sat inside in conversation.

MAE'S CELLPHONE RANG before she was halfway to her parents' house.

"Mae, it's me," Ben said. "Whatever happened over here is being kept real quiet. That's why the unmarked car. They've closed the house to all designers, but they aren't telling anyone why. July actually found Tom Ferris dying."

"The poor thing! Finding Tommy after all these years. How horrible for her. No wonder she wasn't saying much."

"For a woman in your family, it's out of character for sure. I don't have Matthew tonight, so I'll see you at your Mom and Dad's in a few minutes."

Matthew was Ben's four-year-old son. He hadn't known that the boy existed until several months ago, when he was in the middle of the murder case that brought Mae and him together. He had been engaged to Matthew's mother Katie Hudson at one time, but she had eloped with someone else. She had neglected to tell Ben he had a son until after her divorce. Katie had recently returned to Rosedale and they shared custody. Ben usually had Matthew for a mid-week sleepover one week and then for the weekend the following week.

"Mae, are you still there?"

Ben's voice startled her out of thinking about Matthew and his mother, the disloyal Katie.

"I'm here. Wait, how did Tommy die? Why did July think it was murder?"

Ben took a deep breath before he spoke.

"It sounds like someone shot him, although I guess it could have been a suicide. We don't know yet. Drive carefully, babe, okay? We'll get to the bottom of this."

Mae said good-bye and set her phone on the seat.

Chapter Four

—

Mae December

DRIVING TO HER parents' place from the station, Mae recalled the day last spring when July told them she'd landed the Showhouse project for the Booth Mansion. It had been Mae's thirtieth birthday in May. Mama didn't try to name both her girls after their birth months; it just happened. Mae's given name was Maeve Malone December. July couldn't pronounce it and called her baby sister Mae. July was christened Julia Grace, but her parents began calling her July after she renamed her baby sister, and it just stuck.

Sunday, May 20th had been so warm, it felt like high summer. Mae looked out her kitchen window and even the air glowed green. She and Ben had been invited to her parents' for dinner. She called the dogs and went outside with her garden scissors to cut a bouquet of irises for Mama's table. She had been mentally reviewing her wardrobe options when she saw Ben's car coming up the driveway.

He parked and walked across the lawn. The rolled up sleeves of his blue dress shirt revealed the muscles in his forearms. He was a handsome man with blue eyes that could be intense. She dropped the flowers and ran to kiss him.

"Hey, pretty girl," he greeted her. "Happy birthday!"

Mae went back to pick up her scattered flowers and closed her eyes for a minute. Despite all the obstacles in their way, they had gotten together; she could hardly believe her luck.

Mae remembered she had worn her rose patterned sundress and black sandals. She and Ben arrived at her parents' after July and her family. July and Fred had three children, nine-year-old twin boys and a six-year-old daughter, Olivia. July's sons Parker and Nathan, who were lanky like their father but with July's dark hair and eyes, brought their puppies with them. Mae hadn't seen the pups since they went to her sister's house. July had purchased Mae's porgis, Eric the Red and Soot, for her boys' birthdays. The little dogs had grown so much.

"The puppies have been so much fun for the boys, Mae. I'm proud of the kids. They're being so responsible, feeding them, making sure they have water and sleeping with them at night. Although they are a little less interested in the cleaning up after them than I hoped."

"What a surprise." Mae laughed at her sister's naïveté. It was not that difficult to potty train a puppy, but it did require consistency, firmness, and constant supervision. "Have you tried keeping them with you in the kitchen? You can keep a long lead on them and tie it to your waist. That might be sort of tricky with two of them, though."

"I'll try that, but one at a time." July smiled.

They had piled into the house, puppies and all. Mama took charge of getting the puppies into the laundry room. The boys got the dog gear out of the car and brought in their water dishes. Both puppies settled into one dog bed together and Mae smiled to herself, remembering how July's twins used to sleep in one crib. July's husband Fred helped Daddy put the food on the table and everyone sat down.

The December family had a tradition of the youngest person

saying grace, assuming they were old enough to talk. July's daughter Olivia did the honors, finishing with, "God bless Aunt Mae on her birthday. And we need some new children in this family so someone else can say grace. Amen." Fred ruffled his daughter's blonde curls.

"Thank you Livi, that was very nice," Daddy said, after they all quit laughing. "I have some good news. My publisher says my book will be out by Christmas. It's the one that honors songwriters and other behind-the-scenes people in the music industry. It's dedicated to you, Mae."

Ben squeezed her hand under the table. Mae's former fiancé, Noah, was one of the songwriters featured in her father's book. During his career, he wrote several hits, including the Arlen Hunter song "Miss December." Ben knew Mae had mixed feelings about the song and her father's latest book. It brought back painful memories of the night, over a year ago, that the police had arrived at Mae's to tell her Noah was dead.

"I have an announcement, too," July had told them. "I wanted to tell y'all I got selected to design one of the rooms in the Booth Mansion, for this year's Junior League fundraiser."

"Congratulations, July. How did you manage it?" her mother asked. July had tried twice before, but hadn't been selected. *Third time's the charm*, Mae thought, happy for her sister.

"The way the process works is that first you have to be invited to participate. Then you have to submit plans, drawings and finishes for three rooms in the house to the Junior League committee."

Mama's dark eyes sparkled. "I remember when you went through the house last month with the rest of the designers," she said, "before you started your sketches and presentations. I've always loved the old Booth place."

"I submitted for the nursery, a powder room, and the back mud room," July said. "I was hoping to get the nursery, but it went to another designer. Mae, I'm going to need your advice. I'd like to do the mud room with dogs in mind."

"Wonderful. I'd love to help you. So many people have dogs and don't have the right spaces for them." Mae asked for the overall dimensions for the room and offered to do some research on dog washing systems.

Then her father looked at his wife and said, "Suzanne, wasn't it Irene Booth that went skinny-dipping with you on that Fourth of July weekend when you two were in college?"

Olivia's eyes widened. She turned to her grandmother. "Does that mean you were *naked*, Zana?"

The entire family enjoyed the rare sight of Suzanne December at a loss for words.

Fred Powell nodded at his youngest child. "That's right, Livi, skinny-dipping is naked swimming."

"I think it's time we changed the subject," Mae's mother said with a blush.

Mae recalled herself to the present as she drove into her parents' driveway. The crickets chirped loudly in the summer twilight. When she walked in, July was sitting next to Mama on the living room couch. Mae sat down beside her sister.

Ben joined her father in the kitchen, where he was preparing drinks.

"What happened, July? Was it really Tommy?"

"Oh, Mae," July looked up. Mama handed her a tissue. "Yes, it was. I heard a noise and walked upstairs to investigate, though I never dreamed it was anything serious. In any case, I had wanted to see the nursery one last time before the opening. It was his old room." Her voice broke.

Mae exchanged a worried glance with her mother.

"I saw something on the floor and realized it was a man," she shook her head and her eyes went blank.

"Here." Daddy handed her a glass of water.

"I didn't see the blood at first," July went on, her face ashen. "He was face down and I was trying to determine if he was injured or had fainted. He was still breathing, but not very well." She started to shake.

"You called 911?" Ben interrupted.

"Yes, I had my cellphone in my pocket. I sat right there by Tommy and called them. I held his hand. I thought he wanted to tell me something."

"What happened when the emergency crew arrived?" Ben was now in full-on sheriff mode.

"I heard them at the door and ran downstairs. They brought up a stretcher and took Tommy down to the ambulance. I wanted to go with him to the hospital, but they wouldn't let me. The ambulance drove off just before the police arrived. I took the officer up to the room and showed him where Tommy was when I found him. I could hardly look at it. The carpet was soaked in blood," July shuddered and took a big gulp of water.

"Then they asked you to come with them to the police station?"

"Yes, the officer took me there. The police chief talked to me—I think his name was John. I was crying so hard by then, I could hardly tell him what happened. Finally he said I should call someone and I called you, Mae."

"What did you think when you heard the noise?"

Ben seemed to be interrogating her. Although he was being gentle, Mae was not pleased and gave him a sharp look.

"I thought a heavy picture or mirror must have fallen."

"Could it have been a gunshot?"

"Ben, honestly, will you please stop being sheriff for a moment?" Mama held her hand up. "Let July catch her breath."

He nodded, and although he clearly had more questions, he acquiesced to Mama's request, sat back and sipped his bottle of beer.

Mama and Mae took July upstairs. Mama gave her a sleeping pill and she went into her old room for a rest. Mae sat on July's bed for a moment after her mother left the room and patted her sister's shoulder. "Did Tommy say anything to you, July?"

"He said he wrote me a letter, but I'm not sure if he meant recently or a long time ago. Please don't say anything to Ben about it, okay? I really don't want to be questioned anymore."

With some reservations, Mae agreed. She left the room and called her sister's babysitter, Abby, who told her Fred was flying home that night. Mae asked her to stay with the kids until he arrived. Abby said July was supposed to pick Fred up at the airport. Mae told her July wasn't feeling well and that she'd pick Fred up. Luckily Abby had Fred's itinerary and Mae wrote down the time of arrival and his airline. He was due to arrive within the hour, so she said good-bye to everyone and left. Ben walked out to the car with her, and they kissed good-bye.

"Daddy said he'd run you back to my house so you can get your car. While you're there could you—"

"Check on the Tater? Of course I will."

He hugged her, and she could smell his shampoo. His cheek was scratchy, but Mae didn't care. She buried her face in his neck for a minute.

"This must bring back memories for you."

"This is much worse. It's appalling for July. I knew Tommy, but I wasn't the one in love with him. I sometimes wonder— even after marriage and three kids—whether July ever really got over Tommy Ferris."

MAE WAS FIVE minutes from the airport when her cellphone rang.

"Hi, it's Abby, your sister's babysitter. Mr. Powell got here about ten minutes ago. I told him you were on the way to get him. He said he caught an earlier flight. He asked me to let you know he was already home."

Aaargh ... I just drove forty miles for nothing. "Did he say how he got there?"

"No, he didn't. He must have taken a cab."

Mae took the Briley Parkway exit, so she could turn around to head back home.

"Well, thank you for letting me know, Abby." She tried not to sound frustrated. It wasn't the babysitter's fault.

"No problem. Talk to you later."

Mae called Ben to see where he was. He said he had already checked on the puppy and headed to his own house, since he had to work tomorrow. She told him Fred was already home. She had wasted an hour driving out to the airport and back.

"When did Fred get back in town?"

"I don't know. I only talked to Abby, the babysitter. She said he'd been home about ten minutes."

"I'll ask him what time his flight arrived."

"Why, for heaven's sake?"

"Well, his wife's old boyfriend turned up dead today, and he may have been in town when it happened."

"Don't be silly. Fred would never hurt anyone."

"Listen, I need to go. I'm beat, and you should pay attention to the road. Goodnight."

He was gone. That was abrupt even for Ben, who didn't enjoy long phone conversations. Mae drove the rest of the way home in a complete snit. She took the dogs out for a final potty break, and then against all her rules, carried little Tater upstairs and climbed straight into bed with her new puppy.

Chapter Five

——

Sheriff Ben Bradley

THE NEXT DAY, after his morning shower, Ben dressed in his uniform and left for the office at six a.m. It was now seven-thirty. Although the Ferris murder wouldn't be his job, he was on edge and kept thinking about July finding Tom Ferris. He watched from his office window as Miss Dory Clarkson, his office administrator, opened the front door and came in. She looked cool and composed in the August heat. A striking African American woman, she ran his office with a velvet tongue and a laser glance. She appeared to be about fifty years old, but Ben thought she had to be older.

Ben walked into the waiting room and smiled at Dory. The staff secretly referred to her as "Melting Moments." Ben knew she was anything but sweet and yielding. Dory started the coffee, then sat down at her desk and pulled out a small mirror from her purse. She gave a self-satisfied grin. Apparently, her hair and lipstick met her high standards. Her smile grew wider as she glanced down at her red high heels; the color was a precise match for her red and white top. But when she looked up at Ben, the smile vanished.

"It's a good thing I work here," Dory said, looking at Ben askance.

"What do you mean?"

"Without me telling y'all what to do, you men would not have a clue."

Ben could tell Dory was in one of her "men are idiots" moods. He gave her a stern look, got a coffee and returned to his office. He flipped through a couple of "Return Call" slips and went into the conference room. In the next few minutes his two deputies, Robert Fuller and George Phelps, entered the room. Ben could hear them getting coffee. On the heels of the deputies, Wayne Nichols, Rose County's Chief Detective, made his appearance, greeted Dory and joined the meeting.

"Good morning all," Ben said when everyone was in their accustomed places. He looked at his chubby, redheaded deputy. "Let's have reports. George, you're first."

George had opened his mouth to speak when they heard a knock on the door.

"What is it?" Ben called out, frustrated at the interruption. Dory opened the door. He frowned at her. He liked to start staff meetings on time and she knew it.

"It's John Granger on the line from Mont Blanc. You'll want to talk to him."

He walked out to Dory's desk. She had reigned as the undisputed queen of the office for almost thirty years. Sheriffs might come and go, but Dory endured. She took no nonsense from anyone—especially him.

"Okay, which line?" Dory punched a button and handed him the receiver. "Good Morning, John."

"Morning, Ben."

"What's up? I'm about to start a staff meeting."

"What's up is that the death at the Booth Showhouse last

night is being turfed to your shop. Turns out it's in your jurisdiction, not mine."

"I was over at your station last night after your deputy brought July Powell in," Ben said. "She found Tom Ferris dying and called 911. I guess dispatch routed that call to you. Didn't you interview her?"

"I did, just briefly. Dispatch assumed that it was in the Mont Blanc jurisdiction, but I checked this morning and the house is outside the city limits, so you get this one. Sorry, buddy," John sounded anything but sorry.

"Are you sure about the location? As I understand it, the sheriff usually cedes jurisdiction over a murder if it happens in one of the cities with a police department. And since Mont Blanc has a police department, it should be yours."

"Nice try, Ben. You'd be right in most cases, but you're wrong this time. It's yours unless you want to give it to the state boys. I've never handled a murder before and you were successful with the Ruby Mead Allison case last spring, so I'm bowing out."

Ben thought for a moment. "Have you heard from the Medical Examiner yet? Is it possible it was a suicide?"

"I just talked with him. The guy was shot only once—in the back."

"Damn it. Well then, it's murder. I definitely don't want the state cops in here. They could dance around this one for months. They don't know the local history or people. Hang on a minute." Ben looked at Dory. She wasn't even pretending not to listen. He put the call on hold and walked down the hall to his office.

He walked in, closed the door and picked up the phone. "Are you still there, John? Okay, here's my problem. I'm dating July Powell's sister, which might complicate things."

"Oh, man."

"Yeah, I talked about Ferris with my girlfriend yesterday. She said her sister and the deceased were high school sweethearts who still dated in college. I can't see July killing him, but stranger things have happened."

"Well, the good news is that my deputy secured the crime scene, sealed the room with crime tape and the CSI Team worked the scene last night—photos, room dimensions, Luminol, searched for bullets, the works. I got their preliminary reports this morning."

"Did they find anything?"

"Not much. It was right before the public viewing of the house and the cleaning service went through yesterday afternoon. Even if we do find some prints, they'll probably be from the designers or cleaning crew. Apparently, about twenty designers have been working on the place for months—not to mention painters, tile installers, and landscapers. Other than ballistics, the scene won't tell us much."

"Okay, but I'll still need all that information. I assume the CSI guys were at least able to eliminate the ambulance crew." Ben indulged in a little sarcasm.

"Yep, and they were able to lift a print from the victim's hand using that new technology. It's probably the Powell woman's print. She said she held the man's hand until the ambulance arrived. The ambulance took the body to the hospital, where he was pronounced DOA. I understand that the victim owned the mansion where he was found. Anyway, while you wrestle with your personal and jurisdictional issues, I'll ask Doctor Estes to call you."

"I'll need your report, too, John. Can you have the deputy who was on site come over here? I want to talk to him."

"I'll get on it. Good luck."

"Yeah, right. I thought we were friends, John."

He heard John laugh and then hang up.

BEN WENT BACK to the conference room to update his staff and give assignments for their current investigations. He dismissed them from the meeting without mentioning anything about

Tom Ferris' murder. He figured it was probably okay to see the body and read the reports, but he wouldn't interview anyone until he got clearance from the Chief of Police in Nashville.

When the Medical Examiner called, Dory buzzed him. She always screened his calls, and although Ben found this frustrating when he first took office, he now knew better than to try to wrest control away from Dory.

"Hello, Doctor Estes? Are you calling about the Ferris case?"

"Sure am. It wasn't an accident. The angle of the shot was straight, and the victim took a single bullet in the back."

Ben knew Doctor Estes well. He was exacting, fussy and somewhat touchy about his findings. He doubted he would tell him anything more without seeing the body, but he tried.

"Can you tell me anything else?" Ben asked.

"Certainly not," he said, crisply. "If you wish to know more, I'll be in the morgue."

"Do you have the bullet?" Ben asked.

With the supercilious air of one enlightening the ignorant, Dr. Estes declared that he did.

"Could you send it to our lab for analysis?" Ben asked, ignoring the ME's sarcasm.

"Yes. When do you want to see the victim? I have other work to do, you know."

"I'll come over in about an hour if that will work with your schedule."

"It will. See you then." He was gone.

Ben looked up to see his detective standing in the doorway. Wayne Nichols was a big man, quiet and intense. He had hazel eyes with dark eyebrows and thick, graying hair combed back from his forehead. Pushing sixty, as compared to Ben's age of thirty-two, he was very experienced, with an intuitive understanding of the darker recesses of the human mind. Originally Ben had resented Wayne's attempts to be a mentor. However, over the last year they'd grown closer and for the most part worked well together.

"Looks like you have another case, Wayne."

"How so?"

"A man named Tom Ferris was found near death from a bullet wound in the Booth Showhouse yesterday. He died in the ambulance on the way to the hospital. Mae's sister, July, found the body."

"Here we go again." Wayne gave a slight shake of his head. "Did this one have the sense to call 911?"

"She did, right away. Dispatch sent over an ambulance, since she reported that he was still breathing. Ferris was taken to the hospital and pronounced DOA. The emergency dispatcher sent a deputy from the Mont Blanc station and the crime scene guys, so I assumed it was their case."

Wayne waited. It was one of his strengths as an interrogator. Most suspects quailed and caved in that silence.

"But John just called and said that 911 really should have called us. It's in our jurisdiction. Apparently the Booth Mansion is just outside the Mont Blanc city limits."

"Boss, you have to stay out of this one."

"Yeah, that's what I was thinking too, but the house *is* in Rose County, so it's ours. And you work both sides of the street, my friend, so it's yours in any case." Ben referred to Wayne working with both Rose County and the Mont Blanc police station when there was a serious crime to investigate. "If I reject it, John's going to call in the state cops because he's never handled a murder before."

"I'm not talking about jurisdiction. What about your involvement with the December family? Or should I say lack of *objectivity* about the family?"

"I know. I really don't need this. I'm going to call the Chief of Police in Nashville and go over it with him."

"Okay. Just to clarify, do we know for sure it was murder?"

"One shot in the back, so murder definitely. The ME also found something else of interest. He wouldn't tell me what it was. I'm going to go see the body. Want to go with me?"

Wayne nodded, and they went out to his car. He was quiet, and Ben was lost in his own thoughts.

AFTER VIEWING THE body, Ben and Wayne left the cold of the morgue in silence and headed for the car. The scent of disinfectant could never quite cover the smell in what Ben thought of as "the dead zone." Doctor Estes had flipped on the bone saw just as they were leaving. Ben was pretty sure he did it just to see if he or Wayne jumped. The whining sound was horrific. Ben tried to shake off the image of the saw cutting into human flesh.

Enjoying the air conditioning, which gave them relief from the sweltering heat, Wayne drove to the Donut Den on the town square for coffee. Rosedale had changed very little in decades and looked to be the perfect picture of small town charm on this sultry August morning. Two-story brick buildings surrounded the traffic roundabout, which circled an island of green grass. A statue memorializing Civil War casualties stood on the grass. Three flags—U.S., Tennessee, and Rose County— hung limply from the pole in front of the Courthouse. Wayne found a parking space just off the square on a side street near the Donut Den, and the two lawmen went inside.

They found an empty table and sat down with their coffees. Ben looked at Wayne across the scarred Formica surface. He was still dealing with his feelings about the autopsy. As usual, Wayne's demeanor was inscrutable.

"That was rough," Ben admitted. Doctor Estes had told them that Tom Ferris would not have lived very long in any case. He had cancer with advanced tumor progression and residual Hodgkin's in the lymph nodes.

"I wonder if he knew he was dying," Wayne said quietly. "If so, it might have some bearing on his murder. What do you know so far?"

"Mae told me that Tom Ferris was her sister's boyfriend in

high school and college. They were crazy about each other and July expected he'd give her an engagement ring the summer after his sophomore year, but he disappeared in January. That was over fifteen years ago." He thought about the body lying naked on the cold, stainless steel slab, and winced slightly at the thought of the surgical "T" incision and the way the man's skin puckered around the stitches.

"If July Powell found the body, she's a suspect." Wayne was calm but adamant.

"Ferris was alive when the emergency techs got there. He died in the ambulance. They put in their notes that she was sobbing uncontrollably."

"So that eliminates her?" The detective raised his eyebrows. "Come on, Sheriff, you said they were in love. Then he stays away for fifteen years. Then she finds him dying at the Booth Mansion where she just happens to be doing a final check on the space. I have serious doubts about her whole story."

"I can't believe July would kill him. She's a happily married woman with three kids. I've spent a fair amount of time with her since Mae and I got together. She's just not the type." He wondered why he was defending her. Mae had admitted that July never really got over Tom Ferris. Was she as happily married as she seemed?

"Boss, I think your bias is showing. July can't have killed him because you know her and she's *nice*?" Wayne Nichols shook his head. "Let me give you an alternative scenario. What if July knew Ferris was back in town? She was furious he disappeared so long ago. She asked him to come to the Booth house after everyone left, brought a gun and that was that."

"He was shot in the back. We saw the point of entry."

"And a woman isn't capable of shooting a man in the back?" He looked incredulous. "What if Ferris rejected her again, turned his back on her and she pulled out her gun and shot him? Then, realizing what she's done, she calls 911 and breaks down."

Ben was definitely not enjoying this. "If July was coldblooded enough to do that, I doubt she'd have called 911."

"We still have to rule everything out, boss."

Ben sighed. His detective had a point. "I had Doctor Estes send the bullet over for ballistics testing. We need to know anything they can tell us about the gun. I'm also going to talk to the techs who took the fingerprints from John's shop. How about you take your suspicious mind and go question July. Draw your own conclusions."

The big man was on his feet and headed toward the door. Over his shoulder he called, "Sure thing, boss. You can be a Southern gentleman and leave the down and dirty to me."

As he followed his detective out to the parking lot, Ben admitted to himself that Wayne might be right about his seemingly inbred sense that women needed protection. He knew he had shortcomings as an investigator. He was better with non-violent crimes and administrative work.

I probably should have gone to law school. Would have made lots more money and never had to visit the morgue.

Autopsies still made him sick. The scent of pine disinfectant mixed with the smell of formaldehyde never completely covered the odor of death.

On his way back to the office, Ben called Dory to tell her that they would be investigating Tom Ferris' death.

Chapter Six

—

Mae December

FOR MAE, THE day started with a whimper. When she opened her eyes there was a cold wet nose touching her cheek and two puppy feet planted firmly on her chest. She remembered taking the puppy to bed with her the night before. The Tater was awake and crying to go outside. Mae swung her legs out from under the covers and snatched the puppy up before she could fall off the extra high bed. She pulled on shorts, and holding the puppy under one arm, hurried downstairs. After slipping her yard shoes on, she carried the puppy outside and set her down in the damp grass. The Tater looked up at Mae expectantly, wagging her tiny stump of a tail; then she sniffed around in a leisurely manner. The air was already heavy.

"I thought this was a matter of some urgency," she told the puppy. "We're not out here to entertain ourselves. Hurry up!"

Tater tilted her head at Mae inquiringly and sat down. Sighing, Mae returned to the kitchen, where she poured herself a cup of coffee and called the other three dogs before going back outside. She held the door open for Thoreau, who was the last one out as usual. He was getting old, she noticed with a pang. The fur around his face was all white. Titan and Tallulah bustled over to investigate the new arrival, while Thoreau sat down close to her. She nudged the big dog toward the grass.

"Dogs, hurry up."

All three of the older dogs began to take care of business as the Tater looked on with interest. Mae praised them all and gave them each a treat before herding them back inside the house. Walking back to the puppy, she issued the "Hurry up" command for the third time and light dawned in the Tater's eyes. When she was done, Mae praised her lavishly, gave her a treat from her pocket stash and carried her back inside. She put Tater in her crate and refilled her coffee cup.

Knowing she would be working intensively on training the new puppy, Mae had asked the owners of the dogs she was boarding to pick them up before the Tater arrived. She'd blocked out two weeks, so the kennels were empty. She was glad not to have to go out to the barn and do chores on such a steamy morning, but her own dogs still needed feeding. She filled the food and water bowls and went upstairs to shower and dress.

Mae loved her bathroom, with its robin's egg blue walls and claw-foot tub. The bathroom, one of the first remodeling projects she did after moving in, had turned out even better than she hoped. She took a quick shower but didn't linger over hair and makeup; instead she put her curly blonde mop into a ponytail and swiped on a coat of mascara. Stepping on the scale, she noted once again that she hadn't lost ten pounds overnight. Not even one measly pound.

Back in her room, Mae put on her loosest, most lightweight sundress. She was on her way down to the kitchen when the back door opened, narrowly missing her nose, and Mae's best friend Tammy blew in. As usual, she looked like a blonde waif, albeit with perfect hair and makeup.

"What's shakin', Mae-Mae? I'm not interrupting any torrid love scenes, am I?"

Mae shook her head. "You must not be too worried, or you would have knocked." Relieving her of the bakery bag she carried, Mae ushered Tammy into the kitchen. "Thanks for the pumpkin cream cheese muffin. Did you come to see the puppy?"

Her eyes widened. "No, I forgot she was coming this week. Of course I want to see her." She paused to pour herself a cup of coffee and then continued, "I came to ask you about July finding a body yesterday at the Booth Showhouse."

"How did you already hear about that?" She should have known. Tammy's grapevine was impeccable.

"Small town, you know how it is. Three of my mother's ladies came in for early hair appointments today and they were all talking about it. Mom called, and I decided to bring you some breakfast and get the news from a more reliable source."

Tammy's mother Grace owned and operated Birdy's Salon in the historic district of Rosedale. Tammy had her own business—Local Love, a dating service—in the same building. Between the two of them, not much went on that they didn't hear about in a hurry, but this was quick even for them.

"Did you hear it was Tommy that she found?"

"Tom Ferris?"

Mae nodded sadly.

Tammy walked over to Mae's kitchen table and sighed as she took a seat. Shaking her head, she looked out the window and said, "I had such a crush on him when I was fourteen."

Mae sat down across from her. "Who didn't? He was just so sweet."

"Not to mention charming and handsome. Oh, your poor sister. What an awful thing." Tammy rubbed her forehead with a circular motion. They both sat quietly for a few moments. Mae's friend looked like she was going to say something but then thought better of it.

"Tammy?" Mae looked at her, "Did you know Tommy was back in town?"

A wary look crossed her friend's face.

"Did you?"

Tammy put her hand over her mouth. Sometimes she knew things she didn't tell Mae. According to her, it was for Mae's own good. Mae could hear the wall clock ticking and a very faint snore coming from the Tater's crate.

"All right," she capitulated. "I did know he was back. I heard it from Bethany—I mean, a friend of mine—but it's complicated."

"Bethany Cooper?"

"Don't tell Ben, please Mae."

Mae looked at her, frustrated. Her best friend looked like she was about to cry.

"You didn't *tell* me, I guessed, but I should really tell Ben. For all I know, he and Wayne are about to arrest my sister."

"Please don't, Mae. I promised Bethany. And July didn't even know he was here."

Mae gazed at her steadily for a moment, until Tammy looked down. Mae went to the crate, let the puppy out and put a tiny bit of food in her dish. Tammy got out of her chair and crouched down beside the Tater.

"She's so precious," Tammy said, glancing up at Mae. "I'll take her out when she's done eating if you need to call Ben."

"I have a better idea. I'll call Dory later and she can tell Ben. Then it won't come back to you."

"I have to tell you something else, Mae, before I lose my nerve." Tammy bit her lip and got to her feet.

"What is it?"

"I'm in love with Patrick. We've been together for a while now, and he moved into my apartment yesterday," Tammy's words were flying out of her mouth, but she was avoiding Mae's eyes. "I'm sorry I didn't tell you before this. I was afraid you'd be upset."

Patrick was Noah's West's younger brother. Ever since the car accident that took Noah's life, Patrick—along with Tammy—had been almost over-protective of Mae. The three of them had spent hours together, and Mae sometimes felt as if Patrick and Tammy were parenting her. And, of course, she'd noticed the sparks flying between her friends months ago.

"I didn't know you were living together, but the rest of it isn't exactly a news flash," Mae laughed. "I was wondering which one of you was going to tell me. Did you lose the coin toss?"

Tammy lips curved in a little cat-like grin. "Something like that. So you're not upset?"

"No, of course I'm not. I'm happy for both of you. Maybe you'll end up with the mother-in-law I almost had."

"Nobody's talking marriage." Tammy frowned, but it quickly reverted to a smile. "Don't get ahead of yourself. I need to get going, Mae-Mae." Tammy gave her a fierce, sudden hug. "Thank you." The phone rang and Mae turned back to get it.

Chapter Seven

———

Sheriff Ben Bradley

B EN WAS SITTING at his desk when Dory called to let him know that the preliminary ballistics information had come in—astonishing. He couldn't remember when the lab had gotten a report done a day after an incident.

The phone call to the Nashville Chief of Police earlier about his potential conflict of interest in the case had been eye opening. Dispatch routed Ben to a Captain Paula Crawley, who said Ben couldn't interview July or anyone else from the December family. She was okay with Detective Nichols questioning people, but until they had a suspect in custody, Ben's involvement in the case was restricted to reading reports and doing computer research. If someone called in on the tip line, Ben could talk to the person on the phone.

The captain had been perfectly clear she wanted periodic updates and that Ben's job was on the line if he violated her orders. Ben reminded her that he was elected. He didn't think Captain Paula could fire him. She reminded him that she could bring him before the Internal Affairs group or the

Ethics committee. Ben wondered if the IA Department could actually investigate him. Most sheriffs' units had their own IA, but Ben's small unit did not. He wasn't a member of the police force, but if Captain Paula told them to investigate him, they would probably do so. Ben shuddered at the thought. Every cop dreaded an IA inquiry. His father said they were like the KGB in Russia. At the end of their phone conversation, Ben gave her a brisk salute—for his own benefit, of course, since she couldn't see him.

Since it was all right with Captain Paula, Ben read the lab report. John's shop had faxed only the basic data with a brief sentence saying that if he needed more information, he could call their office. The ammo was a Winchester 158 grain semi-wad cutter hollow point. Ben was familiar with this type of bullet. It was one of the expanding types that inhibit tissue penetration. Even shot from the doorway of the nursery, the bullet would not pass through a body. The killer must have known the police would recover the bullet, but without the gun, it would be virtually impossible to find the killer. There were hundreds, probably thousands of guns in Rose County that used the same type of ammunition.

Ben called Detective Nichols, who was on his way to meet with July. He picked up but said he didn't have much time. He was driving into their neighborhood.

"I got the preliminary ballistics report," Ben told him, "The perp used a Winchester 158 grain bullet, most likely for a Smith and Wesson revolver or a Beretta."

"That's the snub-nosed small one," Wayne said. "I've seen the silver and the black models. They're light and small enough to fit in a coat pocket, or a purse."

Ben said nothing, remembering July's devastated face.

"Have John's deputies gone through the trash in the neighborhood in case the perp disposed of the gun?" Wayne asked.

"Yes, no luck. And that gun's about as common as wild tattoos in East Nashville."

"Later," Wayne said and was gone.

Ben walked out to the front office.

"Yes?" Dory said, looking up at him. Her phone rang. "I need to get this," she said and picked up the tip line phone. He stood there for a moment, thinking about the bullet and wondering how he might trace it back to the gun, when Dory held up one finger. It was her signal for Ben to stand by her desk. Far be it from Ben to ignore Dory's non-verbal commands. He waited.

"Thank you, Mrs. Anderson," she said, "I will certainly tell Sheriff Bradley immediately. This will be a big help. Thank you very much for calling."

Dory hung up the phone, turned to Ben and said, "That was Mrs. Laurel Anderson. She's eighty-three years old and lives near the Booth Mansion. She was walking her terrier at the back of the grounds around five-forty last night when she caught sight of a man standing in the house by the French doors that lead out to the side yard. He stepped through the doors, closed them and the full-length shutters across them. He also latched the two shutter dogs."

"Whoa, back up a minute here. First off, get Deputy Phelps out to the mansion right away to see if there're any footprints leading away from that patio. I trust you told the deputies about the case already?"

She just sighed and rolled her eyes. "Do you really need to ask?"

"The Mont Blanc crime scene people looked all around the house last night. They didn't notice any footprints, but it was dark. George needs to start doing the house-to-house check also."

"I already buzzed George. He's calling back."

"Did you get Mrs. Anderson's phone number?" Dory raised her eyes heavenward.

"Okay, okay, sorry. I'll call her back. I need to know whether Tom Ferris had a will. And Dory, what the heck are shutter dogs?"

Dory raised her imperious first finger. "One thing at a time there, boss man," she said as the phone buzzed. It was George and she told him to get out to the Booth Mansion and check the area by the French doors for footprints.

"Start the house-to-house right after that," she told him.

Ben looked out the window. They'd had lots of rain in the past few days. Finding any footprints would be a long shot in the thick, freshly mulched landscape around the Mansion.

"Oh, and George, take some fingerprint powder with you and dust the shutter dogs on the French doors for prints."

Ben was chagrined that Dory would think about fingerprints. He hadn't thought that far ahead. Sometimes Ben wondered if Dory might make a better sheriff than he did. It was also embarrassing that his not-too-swift deputy apparently knew what the hell shutter dogs were. Dory wrote down a phone number and handed him the slip of paper.

"After you've finished talking to Mrs. Anderson, we will discuss the lamentable gaps in your education that have resulted in you not knowing about shutter dogs." She gave Ben an intimidating smile.

Ben went back to his office and called Mrs. Anderson. A frail woman in her eighties made for an unlikely suspect, so he assumed he could talk to her. She described the man she saw as about six feet tall and heavy-set. He was wearing a baseball cap, jeans, and a black T-shirt. She was too far away to tell eye or hair color, but thought she had seen him once before somewhere, either in the newspaper or on television. She might be elderly, but the old lady was sharp as a tack. Thanking her again and telling her to call his private line if she thought of anything else, Ben obediently returned to Dory.

"So?" She was sketching something on a pad of paper.

"Dory, could I have your attention, please?"

She gave him a long-suffering look and gestured to a sketch that showed a window with shutters. The left shutter was kept open by something that looked like a large, fancy "S." He'd seen them before on old houses; most were made of wrought iron. Dory pointed to it with one long, purplish painted fingernail.

"Shutter dog," she said laconically.

Chapter Eight

—

Detective Wayne Nichols

DRIVING INTO THE Powell's driveway, Wayne Nichols was impressed by the impeccably maintained home located at the end of a quiet cul-de-sac. Deputy Robert Fuller had asked to go with him and Wayne was pleased to see that the deputy's car was already there.

The two men walked up to the house together, where they were met by July Powell, who was wearing cut-off denim shorts and a wrinkled T-shirt. Her shoulder-length dark hair was scraped back in a messy ponytail and her eyes were puffy. She offered them both iced tea and they declined.

"Mrs. Powell, I need to ask you some questions," Detective Nichols said. He motioned to Rob. "Deputy Fuller will be taping our conversation."

July looked away. "Let's go into the family room," she said quietly and led them into a spacious room with brown leather furniture and an enormous television.

"I know you're the person who found Tom Ferris yesterday," Detective Nichols said. July nodded. "I'm sorry you had to go through that. Can you tell me about it?"

"It was awful." She stood looking out through the window into her backyard. July bowed her head for a minute and her shoulders slumped. She looked very small and alone, standing in the casually luxurious room full of oversized furniture and the detritus of family life. He waited for her to continue. Finally, she turned around and collected herself.

"Please sit down, Detective, you too, Deputy."

Wayne nodded and sat at one end of the tufted leather sofa. Deputy Fuller grabbed a chair and set the tape recorder on a nearby end table. July Powell took a seat in a chair on the other side of a large, glass coffee table.

"Mrs. Powell, can you run through what happened, starting with when you arrived at the mansion yesterday? Take your time. Anything you can remember will be helpful," Deputy Fuller said.

"Please call me July." Her smile didn't reach her dark eyes. "I got to the house around five. I was doing a final check of my space, which is the back entry to the house. I was just about to leave when I heard a loud bang. Oh, I forgot to tell Ben, I mean Sheriff Bradley, something else I remembered. I heard another noise, too. I think I heard a door closing."

"Do you have a key to the house?"

July blushed lightly. "Yes."

"How is it that you have a key?" Detective Nichols asked.

"I kept it, Detective," she hesitated, "from the time when I was dating Tommy."

"What time do you think you heard the loud noise?"

"It was probably close to six. I thought the sound came from the nursery so I went up the back staircase. It was dark up there and at first I didn't see him. But then I saw a body lying on the floor." She looked away again and dabbed at her eyes with a tissue.

"Go on."

"I got down on the floor and asked him if he was all right."

She shook her head. "I realized then who it was. It was my old boyfriend, Tommy Ferris." She closed her eyes.

"He'd been shot," Detective Nichols said.

She stared at him. "God, I hate it that somebody did this to him. Who could have done such a thing?"

She looked angry now and not so pitiful. He hadn't heard a false note yet. Maybe the sheriff was right.

"I'm very sorry for your loss." The detective looked at her searchingly. "Let's go back to where you were when you heard the bang. There's a staircase from that back entry leading up to the second floor, is that right? One of two staircases in the house?"

July nodded.

"And you can get to the nursery from either staircase?"

She nodded again.

"When you heard the door closing, did you think it was a door to one of the rooms or the main entry door?"

July was quiet for a minute. "I think it was the front door, and I remember being startled that someone was leaving the house. Until then, I assumed I was alone. There was only one other car in the driveway when I got there and I thought it belonged to one of the landscape designers—they wouldn't have been inside."

"It's possible that you heard the person who shot Tom Ferris leave. Among the designers, who tended to stay late at the house?"

"It couldn't have been one of the designers." July looked at him with a knitted brow.

"Why do you say that?"

July shook her head. "I just can't believe any of them would have been involved."

"Did you shoot him?" Detective Nichols kept his voice low and even, watching her carefully.

"No. I would never kill anyone. And it was Tommy. I love him, *loved* him." Tears shone in her eyes.

"Who else could have been in the house?"

"I really don't know, Detective. Have you looked at the video footage yet?" July had regained her poise. "The Booth Showhouse committee installed a closed circuit camera at the front and the back doors in case there was a robbery or something, so they'd know who'd been in the house."

Now she tells me. "Okay, good. I'll get the discs and we'll check it out. Just one last question, did you think Mr. Ferris recognized you?"

She closed her eyes and nodded.

"Did he say something? Anything?"

She paused just a fraction of a second too long and then shook her head.

"Are you sure?"

July nodded her head again but didn't meet his eyes.

"All right, I need you to give me the key now," he told her. After a brief hesitation, July took an iron key out of her shorts pocket and handed it to him. Deputy Fuller turned off the tape recorder. July started to get out of her chair. "We'll show ourselves out," the detective told her, and she slumped back without saying another word.

WHEN THEY GOT outside Rob cleared his throat. The deputy's smooth skin and short, golden brown hair made him look younger than he actually was. The silver frames of his glasses reflected the sunlight. He wanted to become a detective and had informally apprenticed himself to Wayne.

"Do you have a question, Rob?"

"Why did you take July's key away from her?"

"I don't want her going back in there."

Rob nodded. "Do you think she was telling the truth?"

"Yes and no," Wayne answered. "C'mon, it's too hot to stand out here." They walked back toward their cars. A tiny blonde girl wobbled past on her pink bike. The cicadas buzzed in the trees. Wayne put his hand on the car door handle tentatively. It was hot, but not hot enough to burn. He opened the car door to release the heated air from the interior and then turned back to the young deputy.

"She seemed genuine to me," Wayne told Rob.

"Yeah, I thought so too, except at the end. I think the victim said something to Mrs. Powell that she didn't want to tell us. Still, she was obviously upset about him dying."

Wayne clapped him on the shoulder. "You'll be a good detective someday. Trust those instincts. I'll see you back at the office."

DRIVING BACK, WAYNE thought about that tiny slice of time before July denied Ferris had spoken to her. He would bet his last dollar there was unfinished business between July Powell and the victim. And that Tom Ferris had said something to his old girlfriend.

The phone rang.

"Wayne," it was Ben's voice, "are you on your way back?"

"We just finished up with July Powell. I should be there in about twenty."

"Okay. I wanted you to know that I talked with the Chief of Investigations in Nashville, a Captain Paula Crawley. She made it clear that I can't interview anyone connected with the Ferris case until we have someone in custody. I've been thinking about some way to get around her rules and still help with the investigation. She said she'd report me to IA if I got into it." Ben sighed. "I hate this. Apparently, I can look at reports, including yours. You can update me daily and I can talk with anyone who calls on the tip line. She wants you to call her once a week."

Wayne didn't say anything, just gave a brief sigh.

"Anyway, Dory found some information for us. There was a rental car parked at the Booth Mansion the night Tom Ferris was shot. Ferris rented it from Enterprise. They had a cellphone number, a driver's license number and an address, a P.O. Box in Colorado. When the Mont Blanc police went through his effects, there was a volunteer firefighter's card in his wallet, plus a couple of check stubs from a resort in Telluride."

"I was hoping you were going to find a hotel confirmation. One of our problems is that we don't know how long he'd been in town."

"Right. Here's the good news. Enterprise will have a record of where they picked him up, the time and the date. George is there now, checking on the times. When he gets back here I'm going to have him start going over Ferris' cellphone outgoing and incoming calls. It'll take a while, but we could get some leads from the local usage details."

"Excellent. You were right, by the way. I don't get the feeling that July was the shooter, but there's still something she isn't telling us."

"There always is," he heard Ben say.

Chapter Nine

———

Sheriff Ben Bradley

BEN BRADLEY AND Detective Wayne Nichols had looked at the video from the closed circuit cameras a hundred times. They saw July Powell coming in through the backdoor of the house. They could see that the parking lot contained her car—a late model black Chevy Suburban—a green Mini Cooper and a silver Nissan Altima, the car Tom Ferris had rented. They could even see the person who left the front door of the Booth Showhouse at 5:58 p.m. yesterday. That individual was wearing jeans, tennis shoes, and a lightweight rain jacket with the hood up—although it wasn't raining. They couldn't tell if it was a man or a woman, much less identify them.

"Let's get Dory in here," Wayne suggested.

"Okay," Ben agreed, knowing it was impossible to evade his office parents when they stuck together.

Dory walked in and sat down. Ben replayed the video and looked at her questioningly.

"Man or woman?" Wayne asked her.

"That's a woman, of course. Is that *all* you boys needed?"

"Why do you say that?" Ben tried to keep the frustration out of his voice. "Wayne and I couldn't tell."

"The thighs." At their expressions, she added, "She's thin, but she has some weight to the outside of her thighs, her saddlebags. Men don't carry extra weight there."

"How old?" Wayne piped up.

"She moves well, almost like a dancer, but I'd say in her late thirties."

They had wasted two hours, Ben thought, feeling distinctly annoyed with himself.

"What's your certainty level?" His detective was looking at Dory with obvious admiration.

"About eighty-five percent." She smiled up at Wayne Nichols.

Ben cleared his throat, "Do you two mind not having a meeting of the mutual admiration society in front of me?"

"Later, boss man, I'm going home." Dory stood up and left the room.

SHERIFF BRADLEY TURNED to his detective and said, "So we have a suspect—female, late thirties. And since July Powell was still in the room when the emergency medical techs arrived, she's almost definitely not our shooter." He gave Wayne Nichols a pointed look.

"Well, we don't know that the woman who left the Booth Showhouse by the front door was the killer either, but I'm inclined to agree with you about July. Her grief seems authentic. You said Mrs. Anderson saw a man leaving out the French doors on the side of the house. Too bad nobody thought to put a closed circuit camera back there. The perp just about has to be one of those two people—the woman who left by the front door or the man who went out the French doors."

"Right. I'm going to talk with Mrs. December. She's definitely not a suspect and she knows everything that happens in this town."

"Hold on a minute, Sheriff. She's in the December family. Are you sure she isn't a suspect? Remember, you aren't supposed to do any interviews."

"Suzanne's a local reporter, not a suspect."

"I wouldn't be so sure," Wayne said. "Tom Ferris broke July's heart. The woman is very protective of her daughters."

Ben shook his head. "No, it doesn't add up. July is married now with three kids. She moved on long ago and got over her college boyfriend. And I know the Decembers don't have guns. But you're still right, damn it. My hands are tied." Ben thought for a few minutes. "I guess I can do some research on the computer."

Wayne drummed the table with his fingers. "I'm going to interview Miranda Booth Stackhouse. Dory told me she was the chair of the Booth Showhouse Committee and is related to the victim. I'll ask Dory to find out who the nursery designer was and talk with her. I suppose it's too late to do any of that tonight. First thing tomorrow I'll call and see if I can meet with Mrs. Stackhouse."

Ben nodded. "I'm going to concentrate on the background and figuring out what Tom Ferris was doing before he came back to town. We found his driver's license, his volunteer fire fighter's ID and some paystubs from a resort in Colorado. I'll contact those organizations and find out what I can about his life there and any ideas they might have about why he came back now."

Wayne stood up and turned to leave.

"Oh, hang on, Wayne. Did I tell you Fred Powell came home early from his conference? Since he's July's husband, you better be the one to talk to him." Ben frowned, still irritated at Captain Paula's prohibition. Wayne nodded. "I know what I'll do," Ben snapped his fingers, "I'll ask Dory for the local scuttlebutt about the Ferris family."

After Wayne left, Ben dialed Dory's number. He was somewhat apprehensive. Dory did not like to be bothered after she left the office.

"Hello, Dory?"

"Is this Ben Bradley?" She sounded annoyed.

"Hi Dory. Sorry to bother you at home, but I need some background on the Ferris family. Could you find that for me?"

"Overtime, Sheriff. Overtime. Remember that little promise you made to add more staff? Well, until that happens, anything I do for the office after hours I get double time for."

"Time and a half," Ben said.

"Fine." Dory was exasperated. "I'll call you back."

Ben heard the phone smack hard into its cradle.

Dory called back an hour later.

"This is what I found out," Dory said, not bothering to identify herself. "The Booth and Rawlins families—"

"I wanted information about the Ferris family," Ben tried for an official tone.

"Sheriff," she laughed, sounding like a kid. "I know." He had no time for her lightheartedness.

"Dory, I'm working a murder here." Sometimes Eudora Clarkson drove him slap out of his mind.

Dory suddenly sobered, "It's just funny that you don't know that the Booth, Rawlins, and Ferris families are connected."

WHEN THE CONVERSATION ended, Ben ran through what Dory had told him again. If he had the multi-generational family story right, Judge Henry Booth, still remembered as a strict law and order man, had married Charlotte French after law school. They renovated the Booth Mansion, which was a family property. After years of waiting, they finally had one child—a daughter named Irene Booth.

While in her early twenties, Irene married Wade Rawlins; according to Dory, it was against the wishes of her family. He was apparently quite the local playboy. Irene and Wade also had a daughter, Miranda Booth Rawlins, now the chairwoman for the Booth Mansion Showhouse Committee.

Irene, Miranda's mother, died of cancer when Miranda was

almost thirteen. After her death, Miranda's father remarried. Wade Rawlins' second wife was a woman named Joanna Ferris, a divorcee with a son—Tom Ferris. Tom was five when Miranda's father married Tom Ferris' mother.

The last thing Dory said—before she huffily reminded him that digging out this information would cost him big time—was that they needed to talk to Bethany Cooper, one of the designers.

"Why her especially?" Ben asked. "We plan to talk to all the designers to find out if anyone had a reason to murder Tom Ferris."

"Just something I found out from one of my friends," Dory said, enigmatically.

Ben decided not to push it.

As Ben drove through the darkened streets of Rosedale, he briefly entertained the fantasy of spending the weekend at Mae's, while his young son played with the Tater. Matthew would love Mae's new puppy. It was Ben's weekend to have him.

Then he interrupted his own reverie. The weekend he envisioned would not be possible. When there was a murder, they all worked 24/7. He'd have to tell Mae he would be working and Katie that he couldn't take Matthew. Ben picked up his cell to begin the process of pissing off both the women in his life.

Chapter Ten

—

Mae December

B EN SHOWED UP at Mae's door at about ten that night, looking absolutely beat. He played with the puppy for a few minutes and then gave Mae a serious look.

"I talked to Katie on the way over here," Ben said.

The name Katie was rarely followed by good news. She waited.

"I'm not going to be able to keep Matthew this weekend because of the case." He carried the Tater to her crate and shut her inside before sitting down heavily on a kitchen chair.

"Is she upset?" Mae inquired in what she hoped was a neutral voice.

He nodded. "Said she has plans, whatever that means."

Mae had to laugh. "I think it means she has plans. Do you think she'd be comfortable with Matthew staying here? I'm *very* flexible this weekend. I have no boarders at all. Plus, I think my boyfriend is going to be busy, so Matthew could keep me company and play with the Tater."

Ben gave her a grateful look. "You don't have to do this, Mae. Katie and I can work it out."

"I want to do it. We'll have fun, and you can come over when you can get away and have some time with both of us. As long as she's okay with it."

He laughed. "I'm sure she will be, or she'll at least act like she is while she's here."

"Here? Why would she be here?" Mae realized her voice sounded alarmed.

Ben looked at her with a little grin. "Don't panic. She'll have to pick him up from nursery school and bring his clothes and things with him. I'm sure she'll be pleasant."

Mae wasn't at all sure. The truth was, Katie made her nervous and her housekeeping probably wasn't up to the woman's standards. It was tough to keep a perfect house with three, no four dogs inside. Ben's son was a great kid, and it would be fun to spend some time with him. She told herself his mother being there for a few minutes was a small price to pay.

"Why don't you call her and see what she thinks?"

Ben's blue eyes darkened as he reached out and smoothed her hair. "I'll call her later," he said in a husky voice. "Give me a kiss."

She gave him a short but thorough kiss. "Ben, did you find out the reason Tommy came back to Rosedale?"

"No, but Dory gave me a lot of background."

"Did she tell you anything that might help with the case?"

"She said I needed to bring Bethany Cooper in for questioning. Did she hear that from you?"

"Not exactly," Mae looked away, "but I think Bethany knew that Tommy was in town when no one else did. At least that's what I heard."

Ben looked intently at her. "Did your *source* tell you why he was here? We're checking out when Tom arrived at the airport and picked up his rental car, but he wasn't in town long. Was it July who told you?"

Mae shook her head. "No. July would have been devastated if she knew Tommy was back in town without telling her. When I talked to her today, I learned a little more about their relationship. She and Tommy only slept together once—right before he disappeared. They'd been a couple for more than two years. They kept seeing each other after they both went to college—he to Southeast Tennessee State, she to Ole Miss. I know she went and stayed with him whenever she could during freshman year and the first part of sophomore year, but they'd never actually made love. Then finally, while they were both home for vacation, she decided she was ready. Anyway, after that they both went back to college. She never saw him again."

"Did July tell you anything else that might be relevant to the case?" The sheriff's eyes were focused tightly on hers.

"No," she said quietly. She wished she hadn't given July her word not to tell Ben about what Tommy whispered just before he died. It bothered her to keep things from Ben, in particular things related to a case, but her loyalty to her sister was strong.

"So the poor guy dated July for two years before he got her into bed? I can sympathize. God knows it took me a while to get you into bed. I wouldn't be satisfied with one night." Ben grinned.

"Well you're certainly not getting me into bed while Matthew is here," she said, trying to be strict.

"We'll just see about that. I might be irresistible."

"You are *impossible,* not irresistible."

They talked a little longer, and she told him everything July had agreed she could share. It was getting very late when Ben said he needed to go. He was reluctant, but Mae knew the drill. When he was working an important case, he rarely stayed over. She gave him a lingering good-bye kiss.

"Woman, have you no mercy?" He nuzzled her neck, gave it a gentle bite, and headed out into the dark.

Chapter Eleven

—

Sheriff Ben Bradley

Sheriff Bradley arrived at the office so early the next morning that it was still dark. Using the white board in the conference room, he began working on a time line for the last two days of Tom Ferris' life. Ben had informed the staff the previous day that all ongoing cases were suspended until they found out who murdered Tom Ferris. All staff meetings for the foreseeable future were canceled.

The car rental agent had picked up Ferris at the airport on August first, the day before he was shot. By calling all the nearby hotels, Ben found out that a man matching Ferris' description stayed at a Microtel outside Rosedale that night, paying in cash for the room. He glanced at his watch and noted that it was 8:00 a.m.

He buzzed Dory. "Dory, would you mind coming in here and writing things in this grid I made on the white board?" he asked.

"Sure thing," she said. Dory was in a good mood. She came in smiling and holding a sharpie.

"Okay, I divided the board into two columns—a column for August first and second. Tom Ferris arrived at the airport at three p.m. on August first, left the airport in a rented car at four-thirty and checked into the Microtel by six that evening. His cellphone history tells us that he ordered a pizza at seven. After dinner he must have driven around town. There were close to forty extra miles on the car's speedometer."

Dory wrote while Ben concentrated on his notes for the timeline. Had Tom Ferris driven to see someone late on the evening he arrived? Had he gone over to see July? He looked at the white board and said, "You can write 'arrived at Booth Mansion in the late afternoon' and his TOD at 5:57."

Ben raised his eyes from his notes and looked at the board. He was dismayed by how sketchy it was.

August 1	August 2
3:00 p.m. Tom Ferris arrives at Nashville airport	No Information
4:30 p.m. T.F. rents car. Leaves airport for Rosedale	No Information
6:00 p.m. Checks into Microtel.	Arrives at Booth Showhouse
Orders a pizza at 7:00. 40 extra miles on speedometer	TOD 5:57 p.m.

"Thanks Dory, I'll do the rest."

Ben dialed Wayne's cellphone.

"What's up?" his detective asked.

"I've been working on the time-line. Want to meet at Donut Den or the office?"

"Donut Den," Wayne said, sounding surprisingly alert. Knowing Wayne, Ben guessed that he had hardly slept since they got the case the previous day. He often did background work on the victim's known associates late at night, prowling the streets and talking to the people he encountered.

They drove into the parking lot in the alley behind Donut

Den at almost the same moment and walked in together. It was hot and humid again with a low cloud cover. After Ben paid for Dory's blueberry donuts and an assortment for everyone else, he joined Wayne at their usual two-top by the window.

Ben summarized what he had found out about Tommy Ferris' movements before he arrived at the mansion. "I stopped over at Mae's last night after I got the lowdown from Dory," he said.

Wayne shook his head and grinned. "Really? I'm amazed you still have a girlfriend, Ben. I was thinking since we were considering July Powell a suspect, Mae would drop you like a bad habit." His low-pitched laugh rumbled.

"No way. Dory told me that we should talk to Bethany Cooper. I got the feeling that Bethany knew Tom Ferris was in town before anyone else did. I'm wondering why." Ben expected to surprise Wayne with this information, but he just nodded.

"We need to talk with her and her husband, Dan. And I think you should also talk to George Stackhouse, Miranda's husband. Dory said Miranda really wanted that house and was crushed when it went to Ferris after their parents died. I had an idea that Miranda might have pushed her husband to get rid of Ferris, thinking she would get the house if he was out of the picture."

"On it." Wayne was already picking up his car keys.

"Mae also gave me some helpful information. Tom Ferris had a high grade point average at Southeast Tennessee State, and at Christmas he told his parents and July that he intended to go to law school. Mae said his parents gave him a new car for Christmas that year—a red rag top. He returned to school on January third, and that was the last time July ever saw him."

"Ah, the female network," his detective said. "I'm puzzled by the fact that Ferris apparently fell off the face of the earth when he returned to college fifteen years ago. I suspect his disappearance way back then has something to do with his murder."

Ben looked out the window at the hot morning sky. The temperature was in the low nineties already. Heat waves rose off the pavement.

"Just what I was thinking," Ben said. "The kid heads back to school in his new car, his beautiful girlfriend on his mind, and simply vanishes. Then on January fifth, Tommy's parents, Mr. and Mrs. Rawlins, were killed in a car crash. The opposing driver fell asleep, crossed the median, and ran right into them. Something happened on Tom's way back to college, or in the two days between January third and January fifth that made him give up his whole life here." Ben frowned and scratched his head. "Dory found out he didn't even attend his parents' funerals."

"The motive for this killing goes back a long time," Wayne said. "The Ferris murder might be a new case on top of a cold case."

"Right, it's like two sleeping dogs." Ben grabbed the donuts and headed out the door.

ON THE WAY to the office, he called Dory. When she answered, he asked if she could look up the obituary for Mr. and Mrs. Rawlins.

"I want to know if an obit was placed in the student newspaper at Southeast Tennessee State. Can you check?"

"You bet," Dory said.

When Ben walked into the office, he noticed Dory was wearing a purplish top with a gray skirt and some shiny silver and purple earrings. He made a mental note to ask her where she got them. It would be nice to get something similar for Mae, to thank her for keeping Matthew for the weekend.

"Purple earrings," he said, "very nice."

"Aubergine," she corrected him.

Ben sighed.

Dory mentioned she had been on Facebook and Twitter. She'd found a high school reunion search trying to locate Tom Ferris. She sent out an email to the organizer and got a reply saying that they hadn't gotten a response from Ferris, but she had received two e-requests for his contact information. One was from Miranda Stackhouse and one was from Bethany Cooper. Both women wanted to know if anyone had heard from Ferris. The emails were dated July 27th and 29th respectively.

"Here," Ben said, handing Dory the donut box.

"I'm finally getting you trained," she said.

"Where are the spikes this morning?" Wayne asked, referring to her usual stiletto heels. He had walked into the office right behind Ben.

"Under my desk," she said. "They're *fine* lookin' but way too tight." She was looking into the donut box. "Sheriff Bradley, I don't see my blueberry donuts."

"Right here," he said with a cheerful smile, producing a small white paper sack from behind his back. "Just wanted to ruffle your feathers."

"Would the two of you like to know what else I found?" she asked, looking at them indulgently.

"Sure would," Ben said. "Come down to my office. I don't want to be talking about this if anyone besides the staff walks in." Taking the donut box, they went to his office.

"Please sit down." Dory took the chair. Wayne remained standing.

"I checked the gun registry, and neither July Powell nor Miranda Stackhouse owns a gun. But Fred Powell does—an assault rifle."

"Good Lord, an assault rifle." Wayne started to pace. "Why not just buy an AK47 or a Kalashnikov? Well, it's not important for this case, but what people who live in nice suburbs need with that kind of firepower is beyond me."

"Well, the rifle is only used at a special shooting range; apparently, he belongs to a club."

"Good work, Dory." Ben tapped his pencil rapidly on his desktop.

"That's not all. I also located the cabbie who picked up Fred Powell from the airport. He dropped him off about four blocks from the Booth Showhouse at 4:45; that's six miles from his home and ten miles from his office. The driver remembered, because Powell had him drive past the house first and then circle around to drop him at the corner nearby. He also tipped him very well."

"So, if Fred stopped at the Booth Showhouse, maybe to see his wife, it could have been Fred that Mrs. Anderson saw coming out the French doors," Ben said, thoughtfully. "July didn't say anything about seeing him there, though."

"We need to speak with him," Wayne said. "It doesn't sound like he has an alibi for the time of the shooting." Turning to Dory he added, "Have I mentioned lately how much I appreciate you? And that you're looking very lovely this morning? Good toenail polish." Wayne wrapped an arm around Dory's shoulders.

Ben stood up. It was time to end their little love-fest. "Dory, did you say that you were able to get Bethany Cooper to come in this morning?"

"Yes, she'll be here at ten-thirty."

"Can you check the gun registry for her and for Dan Cooper? And put some shoes on. Damn it, woman, I'd like this place to at least *look* professional."

"Yes, sir." Dory rolled her eyes and padded out.

Chapter Twelve

———

Detective Wayne Nichols

DORY HANDED DETECTIVE Nichols the list of his appointments. The first name on the list was Miranda Booth Stackhouse.

"Miranda is the Junior League chairwoman for the charity event, and she holds the keys to the house. While the designers are working at the house, a member of the Design Committee has to let them in. There's a front table and every designer signs in and out. You need to check the ledger. The Committee has to be very careful in case of any allegations of theft."

Detective Nichols jotted this down in his notebook, wondering who else besides Miranda and July Powell had keys to the house.

"Can you find out whether anyone else had a key?"

Nodding, she said, "I'll try. You're going to interview Miranda first this morning. Deputy Fuller will be going with you to her house. Bethany Cooper will be here when you get back."

"She wasn't the nursery designer though, right?"

Dory looked at the notes on her desk. "Right, Bethany

designed one of the nearby rooms. Lacey Duncan did the nursery, but he's not available for questioning."

Wayne's eyebrows shot up. "Lacey is male? And can't be questioned?"

"Right. Lacey is a famous designer who grew up here. Apparently, he developed the plan for the nursery, which he did as a personal favor to Miranda, and then he flew to D.C. to work on a design for the French Embassy. He left several weeks ago. Shauna Lewis, his assistant, finished it to his specs and did the mural." Dory sounded unimpressed as she read from her notes.

"Okay, thanks." Wayne collected Deputy Robert Fuller and they left the office.

AFTER DRIVING TO the eastern side of Rosedale, they entered a new subdivision called Heather Hills and the driveway of a large home at 4891 Heath Drive. Deputy Fuller rang the bell, and a short heavy-set brunette in her forties, wearing a tan skirt and a pale blue blouse, answered the door.

"Hello," she said, "I'm Miranda. Come in." She had dark circles under her eyes and looked tired.

They entered a formal foyer and Miranda led them to an office with an imposing desk and dark, solid looking bookshelves. The books looked like those you see in a law library. The impressive bookcases were made from walnut with curved glass fronts.

"Would you like coffee?" she asked.

"No thank you." Detective Nichols shook his head. Deputy Fuller switched on the recorder.

"Mrs. Stackhouse, you're the Junior League chair for this year's fundraiser, is that right?"

"Yes," she nodded.

Detective Nichols always started with the routine questions—questions he already knew the answers to. "Is that a volunteer position?"

"All the Junior League jobs are volunteer positions, Detective. Chairing the committee for the Showhouse is a lot of work, but it's an honor. I've been working up to it for years. When we got the Booth Mansion for this year's Showhouse, everybody wanted me to be the chair because of my connection to the home."

"Since the Showhouse opening had to be postponed indefinitely, you're most likely aware that Thomas John Ferris was killed at the Booth Mansion at approximately five-fifty seven p.m. on August second." Wayne watched her closely.

Miranda nodded. She closed her eyes briefly and her face paled.

"Did you know Mr. Ferris?"

"Yes, I did. Poor little Tommy. I am ... that is I *was*, his big sister. Actually, I'm his stepsister. His mother married my father when he was barely five. I haven't seen him since he was twenty years old. He must have been about thirty-five." Miranda looked utterly miserable. She took a tissue from her sleeve and blew her nose. "Sorry, it was just horrible news."

"So, he left Rosedale when he was twenty? And returned recently?" Deputy Fuller asked. They knew this already, but they wanted Miranda's confirmation.

"Yes. My husband and I looked for him for a long time. We even hired two private detectives, one when he first disappeared, and one about two years ago. Neither of them came up with much. Our family attorney, Evangeline Bontemps, has always been able to reach him, but she wouldn't tell me anything about where he was. I guess he insisted on that." She threw the tissue into a small brass trashcan near her feet.

"How was your relationship with him when you were younger?" Detective Nichols was getting to the significant questions now.

"Good. I have so many happy memories of Tommy as a kid. I used to take him for rides on the handlebars of my bike, and he would come into my bed at night if there was a thunderstorm," she trailed off and tears came into her eyes. "I remember holding his hand when our parents were married. He was so happy to have a big sister."

"I'm sorry for your loss." Wayne handed her another tissue. "Did you know he was back in Rosedale?"

"On the morning of August second, I got a call from Bethany Cooper. She told me Tommy was in town. I was shocked and hurt that I hadn't heard from him. She said she'd seen him at the mansion, but I never got a chance to speak to him. And now I never will." Tears flooded her eyes.

"What did the private detectives find, do you remember? I need their names, if you still have them. Were they able to tell you what he'd been doing all those years?"

"The first detective, his name was Marc Whitney, did locate him. It was about two years after Tommy disappeared. He traced him to a ski resort in Utah. He met with him and asked Tommy to call me. Tommy said he would not. No, that's not right; he said he *could not* speak with me."

"He wouldn't or couldn't speak with you? Why was that?"

"He told the detective he needed time to recover from the death of our parents and that he would call me or write when he could."

"And the second detective? Did he find anything?"

"No. Apparently Tommy left that town and he found no further trace of him." Detective Nichols met Deputy Fuller's eyes for a moment, knowing Ferris had been working in Colorado.

"I understand that your parents died in an auto accident around the time your step-brother disappeared. When was that exactly?" Detective Nichols asked.

"It happened just two days after Tommy returned to college for his sophomore year from Christmas break. We got the news that my father and his mother had been killed in an auto accident. I called the housemother at his fraternity to tell him, but she hadn't seen him since January third."

"So, it was at that point that your brother disappeared?"

"Yes, in fact when I called her again a few days later to ask Tommy to come home for the funeral, she said nobody had seen him since January third. I called the registrar and they said he hadn't completed registration. The registrar was able to tell me that Tommy was in good standing academically, because I was his only relative at that point, but the school had no knowledge of his whereabouts. The funeral and the reading of the will took place without him."

Detective Nichols was quiet, running through the scenario again. Why would a young man with apparently no academic or financial problems not register for the winter semester? Something happened during Christmas break that made it impossible for Tom Ferris to return to the university, and it wasn't the death of his parents. What could have been worse than that?

Miranda was looking at him with a little frown.

"I'm sorry. I was just thinking. You said there was a will?" Detective Nichols asked.

"Yes, and Tommy got the house." Miranda stared down at her empty hands. "It should have come to me. It was my grandparents' house, in my family for generations. I was the legitimate heir. I was bitter for a very long time about that. I had a trust fund from my grandparents, so I did receive money from the estate, but not the house. I loved that house. I always had." Miranda's mouth was pinched and her fists were balled up on the desk top.

"It must have been a terrible blow," Wayne said, keeping his voice gentle and kind.

"I felt so alone then, no parents, no grandparents, no little brother. I realized later that I experienced a clinical depression. I finally got treatment. Then I met my husband and we used my inheritance to start his business. But I would have traded it all, every dime of it, to own that house." She was looking past him now with her arms crossed tightly over her chest.

The ferocity of her feelings struck Wayne hard. He wondered if her desire for the house was strong enough to make her kill Tom Ferris. Wayne knew that women sometimes had much stronger attachments to homes than men did. Or perhaps the fact that her stepbrother had been in town and hadn't contacted her pushed her over the edge.

"Where were you between five and six p.m. on August second?"

"My husband and I met some friends for dinner that night. We were driving to the restaurant at that time."

"Okay," the detective said, thinking that if her alibi was confirmed, she would be off his list. While he still intended to talk with her husband, if they were together and their friends confirmed it, neither one of them could have killed Tom Ferris.

BETHANY COOPER WAS waiting when they got back to the office. Dory slipped a note into Wayne's hand.

"Read that before you talk to her," she whispered.

Deputy Fuller and Detective Nichols walked into the conference room and introduced themselves to Mrs. Bethany Cooper, who rose to her feet when they came in. She was an attractive woman, slender, with a small waist and flaring hips shown to good advantage in her sleeveless tunic and dark leggings. She wore her long dark hair loose. She reminded him of someone, but he couldn't think who it was. He indicated that she should sit, and admired the graceful way she slid into the chair. Wayne remembered Dory saying the woman who left the Booth Showhouse at the time of Ferris' death walked like a dancer.

They had recently installed audio capture equipment at the office. The deputy clicked the audio button, turning on the system.

"Mrs. Cooper, would it be okay if I called you Bethany?" Detective Nichols asked.

"Certainly."

"I understand you designed the upstairs bedroom closest to the nursery, correct?"

"Yes, the grandparents' suite was my project." She sat with her back ruler-straight. Her legs were crossed at the ankle.

"As you know, Tom Ferris was found dying in the nursery of the Booth Showhouse the evening of August second."

"Yes, I know," she swallowed, and he saw her throat constrict.

"Did you see Mr. Ferris before he died?"

"Yes, I did. I came over to take a look at the nursery and he was there. He told me that room had been his bedroom when he lived in the house."

"When was that?" Wayne was getting the distinct impression that Bethany Cooper was holding back.

"It was after five o'clock on August first. I planned on going to the Booth Showhouse the next day for a final check, but when I got to the house, I realized I was running late. My husband was expecting me, so I left."

"How did you expect to get in the house? I thought only Miranda Booth Stackhouse had the keys."

She paused. "I expected some other designers would probably be there and if I rang the bell they would let me in."

"We know you were in the house on August second also, Mrs. Cooper. Who let you in?" Deputy Fuller asked.

She was obviously trying to make up a story. "The front door was unlocked."

"Weren't you upset about that? I thought security was supposed to be very tight."

"I saw cars in the parking area, so I figured somebody else had left it open."

The detective looked at her doubtfully. "Are you holding something back, Bethany? Did you meet with Ferris anywhere else?"

Bethany Cooper shook her head but didn't meet his eyes.

"Don't lie to me, Mrs. Cooper; I can't help you if you lie to me." His voice was very quiet, almost tender.

She didn't say anything, so after a pause Wayne continued, "Where did you go after you left the Booth Mansion on the second?"

"I went home." Bethany stood up abruptly and reached down to the floor for her purse. "Detective, I heard that Tommy died there. Is that true?"

It was the second time she had referred to him as Tommy, and Wayne wondered whether everyone called him that, or only women who knew him intimately. Both July Powell and Miranda Booth Stackhouse had called him Tommy and now Bethany Cooper.

"Yes. He was shot and died there," Detective Nichols told her. He considered telling her that Tom Ferris died from a bullet in the back, just to see her reaction, but they'd kept that quiet.

She said nothing, just exhaled and closed her eyes for a second.

Deputy Fuller rose to his feet. "You're free to go, Mrs. Cooper," he said. "Thank you for your time."

"No, wait a minute," Wayne interrupted. "You're a married woman. Why were you meeting with a man alone at the Booth Showhouse?"

She didn't answer, just shook her head. Standing, she tucked her hair behind her ears and left the room.

"What was that about?" Rob Fuller asked. "You made me look like a jerk. I told her she was free to go and then you asked her another question."

"I made you look like a nice guy. I made myself look like a jerk. I wanted her off balance." Wayne pulled the sheriff's note from his pocket and spread it on the table so the deputy could see it. Ben had reminded Wayne to ask Bethany about the nature of her relationship with Tom Ferris. She apparently was the first person who knew he was back in town. They still didn't know why.

"Well, now I feel like a jerk," Rob mumbled.

"It's all right. I didn't have time to let you know beforehand.

You were fine. We'll be talking to Mrs. Cooper again."

Bethany Cooper was just leaving the building as the men entered Dory's area.

When the office door closed behind Bethany, Wayne said, "Dory, take a look at Mrs. Cooper, will you?"

Dory stood up and watched Bethany Cooper walk out to her car.

"Do you think Bethany was the person we saw on the video leaving the Mansion on the evening of the murder?"

"She could have been. She walks like a dancer. Let's look at the disc again."

They could see the woman in the hooded jacket entering the house at 5:30 on August second and leaving at 5:59. After reviewing it several times, they were sure. It was Bethany Cooper, and she had been in the house for almost twenty minutes, much longer than she had admitted.

"I need to talk with her husband, Dan Cooper," Wayne said.

"How come?"

"Don't play coy with me, Miss Clarkson. No doubt you opened Ben's note to me," he said, looking sternly at her.

"Not a doubt in the world," she said cheerfully, not looking in the least abashed or impressed with his deductive powers.

"You're incorrigible. I want to find out whether Bethany told her husband that Tom Ferris was in town. There's something funny about her demeanor, and I don't think it's because she and Ferris were in a relationship. Either she's holding something back or she's protecting someone, maybe her husband. And I'd like to talk with July's husband, Fred Powell. Today if possible."

"It's getting late. I was about to leave," Dory said, but at his flat stare, she called Fred Powell on the phone and handed the receiver to Wayne.

"Hello, Detective," Fred said. "I understand you talked to July yesterday. My wife is still pretty upset about your visit. Furthermore, she said you might need to talk to her again." His voice hovered on the edge of anger.

"I may." Wayne paused. "I'd like to talk to you too. Do you have time to answer some questions?"

"On the phone or do you want to come over here?"

"I'll come on over to your office."

"Okay," he said. Dory wrote on a pad of paper that Fred worked at IT Fixes Now—a business located in a large office building just off the highway between Rosedale and Nashville.

"Sheriff, I'm going to go talk to Fred Powell," Wayne called as he walked by the sheriff's office. "I just spoke with him on the phone."

"I already got a search warrant for their house, so I'll get George and Rob to start the search while you're talking to him," Wayne's young boss said.

When Wayne got into his car, he noticed that the temperature display on the building read 92 degrees. High temperatures made him short-tempered. *Watch yourself, Wayne Nichols. Keep your cool.* Solving this one would take every ounce of his mind and ability—until they nabbed the killer, or moved it to the cold case file where it would be a reproach to him for the rest of his life.

Fred Powell met him in the entrance to the large building saying, "I thought I'd watch for you. You probably haven't been here before, have you? I'd be happy to show you around."

"Do you have a conference room where we could talk?" Detective Nichols asked.

"Sure," he said. "What's this about?"

Wayne just looked at him, irked that Fred would offer him a tour of the building. Fred Powell knew perfectly well why the detective was there. The man was playing games. Fred kept his expression impassive. The two men walked down the marble tile floored corridor to the impressively furnished conference room. As they sat down, Fred gestured to the sideboard that was loaded with a variety of coffee machines and an urn filled with coffee. It smelled burned; clearly it was the last coffee of the day. Wayne shook his head.

"Mr. Powell, what time did you get home on August second?"

"I got an earlier flight, flew standby. The conference I was attending ended a little early and I wanted to get home. I never sleep well when I'm not in my own bed."

"What time did you get to the Nashville airport?"

"It was right about three-thirty."

"So did you call someone to pick you up?"

"July was supposed to, but I knew she had to finish up her project, so I took a cab. I did send her a text, but I never got a response, so I don't think she saw it."

"Did you go straight home?"

"No, I came here to the office. I didn't get home until about seven-thirty. That's when I found out about Tom Ferris' murder. July was still at her parents' house."

Detective Nichols set his hands on the table, palms down. His voice trembled with repressed fury. "Don't lie to me, Mr. Powell. We know you took a cab to the Booth Showhouse." Fred's eyes darted sideways. "You arrived there around four-thirty. The victim died of a gunshot wound at five fifty-seven. Do you own a gun?" Wayne watched his face carefully. He knew the answer to this one and wanted to see if Fred would confess to owning a semi-automatic.

"A gun? For hunting, you mean?"

"For any reason."

"Surely you aren't suspecting me of this murder, are you?"

"We have to get the whereabouts of everyone who may have been involved. Your wife found the victim dying, and she and Ferris were very close at one time, as I'm sure you know."

Silence. Fred looked at Detective Nichols and he looked back. Neither of them blinked.

"Yes," he said, finally. "I own a gun, but I keep it locked at the Rosedale Gun Club. I resent you even asking me that question."

"Did you know Tom Ferris?"

"No." Obviously Fred had decided that he was going to reply in single syllables.

"Never met him?"

"No."

"You were aware that he and July dated in high school and college?" the detective asked, hoping to detect Fred's level of jealousy, if it indeed existed. "I understand it was a serious relationship and that July expected it would culminate in marriage."

"I'm aware of that, Detective." The pupils in Fred's ice-blue eyes contracted to pin dots. "It was before she and I met."

"Did either of you have any contact with him since that time? He left the area about fifteen years ago, in January of '98."

"I didn't. July may have."

"Did you think she was in touch with him?"

"I don't know," he said, exhaling sharply. "With all this damn Facebook, Twitter and all, you can find just about anyone these days."

"Why did you go to the Booth Mansion when you returned from the conference?"

Fred took a deep breath. "The truth is I was checking up on July. She'd seemed distant lately. I even wondered if she could be having an affair." He exhaled slowly; it was a big admission.

"You must have seen her car in the parking lot of the Booth Showhouse and known she was there," Detective Nichols said.

"Yeah, I did. The only other car in the lot was a rental. It was unlocked, so I looked in the glove box and saw it had been rented by Tom Ferris the previous day. I waited a while for July to come out. Another woman showed up in a little green car and went in the front door. After she left, around six, all hell started breaking loose and an ambulance roared in. Two guys ran inside and another one stayed in the car. I talked with the driver and asked him why they were there. He said there'd been a shooting. A few minutes later, they brought a guy down on a stretcher. I asked who it was and he said the man's name was Ferris."

"That must have shaken you up."

"Definitely. I probably should have gone inside to see if July was okay, but I knew she'd be furious, thinking I was checking up on her. I called a cab, went back to the office and then later called another cab to take me home."

"I'll have to check your story, Mr. Powell," the detective told him. "We'll be in touch. Just don't leave town."

Fred Powell nodded. "I'm not going anywhere," he said quietly.

Chapter Thirteen

—

Mae December

AT THREE O'CLOCK on August fourth, Katie Hudson pulled into Mae's driveway. She was bending over Matthew's car seat to release the harness when Mae walked down her front steps to greet Katie and her son.

"Hi, Miss Mae." Matthew's voice was deep and husky for a little boy of only four. With his light brown curly hair and bright blue eyes, he was Ben in miniature—with chubby cheeks.

"Hi Matthew. Hello Katie."

Katie pulled the harness over Matthew's head and hoisted him down.

"Hello, Mae," she said, straightening up. "Thanks for agreeing to keep him this weekend. I've got plans that I didn't want to change."

Katie was looking thin and stylish. Her short brown hair was sleek and straight, even in the heat and humidity of a summer afternoon. Her hazel eyes looked almost golden in the sun. *Her rear-end and her hair are both half the size of mine.*

"You're welcome. Can I help you carry anything in?"

Matthew crawled into the driver's seat and grabbed a small suitcase decorated with dinosaurs from the passenger side. He dragged it across the seat and out onto the driveway, where it flipped onto its side.

"I need to unhook his car seat and put it in your car," Katie said. "He can get his backpack and bring that in."

Matthew dove into the backseat again, emerging with a backpack that looked like a small, green brontosaurus.

Katie looked down, smiling at her son. "Are you sensing a theme here?" she asked.

"Uh-huh. I'm betting there are some dinosaur jammies in that suitcase."

"And T-Rex underpants!" Matthew began unzipping his suitcase to demonstrate.

"Let's do that inside, okay, Matthew?" Mae picked his suitcase up and walked up the porch steps. "Come with me and I'll show you where you're sleeping this weekend." She turned to Katie. "Do you want to set the car seat inside? It's awfully hot out here. I can put it in my car later on."

"Okay. Or Ben can do it when he gets here. He called to say he'd be here soon. They're hard to install if you aren't used to doing it." Katie grabbed the car seat with her well-manicured hands. Mae noticed that she had muscular arms for such a thin woman and guessed it was probably from carrying that solid little guy of hers around.

Mae led them inside. Depositing the car seat in the entryway, Katie took Matthew by the hand.

"Did your Daddy tell you about the Tater?" Mae asked him. He nodded his head.

"She's in the kitchen. C'mon, I'll introduce you."

Nervous about Katie seeing her house, Mae had cleaned most of the day. Her remodeled one-hundred-year-old farmhouse was looking its best. Katie followed Mae and Matthew into the kitchen without comment. Mae released the Tater from her crate and the fluffy, gold and white corgi bounded out.

Her oversized ears stood up straight and her stubby bottom wagged, taking her entire body along with it.

"That might be the cutest puppy I've ever seen," Katie said.

"That's not a puppy, Mommy." Matthew sat on the wide-plank pine floor and the Tater swarmed into his lap. She planted her front paws on Matthew's chest and began to lick his face. Giggling, he lay back. "It's a fox. Or a teddy-bear."

Mae looked up from the gleeful pair and into Katie's eyes, which looked too bright, as if she was about to cry.

"Your mom's right, Matty, she's a puppy. A corgi puppy. She does look like a chubby little fox, doesn't she? Katie, can I get you a glass of water?"

"Yes, please." Katie sniffled. "Could I use your bathroom?"

Mae nodded. "It's down the hall to your right."

When Katie emerged from the bathroom with a red nose and less eye makeup, Mae handed her a glass of ice water. Katie pointed to the large painting that hung above Mae's kitchen table.

"That's beautiful. Is Malone a local artist?"

"Thank you. Malone is very local." Mae smiled. "Malone is me; it's my middle name."

"Oh, I thought you were a dog breeder, not an artist."

"Well, I'm both. I took a hiatus from painting for about a year. Ben talked me into picking my brushes up again a month or so ago. I really missed it."

Katie walked closer to the painting. "You're very talented." She looked down at Matthew and the Tater, who were rolling around on the floor.

Mae cleared her throat. "Thanks. If you have a minute, I'll give you a tour of the rest of the house."

Katie took a big gulp from her ice water and nodded her head. "I'd like that. Can you show me where Matthew will be sleeping?" Her eyes suddenly teared up and her voice quavered.

"Sure. Or maybe we should go sit down on the porch for a minute and talk."

"I'm sure your porch is beautiful too," Katie said, with a pitiful attempt at a smile.

Mae indicated her screened porch with a wave of her left hand, wondering where the heck Ben was. "After you."

Katie sat down on the red cushioned glider facing the doorway. She set her glass of water down on the small iron and glass end table and looked at Mae. Her chin was trembling as she reached into her purse for tissues.

"This is harder than I thought it would be—leaving my son with Ben's girlfriend. You seem like your life is so together. Mine is such a mess right now."

"Katie, my life's not nearly as together as it seems. I cleaned all day before you got here because I thought you'd judge me for my messy house."

She smiled, sniffing and wiping her nose. "Your house may not always be this clean, but it's really something. Matty and I live in a tiny condo right now, and it's pretty cruddy. Anyway, I love this porch. Did you design all this yourself?"

If she was trying to lighten the atmosphere, Mae was fine with that.

"Most of it. My sister is a designer and she gave me some ideas for the porch. She told me to use the black and white cowhide as a tablecloth and go with a distressed look to play it up. I was going to do something more traditional out here, but I think she was right."

Mae's cellphone buzzed in her shorts pocket. "Excuse me, Katie." She stepped into the hallway.

"Hi, July, I was just talking about you."

July's loud, agitated voice poured out. "Your boyfriend sent his deputies to my house with a search warrant. Did you know he was doing that?"

"I had no idea. Were the kids at home?"

"No, thank God. Fred's at work, Olivia's with Mama, and the boys are at sports camp. I'm here by myself watching them tear my house apart."

"I'm so sorry. He didn't say anything about it to me. He should be here soon. Believe me, I'll ask him about it."

Matthew materialized at her side, holding the Tater. Mae sighed.

"July, I've got to go. I have his mini-me here beside me."

"Matthew's there?"

"And his mother."

"And they're both listening to you right now?"

"That's right. Oh, hell!" The Tater was slipping out of Matthew's hands. "I'll call you back when I can."

Matthew's eyes were wider than usual. The puppy was squirming against his chest, about to fall.

"Daddy says that word too, but Mommy doesn't," Matthew informed her.

Of course she doesn't. "Can I have the puppy, please, Matty?" Mae relieved Ben's little boy of his wiggling burden. "Why don't you go out on the porch with your mom, okay? I need to take the Tater outside for a minute."

Chapter Fourteen

———

July Powell

JULY PRESSED THE end call button on her cellphone and smacked it down on the granite counter in her kitchen. She heard Fred coming through the front door.

"July, what the hell is going on?" He blew into the kitchen and set his briefcase down. His normally smooth, white-blond hair was standing on end and his shirt was soaked with sweat. "Did you just let these people ransack our home?"

July looked around. There were dark marks from where the techs had dusted for prints. The red-haired deputy was in her pantry, looking behind the cereal boxes. Two other officers were pulling dishware out from her china cabinet.

She glared at her husband of twelve years. "They had a warrant; I didn't just *let* them in. And it's your fault they're here!"

Fred's blue eyes widened and a vein in his temple stood out against his fair skin. "How is this possibly my fault?"

"Because you came home early from California to spy on me. Now they've asked me for the clothes you wore home from the conference. They're looking for blood stains. Fred, you're a suspect in a murder case." July was almost screaming now. Somewhere inside of her, the walls were breaking. The three people from the sheriff's office were staring at her and so was Fred. She didn't care. "Mind your own damn business," she snapped at them. "Hurry up and get out of my house."

Whirling, she ran down the hall to the master bedroom. Fred was right on her heels.

"We're not done yet," Fred started to say.

She slammed the door in his face and locked it. "Oh yes we are," she yelled through the door. "I can't take your jealousy and suspicions anymore." She sat on the floor, leaning against the wall. The doorknob rattled. "Just go away, Fred."

There was a short silence. "Where are the kids?" he asked. "I don't want them to see this—us fighting, our house torn up. Me locked out of our room." His voice was high and tense.

"The kids are fine, Fred. Olivia is with my mother and the boys are going home with a friend after sports camp today. When Ben's goons are gone, we'll be alone."

"They're not goons; they're just doing their jobs. Be reasonable, July. Unlock this door so we can talk. July, did you hear me?"

Fred's volume was rising again. July stood up, pulled a suitcase out from under their bed, and began filling it with shorts, swimsuits, and T-shirts. "I'm going to the lake house," she yelled over her shoulder. "I need a break."

"What about our kids?" Fred was shouting now. "You know I have to work."

July swept her makeup and bathroom supplies into a small tote. Carrying her suitcase and pulling the tote-strap over her shoulder, she opened the bedroom door and walked past her startled husband.

"I'll figure something out for the kids—and the dogs, and the plants—like I always do. The housekeeper will be here in the morning. Get your own damn dinner."

Fred shook his head. "Don't go, honey. I'm sorry." He reached out to her, but she backed away.

"Don't touch me right now. I'm going to fall apart if you do. Please, just let me go." She had tears in her eyes.

Fred's face crumpled. Without another word, he walked into their bedroom and went to the window, where he stood with his back to her, staring out at the yard.

July went back into the kitchen.

"Can I take these bags, or do you need to search them? What was your name again?" she asked the red-headed deputy.

"Phelps, Ma'am. Deputy George Phelps. Are those items from your bedroom and bathroom?"

"Yes."

"You can take them. We searched those rooms already."

"Thank you, Deputy. You can let Mr. Powell know when you're finished."

She went out to the garage and loaded her bags into the car. She opened the side door out to the backyard and called the dogs. "Soot, Ricky, come here."

The two porgi puppies came tearing around the corner. She led them into the garage and picked them up, putting both of them in the backseat. Going back into the kitchen, she grabbed their leashes, dog food, and beds. Deputy Phelps was holding her purse in one freckled hand.

"Can I have my purse?" July asked, glaring at him.

The chubby deputy blushed. "Yes, of course, Mrs. Powell. Do you need some help carrying all that?"

"No. Just set my purse on top of this dog bed and hand me the keys from that hook over there. Wait, I need my cellphone, too. And my charger. Never mind, I'll make another trip."

Deputy Phelps set her purse down on the counter beside her phone. "Sorry," he mumbled, and walked into the dining room.

After several more trips in and out of the house, July was ready to go. She pulled out of the driveway and turned in the direction of the lake house, then changed her mind and drove to Mae's place. She intended to ask her sister to keep the puppies for a week or so. She would ask her mother to bring the kids to the lake house tomorrow.

Chapter Fifteen

———

Mae December

Mae took the Tater outside, with Matthew close behind. She set the puppy down in the soft grass. The Tater sniffed around and then wagged over to Matthew. He started to pick her up.

"Leave her on the ground, please," Mae said. "She needs a potty break."

Matthew sat down, and the Tater claimed his lap. "I don't think she needs to go potty, Miss Mae," he pointed out. "She just wants to play."

Mae sighed. "Maybe if you stand up, I can persuade her. Then we can go check on your mommy, okay?"

He nodded and stood back up.

"Hurry up." Mae commanded. The Tater looked at her alertly and took care of business. After lavish praise, Mae handed Matthew the dog treat. "Tell her how good she is and then give her the treat."

"Good Tatie." The puppy took the treat from Matthew's

chubby little hand. He looked up at Mae, his blue eyes bright. "Can I see my room now?"

"Sure thing, sweetheart. Let's go get your mom. That way you and she can both see where you'll be sleeping."

She picked up the Tater in one hand, held Matthew's hand with the other, and went back inside. *Seriously, what's taking Ben so long?*

"Katie," she called out. "Want to come see Matthew's room?"

"Yes, please," Katie's voice came from the kitchen. She joined them in the front hall. Matthew wiggled his hand out of Mae's grasp and picked up his backpack from the bottom step. Then he went to stand beside his mother.

"It's up here," Mae told them. Katie picked up Matthew's suitcase, and she and her son started to follow Mae upstairs. Mae heard a car in the driveway and paused. It had to be Ben. Finally.

"You two go ahead. It's the second door on the right. I'll join you in a minute." When Mae opened the back door, Ben's truck wasn't in her driveway. Nor was there a squad car. Instead she was confronted by the sight of July's Suburban. Her sister was coming up the steps with two porgi puppies, one black and one red. The pups were leashed, and July was carrying dog beds and a bag of kibble. Mae took a deep breath.

"Hey, July. What's up?"

Her sister's eyes were red and the skin of her neck was blotchy.

"Can we come in?" She looked at the Tater, still in Mae's hand. "Oh, I forgot about your new puppy."

Mae opened the door all the way and relieved her older sister of the two dog beds. "This is the Tater. Let me help you."

She pushed Matthew's car seat out of the way. Carrying the dog beds under one arm and the Tater wriggling in the other, Mae walked into the kitchen. Popping the Tater into her crate, she asked her sister, "Should I put these two in the laundry room with the other dogs?"

"Yes, please." July was avoiding her eyes. "I was hoping you could keep them for me for a week or so."

Or so? Could this day get any better?

July followed her into the laundry room with Soot and Ricky. The puppies jumped happily on Tallulah, their mother, who was napping in her bed beside the utility sink. Tallulah growled. Mae set the dog beds down on the other side of the room.

"Listen, July, this might not be the best time. Matthew and Katie are upstairs right now and I'm expecting Ben any minute. I've got the Tater to potty train and Matthew's here all weekend."

"I'm sorry, Mae," July said. Her face was tight. "I'm going to the lake house. I need a break from Fred." She was frowning. "If you can't keep them, I understand. I just don't have a fenced area for them at the lake. The man who was going to build it can't get to it until September. He's all covered up with work this summer." July leaned against the wall and began to cry.

"Its fine, July, don't worry. I can keep them." Mae looked at her sister with alarm. July hadn't cried in front of her in years. Now, for the second time in three days, her normally self-contained big sister was dissolving in tears. July put the bag of kibble on top of Mae's dryer, unhooked the leashes from her exuberant young porgis and turned to leave the room.

Ben appeared in the doorway with a quizzical look on his face. "Hey, July. Thought we said 'no backsies' when you took these two in the spring."

"Funny," July said. She did not sound amused. Two spots of color appeared on her cheeks. "You know what, Ben? I sure would have appreciated a heads-up on the fact that you were sending your people to trash my house today."

Mae stepped forward, hands on hips. She glared at her boyfriend, who was staring at her sister. "Hello, Ben. Your son and his mother are upstairs. And I would have appreciated some notice about you having July's house torn up, too."

Ben looked at Mae. His face began to flush. "You can't be serious—either of you. This is a murder investigation. I don't let suspects know that we're going to be showing up with a warrant. That gives them time to hide evidence! I'm not going to compromise an investigation that I'm already getting grief about for my involvement with *your* family."

Her sister stepped around Ben as if he wasn't even there and walked out. In the silence, Mae heard the slam of the door.

"Where's she going?" Ben asked.

"Is she really a suspect, Ben?"

"No," Ben admitted. "Her husband might be, though. July's certainly a witness. She shouldn't be leaving town."

"She's not going very far. You'll be able to get ahold of her if anything comes up. She's just going up to their cabin on the lake."

Katie and Matthew appeared in the laundry room doorway. "Hi, Daddy! Did you bring us more puppies?"

"Hi, sport. Miss Mae's sister just dropped her two off." Ben patted his son's head and looked at Katie. "Everything all set for him?"

Katie glanced from Mae to Ben. "Yes. Matty and I just put his things away upstairs. Would you mind putting his car seat into Mae's car? I really should go."

"No problem," Ben said.

Katie quickly walked over to Mae and gave her an unexpected hug. "Thanks for keeping him. Ben can give you my cell number." She bent to give her son a kiss and a lingering hug. "I love you, Matty. Be good. I'll see you in two days." Nodding at Ben and Mae, she left the room.

Matthew looked up at Mae. "Can I take the puppies up to my room?"

"Sure. The reddish one is Ricky, and Soot is the black one."

"C'mon, Wicky. C'mon, Soot!" He ran out, with the puppies close behind.

Ben laughed. "He sure won't be bored with three puppies to play with. Why did Katie hug you?"

"I'm not sure."

Ben reached out for her. "I'm the one who should be hugging you."

"Not now, Ben." She backed away. "I'm still upset over all of this with my sister. Could you put that car seat in for me before you go?"

"Am I dismissed? Don't be like that. My job's on the line here, you know? I was told to limit my investigation—basically, I've turned everything over to Wayne—because of our relationship and being close to your family. If I'd warned Fred or July before their house was searched I'd be in a lot of trouble. Plus, I've barely seen Matty, and I have a couple hours free."

Mae could feel herself softening. "Let's go check on him, then. I guess we can talk later."

Matthew, Soot, Ricky, and the Tater were all in a pile on the bed together by the time Ben and Mae got upstairs.

"I guess Matthew figured out the latch on the Tater's crate," Mae said. She grinned at Ben and walked over to the bed.

"Stop!" Ben cried. Something warm and wet squished between Mae's bare toes. She looked down at the puppy poop she was standing in and the three puddles that surrounded her. "Would you grab some paper towels out of the hall bathroom for me, please?" Ben nodded, biting his lip.

Matthew smiled up at her angelically from the pile of puppies. "They all know what hurry up means," he informed her. "I said 'Hurry up,' then they went potty. I said they were good doggies, and then we played on the bed."

Mae raised her eyes to heaven, counted to ten in her head, and looked back at Matthew. "Just take them outside next time before you say hurry up, okay?"

Chapter Sixteen

—

Sheriff Ben Bradley

"WILL YOU PLEASE stop pacing, Sheriff?" Dory asked. "It's like having a wild animal loose in my work area."

"I'm sorry," Ben said. "It's driving me crazy that I can't interview anyone." Ben's jaw ached from clenching his teeth. Being tied to the office wasn't the only thing that was driving him crazy. He was still upset that Mae was mad at him, although he'd been completely justified in having July's house searched yesterday without telling her. He strode back to his office and got busy on the computer. Accessing the Southeastern Tennessee State Library site, he pulled up the newspapers from fifteen years ago in January.

About a half hour later, with a headache from peering at scanned microfiche, he had it. A young man named Ryan Gentry, also a pre-law major, had fallen to his death from the Sigma Chi Fraternity House window on January 3, 1998.

He buzzed Dory.

"Hey, I just had an idea. Can you come back here?"

"On my way." She appeared in his doorway in seconds.

"Nobody told me I couldn't investigate the reason Tom Ferris disappeared." Ben smiled with satisfaction. "I can work on that while Wayne focuses on the Ferris murder."

"Pretty proud of yourself, thinking of that idea," Dory said, her lips twitching.

"Wayne and I both think the Ferris killing is tied to something that happened right before he disappeared. I found an article in the student newspaper about a suicide; the kid's name was Ryan Gentry. He jumped from the window of the Sigma Chi House to his death on January third, 1998. I want to talk with the detective who investigated that case. Can you use your contacts to find out who he was and get me a phone number?"

"No problem, boss," Dory said. Although Dory frustrated Ben periodically, she was a whiz at finding information he needed.

About an hour later, Dory buzzed Ben. "I have the information you wanted about the original investigating Detective," she said. "He's retired now, but his name is Patrick Devlin Pascoe, known as PD. I've got the address and phone number." She read off the information.

Ben called but there was no answer. He left a message about his hunch that the recent murder of Tom Ferris was linked to Ryan Gentry's death. The phone rang about twenty minutes later; it was Detective Pascoe. Ben asked if he remembered the case.

"How could I forget?" he said. "It was a bad one."

Every cop or detective had the types of cases that they couldn't get over. Often it was the young victims that haunted them. "Would you be willing to talk to me about the case?" Ben asked. When Detective Pascoe agreed, Ben made arrangements to drive out to his house later in the day.

"Do you have pictures? Crime scene stuff?"

"I've got the whole case file. Took it with me when I left.

Against the rules, but the Department knows where it is if they need it. I'll be waiting for you."

"I get the feeling you had doubts about it being suicide," Ben said.

"I sure did," the detective said. "I still do."

DETECTIVE PASCOE LIVED alone in a small cabin off a long graveled two-track, two hours east of Sheriff Bradley's office. Much of the mile-long driveway had eroded from rain. The sheriff's police cruiser hit each and every pothole. He could feel the springs bouncing. When he drove up to the little place, Ben was reminded of the cabin that had been his grandfather's and where he spent many happy days as a kid.

Detective Pascoe opened the door to let the sheriff in before he knocked. The old man was in his early seventies and pale, but he still looked strong.

"Wondered if you would show up," The detective said gruffly, standing in the open doorway.

"Took me a while to get here from Rosedale. I'm Sheriff Bradley. Call me Ben."

He held out his hand and the old man took it in a bone-crushing grip.

"I'm PD. Come in, I have some coffee on. How do you take it?"

"Black," Ben said. He walked inside the large open kitchen and saw a small table covered in papers and photos. "Is that the file?" he asked.

"Yes. I was taking another look. I made you a copy." He handed Ben a neatly stacked pile of papers clipped together.

"Treat this confidentially," PD said.

"Of course. Thanks for doing all this."

"Sit down." He handed Ben a mug.

"So you didn't think Ryan Gentry committed suicide? Any evidence?" Ben asked.

"Pretty thin, but I knew. Something hinky with the case from the get-go. The family was wealthy. The kid had some trouble with drugs that the father covered up. It happened four years before he died. When he got picked up for the drug offense, he was only sixteen. Dad sent the kid to military school until he was eighteen and could start college."

"Was he dealing dope?"

"It was pills. Oxycodone had just come on the market. Sometimes kids shared them with their friends. I never heard about any money changing hands."

"Did the pathologist find any in his system?"

"That's just one of the things that was off in this case. The family refused an autopsy. The old pathologist, Doctor Lewis, wouldn't push for it. I tried talking with Gentry's mother and his older sister. They were willing, but the father was completely opposed. He said he had religious scruples." The old man snorted. "That man hadn't seen the inside of a church since he was christened."

"Was there a suicide note?"

"No note. College kids were just getting computers in those days and we checked Ryan's. There wasn't a printer in the room and nothing was on the screen." He took a deep breath and looked out toward the sun-dappled woods, clearly discouraged.

"The pathologist saw the body and wrote a report, I assume?"

"He did. Three lines. I can still quote the report. 'Body of a young white male. Died from consequences of a fall from upstairs window. Bruises around his waist.'" Detective Pascoe made a disgusted sound.

"What did you make of that?" Ben asked.

"I thought Ryan Gentry was looking out the window and somebody came up from behind him and heaved him out. The screen was underneath his body." PD shook his head. "I've never seen anyone kill themselves by jumping through a window screen."

"Who did you suspect?"

"Well, I talked with his roommate, Tom Ferris, but I

dismissed him as a suspect right away. He'd just gotten back from Christmas break, and he said he didn't believe Ryan would kill himself. There was something odd about his demeanor, though. He seemed frightened of something or someone."

"Was there bad blood between Tom Ferris and Ryan Gentry?"

"No, the opposite. Ferris was almost in tears, all shaken up. The Gentry kid's father was friends with the police chief and I got a not-so-gentle warning to back off. I tried for another couple of weeks. I talked to the housekeeper—her name was Nellie Franz—and later the housemother, a Mrs. Trula Godfrey. She was the person who told Tom Ferris about Ryan's death. She moved his room that day. Didn't want him looking out the window at all the police activity, she said. Both women's addresses are in the case file."

"What did the housemother say about the suicide?"

"She was totally confused by it. She told me Ryan was a nice kid, good grades, plenty of friends. She never had a clue he was depressed."

"What about the housekeeper?"

"She just kept going on about her bucket being moved. She said she'd been mopping the hall when it all went down. She ran downstairs to see what happened. When she came back upstairs, the bucket was in a different place."

"What'd you think about that?"

"I assumed there'd been a struggle and somebody tried to clean up. We didn't have Luminol with us. And by the time I got around to talking to the housekeeper, she had dumped her pail out. No chance to test it for blood."

The men sat quietly, sipping their coffees. It had clouded over and there was distant thunder. A few minutes later rain pelted against the windows, looking like tears as it ran down the panes.

"Did you know Tom Ferris left town right around then and hadn't been back for fifteen years?" Pascoe nodded. "When he returned he visited his parent's old house, where he was killed—shot in the back."

PD looked into Ben's eyes. "I read about his death in the paper. If you hadn't called me I was going to try to reach you. There has to be a connection."

"Why did you think Ferris left town?" Ben asked.

"I think he saw something incriminating. Someone must have warned him off and he got the hell out of Dodge."

"Sounds about right," Ben said. "Any idea who?"

Detective Pascoe handed Ben a list of the names of the thirty-five college men living in the Fraternity. "One of these guys is a murderer," he rasped out.

"And now he's struck again," Ben said. "Ferris' murder was done to silence him."

"Yup," Pascoe said. "Hope you can find a connection between the guys on this list and the people in the house when Tom Ferris died."

"That's my intention," Ben said. "You've been very helpful. Thanks for all this."

"I want to be there when you get him," Detective Pascoe said. "I could die a happy man if you solve it. I haven't got long." He ran a jerky hand through his hair. He had a distant, empty stare.

"Are you sick, Detective?"

"Prostate cancer. I'll be dead before the year is over."

"Sorry to hear that, sir."

PD nodded his head. "Just get this solved."

Driving back down the twisting washboard driveway, Ben felt something starting to give in this case. They had dismissed the Powells as suspects. There was no gun in July and Fred's house and no blood or gunshot residue had been found on any of Fred Powell's clothing. Fred's semi-automatic had been locked in the shooting club when Ferris was killed. The lab was processing the materials, but it looked like he was in the clear.

Miranda Stackhouse had also been eliminated as a suspect

almost immediately. She was on her way to dinner with her husband and friends when Ferris was shot. Wayne had talked with George Stackhouse, thinking he might have resented his wife pouring out thousands of dollars in a fruitless search to find Tom Ferris and get him to sign over the house. However, the man was completely under the thumb of his wife, Miranda. Plus he still felt guilty that her inheritance had paid to start up his business. He figured he owed his wife, and if private detectives made her happy, he was content to pay for them. Both Miranda and her husband had been crossed off the list.

His remaining suspect, Bethany Cooper, had been in the Booth Showhouse the day before Tom Ferris was killed and again on the day of his murder. They still didn't know why, but Wayne was pushing on her hard. She would crack soon and tell them the reason she was there, but neither he nor Wayne felt she was a likely killer. They still had to talk with her husband, Dan.

Thanks to Detective Pascoe, Ben now had a new direction. Somebody in that fraternity fifteen years ago was connected to someone in the Booth Showhouse. Maybe the man was married to one of the designers. A tiny hunter's grin lifted one corner of Ben's mouth. He was getting closer. It would be a distinct pleasure to inform Captain Paula of their "solve."

Now if he could only get back into Mae's good graces. He dialed her number and left a long message. After he'd helped her clean up the puppy messes, they hadn't discussed the search of her sister's home. She'd been very short with him all evening, so after Matthew was in bed, Ben went home. Mae wouldn't give him a good-bye kiss and she hadn't answered his calls today. Hopefully she and Matty were having fun, he thought, and headed back toward the office. He wanted to be there for the second interview with Bethany Cooper.

Chapter Seventeen

——

July Powell

AFTER CLEANING THE lake house and starting a load of laundry, July called her mother.

"Hi, sweetheart." Suzanne's warm voice flooded her daughter with remorse.

"I'm sorry, Mom. I should have called you earlier. How's Livy doing today?"

"She's good. How are you?"

July closed her eyes. "I've been better. Could you do me a favor?"

"Of course. What do you need?"

"I'm out at the lake house. Can you pick Nate and Parker up from the Beckwith's and bring them out here with Livy? I'd need you to go by my place and pack some clothes for them, too. My housekeeper, JoBeth, is there cleaning this morning. I assume Fred's at work."

"No problem. I'll go get their things together now. Can you call and let Carol Ann know I'm coming?"

"Thank you so much, Mama. I'll call her as soon as I'm off the phone."

"Hang in there, sweetheart. See you in a couple hours."

SUZANNE PULLED INTO the lake house driveway just after lunch. July watched from the kitchen window as her lanky, dark-haired twins exited the car, followed by their six-year-old blonde sister. Nate and Parker had turned nine in June. Lately they both seemed to grow an inch a week. The two boys jostled each other and ignored their little sister, as usual.

"Where're the dogs?" Nate called out.

"Where's Dad?" Parker asked, in an even louder voice.

Olivia and her grandmother walked in, each carrying a suitcase. "I'm helping, Mommy," Olivia announced.

"Hi Livy, I can see that." July smiled at her youngest. "Boys, go get the rest of the bags out of Zana's trunk please." She turned to her mother. "Any problems?"

"Of course not. Your housekeeper was very helpful. She said the place was a disaster when she got there this morning, though." Suzanne raised her eyebrows and looked questioningly at her oldest daughter. "Anything I need to know?"

July nodded. She cringed inside but knew she couldn't keep her mother in the dark. "Let me get the kids settled in. Do you have to go back right away?"

"I turned my column in yesterday. Your father's on a fishing trip, and I asked my neighbor's teenage daughter to take care of my dogs this afternoon. I can stay as long as you want."

The boys came back in with the rest of the bags. There was a loud crack of thunder and then a sudden summer downpour. Rain blew in through the half-open door.

"Close that, Parker. Please take your stuff to your bedrooms. I'll start a movie for you downstairs, okay?"

"Okay, but where are Daddy and the dogs?" Nate looked confused. He bit his lower lip.

"Your dogs are at Aunt Mae's, and your father's at the office, sweetie. I thought we'd come out here for one last time before school starts, that's all." Three pairs of eyes, the twins' dark and Olivia's light blue, regarded her with confusion.

Suzanne shooed them away. "Go on—all of you," she said with a smile. "I'll make you some popcorn."

AFTER HER THREE kids were settled in front of the basement television with popcorn and juice boxes, July looked around the room. She was glad they'd left the lake house as it was when they bought it—aside from some fresh paint and new carpet for the basement. The basement was a walkout, and through the rain she could see their dock and a little bit of the cove.

In contrast to their palatial house in town, the lake house was small and rustic, with the only TV in the basement. There were no videogames here, so the focus was on outdoor activities. The kitchen was original to the forty-year-old house, and there were only two bathrooms, as compared to six in their Rosedale house. July always found it restful at the lake.

She walked back up the narrow, pine-paneled staircase to her waiting mother. "Let's go sit on the porch and watch the storm. I need to talk to you."

Suzanne grabbed a bottle of white wine out of the refrigerator and opened it. Filling two generous glasses, she handed one to July. "It's a bit early in the day, I know, but you look like you could use a drink. I'm right behind you."

It was cooler on the screened porch. The pouring rain had already lowered the temperature to a much more comfortable level. It was still coming down at a steady clip. July sat on the old glider and cleared her throat. She took a long swallow of her wine and looked at her mother. It was like looking into a mirror and seeing herself in the future. Like July, Suzanne had dark eyes and smooth, dark hair. Suzanne's was cut shorter and just starting to show gray at the temples.

"What's wrong, July?"

"I don't know where to start."

"Are you and Fred having problems?"

"Yes, but that's not the reason I wanted you to come out here."

"Is it about Tommy?" Suzanne looked intently at her daughter. Then, in one of her characteristic flashes of intuition, she asked, "Did he say anything to you before he died, honey?" July didn't answer. "You can tell me if he did. I won't tell anyone, you know."

July sucked in her breath. "He said he was sorry and that he'd written me a letter."

"Did you ever get a letter from him?"

"No, I never did. Mama, you know I thought we were going to get married. We slept together, right before we both went back to school. And I never saw him again," tears sprang to her eyes, "until I found him dying on the floor."

Her mother was looking at her with such pity in her eyes.

It was hard enough to tell her that we slept together. I can't stop now. "I hadn't heard from Tommy in almost six weeks when I found out I was pregnant. His parents had died. I had no way to get in touch with him. He'd disappeared. I didn't know what to do. I waited a few more weeks, and then I started bleeding. One of my friends took me to a doctor, and he said I'd lost the baby."

July's mother came over and sat next to her daughter. Putting her arms around her, she said, "We always wondered what happened, July. You were so thin and pale when you came home that spring. You never wanted to talk about Tommy, and we didn't want to force the issue. We thought you were still grieving over him disappearing. You wouldn't go back to Ole Miss in the fall, and you were just so quiet until you met Fred."

"And now Fred's a suspect in Tommy's murder," July blurted out. "Our house was trashed by people Ben sent from the sheriff's department. They had a warrant. They were looking for blood stains on Fred's clothing."

"Oh my God! That's why it was such a disaster when your housekeeper got there."

July nodded. "When Fred got home last night we had a huge fight, and I left and came out here." Her mother released her, and July leaned back into the faded cushions with a green ivy design. They were both in tears.

"Oh, Mama, what do you think I should do?"

"Do you believe Fred could be involved in Tommy's murder?"

"No, but he's been acting strange for a while. I caught him going through my email a few weeks ago, and he keeps asking me questions. It's like he doesn't trust me anymore." July sniffled. "I'm going to get a box of tissues."

When July came back to the porch her mother hadn't moved. She was staring out the window at the sheets of rain streaming down, her glass of wine untouched on the table in front of her. July set the tissue box down in front of her mother, picked up her own glass and took another gulp, without really tasting it.

"How long will you stay here, July?"

"The kids' school doesn't start until the sixteenth, so we can stay at least a week, maybe a little longer."

"What about Fred?"

July frowned. "I'm here to get a break from Fred. He knows that."

Suzanne tilted her head. "Do the kids need a break from him too?"

"Of course not, but he's at work every day. Now that I'm done with the project at the Booth Mansion, I don't have another design job until after Labor Day." She was silenced by a vehement head shake from her mother.

"I don't think it's fair to your husband not to give him a chance to work things out with you or see his children. You need to remember how you felt when Tommy disappeared. Is that how you want Fred to feel?"

July stared at her mother in shocked disbelief. "You can't possibly compare the two situations, Mama. I still don't know why Tommy left, or where he went. Fred knows perfectly well why I came out here, and I told him where I was going."

"All right," Suzanne held her hands up. "Just tell me you'll call him soon and give him a chance to explain himself."

July sighed. "I'll think about it. That's really all I can promise right now."

Chapter Eighteen

——

Detective Wayne Nichols

Dory buzzed Detective Nichols' intercom.

"Detective, Dan Cooper is here to talk to you."

"On my way," he said. He opened his office door to take a look at the man walking down the hall toward him. Dan Cooper was slender and wore his light brown hair in a military cut. He was dressed in a suit and tie, looking every inch the executive.

"My wife, Bethany, said you wanted to talk to me," he said. Wayne thought his manner verged on belligerence.

"Yes. I did. Thank you for coming in, Mr. Cooper. Let's go into the conference room. Would you like a coffee?" Wayne flipped on the audio system.

Dan Cooper shook his head.

"Please be seated. As you know, Mr. Cooper, we're investigating Tom Ferris' murder three days ago. Ferris left this town fifteen years ago and came back on August first. He visited his parents' old home and was shot to death in the house on August second. Your wife was apparently the only person who knew Ferris was returning to Rosedale. Do you know anything about that?"

His response was short. "She told me they were Facebook friends."

"Had they known each other from Rosedale before he left?" Wayne was feeling his way.

"I don't know," Dan said. Again the detective found his responses curt to the point of rudeness.

"We consider your wife a suspect in his murder."

Dan frowned, but waved a hand, seeming to totally dismiss the detective's suspicions.

Wayne smacked his hands down on the table hard. "Are you listening to me, Mr. Cooper?"

"Suspecting my wife is ridiculous." Dan Cooper's face flushed. "Bethany wouldn't kill anybody. You're way off, Detective."

"Where were you between five and six p.m. on August second?"

"I was at work. I'm in charge of Quality Control for Pharma. It's in Murfreesboro. There are ten people who can vouch for my whereabouts."

"We'll need to check that out, Mr. Cooper. Wait here. I'll place a call."

Wayne walked out to the front office and asked Dory to check Cooper's alibi.

Returning to the conference room, Wayne said, "Your wife says you have a gun."

"I do. It's registered. I keep it under lock and key in a cabinet in my home office."

"We'll want to see that gun." They continued talking for a few more minutes until Dory knocked on the door and Wayne said, "Come in."

"Alibi checks," Dory said quietly.

"Mr. Cooper, I'm going to have a deputy escort you to your house and pick up your gun."

Dan Cooper looked irritated, but nodded.

An hour later, Wayne got a call from Deputy Rob Fuller. He had obtained the Cooper gun and dropped it off with Emma Peters, their CSI Tech in the lab, who had said it didn't smell as if it had been fired recently.

"Thanks for the update, Rob. Mrs. Bethany Cooper is coming in again shortly. I'd like you here for that."

Wayne walked down to Ben's office. He had just gotten back from his road trip to see the old detective who had been lead on the Gentry case. They discussed the upcoming interview with Bethany Cooper and agreed that Wayne and Rob Fuller should be the ones to question her. Ben, Dory, and George would watch through the one-way view mirror. They could see and hear the conversation, but Bethany could not see them.

Ten minutes later Dory buzzed Wayne to say she was bringing Bethany Cooper to the conference room. Both Detective Wayne Nichols and Deputy Rob Fuller were waiting when she came in.

"Thank you for coming back in, Mrs. Cooper," Deputy Fuller said cordially. He pushed the button to turn on the audio equipment. "We'll be taping this interview," he said. "Would you care for coffee or water?"

"No thank you," Bethany said quietly. She wore her hair in a ponytail today. It was still very hot outside and she had chosen to wear a brightly patterned red and blue sundress and sandals. She looked pretty and innocent.

"Detective Nichols and Deputy Fuller interviewing Bethany Cooper, August fifth," Wayne said for the recording. "I want to show you something, Bethany. It's a video from the closed circuit television cameras at the Booth Showhouse the day Tom Ferris was murdered. Before I start the tape, I want you to know that we're treating his death as a felony murder. That carries an automatic life sentence in Tennessee." Wayne's voice was deep with veiled threat. Bethany's eyes widened.

Deputy Fuller opened the laptop in front of him. He turned the screen so Bethany could see it and punched a button. The front door of the Booth Showhouse, gabled in climbing yellow roses, filled the screen. A woman dressed in a rain-jacket and jeans walked up to it. Looking around furtively, she pulled out a separate key, opened the door and walked in. The door closed behind her.

"That's you, isn't it? Please note the time, Mrs. Cooper," the deputy said, pointing out a strip at the bottom of the screen where the time showed. It was 5:29 p.m. "Where did you get the key to the house?"

"It was my mother's." Bethany jammed her hands into her armpits. Her lips and chin were trembling. Her face looked stricken as she turned toward Detective Nichols.

"You lied to me, Mrs. Cooper," the detective said, looking at her intently. "You were in the Booth Showhouse from 5:29 until you left at 6:03. That encompasses the time in which Mr. Ferris was shot dead. Why did you kill him?"

"I didn't kill him. I didn't," she said. "I know it looks bad."

"Where's the gun?" The detective's eyes penetrated hers. The tape continued to play, showing only the closed door and the windblown climbing roses as the minutes ticked by.

"Honestly, Detective. I didn't kill him. My husband has a gun, but I don't even know how to use it. You have to believe me." Her voice was high and pleading.

"Bethany, we know you've been in the house several times recently. What were you doing there?" The detective's voice sounded like he was deliberately controlling his anger. "And don't tell me you were finishing the space. You made several visits long after your space was completed. Mrs. Stackhouse said you signed off on your space over a week before."

Bethany Cooper took a deep breath. "I'm sorry I lied to you, Detective."

"What happened? If Tom Ferris attacked you and you defended yourself or if his death was an accident, that would reduce the amount of time you serve in prison."

"What? No. I didn't kill him. I was in the house, you're right, but I didn't kill Tommy. I wouldn't. He was my stepbrother."

Wayne sat back in his chair. *Didn't see that coming.* He glanced at Rob, who looked equally stunned.

"Tell me," he said gently. His placed his big palms down on the table.

Bethany straightened her shoulders and inhaled deeply. "Wade Rawlins, Miranda's father, is also my father. I'm Miranda's half-sister and Tommy's stepsister. My mother and Wade Rawlins had an affair." She looked away, coloring. "I never knew until I turned thirteen. Mother told me then that Wade Rawlins had fathered me. I was disgusted with her, with both of them." Bethany's lips curled down.

"I see," the detective said. "So what were you searching for in that house? Proof of paternity?"

"Yes, exactly. My mother listed my father as 'unknown' on my birth certificate. She did it at Wade's request. She said he later signed a Declaration of Paternity but never gave her the document. He told her it was in the house. I know he gave her money for my support. Probably money for groceries from time to time. He paid for me to have dancing lessons. Unfortunately, his support was always in cash, so there was no trace. My mother thought Wade would marry her when Irene died. It broke her heart when he married Joanna Ferris."

"Did Tom Ferris know about you being Rawlins' daughter?

"Yes, I finally found Tommy on Facebook and gave him my email. This was several months ago. I told him I was his stepsister. Miranda Stackhouse inherited almost a million dollars from the estate. I should have gotten something. I told Tommy he should sign the house over to me."

"Did he refuse? Is that what made you angry enough to kill him? "

"I didn't kill Tommy. You have to believe me, Detective." Bethany's face was full of anguish, and her eyes were overly bright.

Detective Nichols never took his eyes from hers as he said,

"Bethany Cooper, you had the opportunity to kill Ferris. You were in the house at the time of his murder. You had a motive—his unwillingness to recognize you as a family member or sign over the house. That must have made you furious. Finally, you had the means. Ferris was killed with a Smith and Wesson pistol like your husband's."

Bethany's eyes were wide with terror. "No," she whispered, "no." She raised her hands to her face. Her cheeks were ashen.

"Bethany Anne Cooper, you are under arrest for the murder of Thomas John Ferris. Anything you say can be written down and used as evidence against you in a court of law. You have the right to an attorney. If you cannot afford one, one will be provided for you." The words rolled off his tongue, sonorous and damning.

Bethany Cooper started to cry as Deputy Fuller stood up and asked her to stand.

"I need to put the cuffs on you, Mrs. Cooper," he said.

"Please stop," she begged. "Please, Detective. I didn't tell you everything."

Wayne motioned to Rob, and they sat down again. For a moment, she seemed unable to speak. The deputy handed her a glass of water and she gulped it; her knuckles were white.

"When I found out that I was Miranda's half-sister, I wanted desperately to be a part of their family. My mother and I were just barely getting by. We lived in a small, grimy apartment. Mom worked so hard just to pay for my clothes, so I wouldn't feel like the poor kid. She held Wade Rawlins responsible for our poverty. My life was so different from Miranda and Tommy's. Whenever I saw them riding their bikes together, or walking in the park, I only wanted them to acknowledge me." Bethany began to cry.

"So it wasn't about the money then?" The big detective frowned. "What did you want, Bethany?"

"I just wanted to be part of their family. I wanted holidays and birthdays and I wanted to have a little brother. I wanted to play hide-and-go-seek with Tommy. I wanted to go clothes shopping with Miranda. So I went to see her and told her I was her sister."

Detective Nichols felt his whole body start to unclench. He remembered that day, so long ago, that he had left his foster family. A face flashed in front of him—the face of his small foster-brother, begging him to stay. He knew about wanting a family, wanting a little brother.

"When was this?"

"Around the time I got my assigned space for the Booth Mansion project. I showed up on Miranda's doorstep and asked if I could come in. She took me into the kitchen and offered me a cup of coffee. When I told her Wade Rawlins was my father, she called me a money-hungry bitch. She said her father would never have had a relationship with a woman like my mother. She called my mother a whore. It was just awful." Harsh sobs shook Bethany's entire body.

"There's a way we could prove you're Wade's child," Deputy Fuller jumped in, excitedly. "If we got a cheek swab from you and from Miranda, we could find out if you have the same father."

Wayne gave the young deputy such a fierce look that he sat back as if he had been struck.

"I already thought of that," Bethany said, swiping the tears from her cheeks. "I asked Miranda about it. I thought she would want to be certain, but she said she would never take a DNA test. It was terribly awkward working with her after that."

"Wait here a moment, Mrs. Cooper," Detective Nichols said. Rising to his feet, he left the room.

Once outside he said flatly, "I don't think she did it." The sheriff, Deputy Phelps, and Dory waited for him to continue. "All that the woman wanted was a family—a sister and a little brother. Obviously, we'll wait for the tests on her husband's gun, but she didn't shoot Tom Ferris in the back. I'd stake my reputation on it."

"I agree," Ben said, "pending the lab's report, of course."

Detective Nichols walked back into the conference room and told Bethany Cooper she was free to go. Mentally, he crossed her off his list. Unless something turned up on Dan Cooper's gun or on Fred Powell, they had reached a dead end in the Ferris case. He shook his head at the sharp pang of memory, wishing he'd taken his little brother with him on that fateful morning he had left their foster home.

Chapter Nineteen

—

Sheriff Ben Bradley

B Y THE TIME the sheriff arrived at his office the following morning he was already exhausted. His air conditioning had conked out the night before. He had hardly slept, what with the heat and obsessing over the quarrel with Mae and sifting through what they had learned so far about the Ferris murder. He started the coffee machine and stood beside it, taking in the delicious scent of the first cup of the day.

The front door opened and Dory walked in.

"Good Morning, Dory."

"Good morning, Sheriff," Dory was fresh as a daisy. Apparently her air conditioner was working just fine.

"I got a list of the men who lived at Sigma Chi from Detective Pascoe. We need to start working through it."

He and Dory discussed how to obtain the phone numbers, and she offered to call the University Alumni Office and get current contact information. She said it might take a few days.

"We don't have a few days. Go ahead and request that

information, Dory, but while we're waiting, I'd like the deputies to see what they can find."

As soon as Deputy Phelps and Deputy Fuller arrived, Sheriff Bradley handed them the lists and said, "Once you have a phone number, I want you to make contact with the person and ask where he was on August second."

"Can't we just eliminate the ones who don't live in Tennessee?" Deputy George Phelps asked. *Where's that "no whining" button? I'd like to glue it to George's forehead.*

"No, George. I want to be sure. Get started and remember that you could be talking to a murderer. If you find someone who makes you uneasy or curious, jot down the name. People travel and it could even be someone from out of state. Whoever killed him wanted Tom Ferris dead very badly. He could easily have flown in to pursue him."

Ben returned to his office. A few minutes later Dory stuck her head in.

"You'll be happy to hear that Tom Ferris' attorney is coming in this morning. She called yesterday to see if you'd be available."

Half an hour later Ben was looking out his office window when he saw a slim black woman walk toward the door to the station. She looked to be in her late forties, but like many women of color, her face was unlined. She wore a tan linen suit and high heels. The suit jacket was unbuttoned and beneath it she wore a silky blouse in a café au lait color. She wore dangling amber earrings. Despite the heat she looked cool and fresh. He opened the door from his office to the waiting room and was about to walk out to greet her when he got a text. He stopped to read it. It wasn't from Mae, as he had hoped, but from Wayne, saying they were processing the materials from July and Fred's house but coming up empty.

"Good morning. Are you Ms. Bontemps?" Ben heard Dory ask.

"Please call me Evangeline," he heard the woman reply. "You must be Dory Clarkson. I've heard a lot about you."

"I'm not going to ask what you've heard. It's probably all lies anyway," Dory chuckled. "So is Bontemps your married name?"

"I'm married, but I didn't take his name. Hate to give a man that much power. Besides, Bontemps means good times. My parents were from New Orleans and we sure had lots of good times when I was a kid."

"I'll show you into the conference room," Dory said. "Let's get some coffee. I sent our detective out for donuts. You're welcome to have some with your coffee when he gets back."

Ben trailed after the two women. As they neared the conference room, Evangeline looked over her shoulder at him. Still talking to Dory she said, "I like a woman who can boss around an armed man." She grinned, showing a beautiful smile.

Dory ushered Miss Bontemps into the room and flicked on the light. She acknowledged Ben with a tiny nod.

"By chance do you like blueberry donuts, Miss Evangeline?"

"Why, yes I do. They're my absolute favorite."

Ben cleared his throat. "I'm Sheriff Bradley." He held his hand out. "Thank you for coming in today, Ms. Bontemps. It's good to meet you."

"It's good to meet you too, Sheriff."

"Please have a seat," Dory said, as Wayne walked in. He held the donut box out like a peace offering.

"Extra blueberry donuts, as requested." He set them on the conference table. Dory favored him with a gracious smile.

"Evangeline, I'd like to introduce you to Wayne Nichols, our chief detective. Wayne, this is Ms. Bontemps, Tom Ferris' attorney."

"Ma'am." Wayne nodded his head. He looked at Ben. "I've got some things to do, boss. I'll be back in an hour or so."

Dory opened the box of donuts and bustled around with plates and coffee cups as long as she could, but Ben finally prevailed and evicted his office manager.

Sitting across from Evangeline Bontemps at the conference table, he said, "I understand you were Tom Ferris' attorney."

"Yes, I was. I read about his death in the paper. He was a nice young man. I was the attorney for his parents too—Joanna Ferris and Wade Rawlings. The accident that caused their deaths was a tragedy. As it happened, I saw Tom Ferris on the day he died."

"Did he have an appointment?"

"Yes, he called last week, told my secretary that he was returning to Rosedale and requested an appointment. I met with him at ten a.m. on August second for a little over an hour."

"What was the reason for the appointment?"

"He wanted to clear up a few things that still remained from his parent's estate, but when he came in, he seemed off-kilter. He was pale, but I assumed that was due to his illness. He jumped from topic to topic, as if he was distracted. I had a hard time even getting him to sit down and tell me what he came to see me about."

"So you knew he had cancer, Ms. Bontemps?"

"Please call me Evangeline, Sheriff." She tilted her head, smiling.

Oh, she's good. Not answering my question, though. "Then I insist you call me Ben. How long was he ill, do you know?"

"He had lymphoma for at least eleven years." She looked down at the table and cleared her throat. "He came to see me right after he was diagnosed. It was really sad. He was so young, and he'd already been through so much. He wouldn't let me tell Miranda he was in town, or that he was sick. He needed money for his treatment, so I suggested he sell the Booth Mansion, but he refused."

"Why wouldn't he sell?" Ben asked. "He wasn't going to live there."

Evangeline nodded. "You're right, he wasn't. He wanted to keep it in the family, so he asked me to find a lease-management company and rent the house. I have his power of attorney, so the lease-management firm has sent me the rental income every month, minus expenses, and I've put the money into Tom's account."

"Who rented the house, Evangeline?" The sheriff leaned forward in his chair.

"The Shacklefords, L.J. and his wife Nancy. They love the place, raised five kids there." She smiled, "It's a big house, as you know. L.J. and Nancy really wanted to buy it. They've got plenty of money, but Tom would never agree."

"So the Shacklefords moved out for the fundraiser?"

Evangeline gave her head a brisk shake. "No. They gave up after twelve years of renting and built their own house. That's when Miranda contacted me on behalf of the Junior League and asked if they could use the Booth Mansion for their 2013 fund-raiser."

"So you were the go-between, then, between Tom and Miranda?"

"Yes, I encouraged Tom to let them use the house for the event." She rolled her shoulders and leaned back in her chair.

Ben was confused. "Why? He wouldn't get any rental income, right? Did the Junior League pay him for the use of the house?"

"Not exactly, but they take ownership for a year and use their connections, get contractors to donate time or give them deals for all the repairs and upgrades to the house." She widened her eyes. "It's a big, old house. Very expensive to maintain. Once the contractors are finished with plumbing, electrical, etcetera, all the designers have three months to put on the finishing touches, and then people pay twenty-five dollars a ticket to tour it, so they raise a lot of money. Afterward, the house is in great shape." Evangeline glanced at her watch.

"I won't take much more of your time, but did you ever get to the business he wanted to deal with?"

"Yes. He said his doctors told him to get his affairs in order. He made his Last Will and Testament."

"Can you tell me about the will?"

"Not yet. Once it goes through probate, it'll be available."

"You aren't bound by confidentiality now, are you? Ferris is dead."

"There are a series of steps I'm required to complete before I can provide the will to probate court. The funeral takes precedence and we haven't had that yet. All heirs must be located and notified and I need to obtain a certified copy of the death certificate." She paused. "My policy is to respect the wishes of my client above all. Tom wanted me to wait until after the tours of the mansion were over before discussing the estate with his heirs. He was quite specific on that point." Evangeline's voice was gentle, but firm. "So, I'm sorry, Ben. You'll get it soon, but not yet."

"I wondered if there was something in the will that might provide a clue to his killer," he said. "If there is, you really need to tell me."

She pursed her lips. "I don't believe so. I would tell you if I had any inkling that the disposal of Tom Ferris' personal property had a bearing on the case. I just wanted you to know that he was on edge. Maybe he even saw his killer on his way in to my office. I sensed some fear, but he almost looked resigned, as if something he had expected for a long time was about to happen."

"That's interesting. What building is your office in?"

"It's that old two-story brick building at 3448 Main Street. I think it was built in 1890."

"Besides your office, what other businesses have offices there?"

"There's another law office—the Osbourne, Townsend, Phillips and Coniglio firm. There's also a commercial insurance agency and the Rosedale credit union."

"We'll definitely look into who Mr. Ferris may have encountered. One other thing. Miranda Booth Stackhouse, the judge's only granddaughter, didn't inherit her grandparents' house. Do you know why the house went to Tom Ferris, instead of to Miranda?"

"Yes, the transfer of ownership was legally complex. Wade and Joanna Rawlings were killed in a car accident. The money from the Booth family estate came to Miranda upon Wade's death, but the house wasn't included in the trust. Miranda's mother, Irene, left the house to her husband Wade, outright. Wade died instantly in the accident, but Joanna outlived Wade by several hours. Wade's will gave the house to Joanna. Because Joanna lived longer than Wade, she owned the house at that point. When she died, she left everything to her son, so Tom inherited the house from his mother. I understand Miranda didn't take it well."

"Apparently not," Ben said, deep in thought. "Thank you, Evangeline. Call me if you think of anything else that would shed some light on this."

"I certainly will." She stood up and gathered her purse and attaché case.

Ben showed her out of the conference room and watched her walk back into the reception area. She stopped by Dory's desk.

"Anytime you'd like to go to lunch or dinner, please give me a call," she said and handed Dory her business card.

Ben turned and went back into his office, where the murder board was posted. He wrote in "met with attorney" in the 10:00 a.m. time slot on August 2nd. Then he called his detective and told him what Ferris' attorney had said.

"Too bad she's hanging tight to the will," Wayne said. "I'd like to know if his assets enter into this."

"She and Dory really hit it off," Ben said. "Maybe Dory can get some more information out of her. I also wanted to tell you more about my meeting with Detective Pascoe. He was lead detective on the old Ryan Gentry case. He didn't buy the suicide story, thought it was murder. He had the case file with him and gave me a list of the names of the guys in the frat house. I've got George and Rob started on finding out if anyone from that list has any connection with the Booth Showhouse."

"Good work," Wayne said, and Ben didn't detect any sarcasm at all in his voice.

Chapter Twenty

———

Sheriff Ben Bradley

LATE THAT AFTERNOON the Sheriff walked out to Dory's desk. "I have something I want you to do," he told her.

Dory looked at him askance. "What do you want now, boss?"

"I want you to go to dinner with Evangeline Bontemps."

"Well, that's a pleasant change," she smiled. "If this is business, I should be reimbursed."

"Dory, Dory, Dory, this is your first time out as a snoop and already you're asking me for money," he said, shaking his head.

"So, what do you want me to pry out of Miss Evangeline?"

"Tom Ferris met with her to draft his Last Will and Testament. If we wait until it goes to probate, it'll be weeks. I want to know what's in that will and whether anyone else in her office might have read it. Better check to see if she has a legal secretary and if she types up the wills. Think you can get Evangeline to talk?"

"You already know the answer to that," she said and grinned. "Hand over the credit card, Sheriff."

Ben did so and went back to his office. Through his open

door he could hear Dory making dinner plans with Ms. Bontemps. He wondered how much money Tommy Ferris had in his estate and whether he had left the Booth Mansion to Miranda or possibly to Bethany Cooper. He wondered if either of those women had a connection to Evangeline Bontemps or someone who worked for her.

He picked up his phone and called his Chief Detective's cell. "What's up?" Wayne sounded distracted.

"I've been thinking about the mileage on Ferris' rental car. He drove about forty miles on the evening before he died. He could have gone to see Bethany, Miranda, or July that evening."

"We checked the women's alibis. Miranda Stackhouse and her husband were with friends. They didn't get back until past eleven o'clock. If Ferris drove to her house, they wouldn't have been home. July Powell would have been home with her kids all evening, and her husband was out of town. If Tommy showed up there, she would have been surprised, but she would have let him in. However, I doubt seeing Tom Ferris the night before he died would have turned July Powell into a killer. The materials from the Powell house are still in the lab, but it looks like both the Powells are in the clear."

"Did you call the lab and ask Hadley what he found?"

"Yes. No blood on any of July or Fred's clothes, except for that one spot on the blouse July was wearing when she found Ferris dying."

"Okay. What about Bethany? She admitted seeing Tom Ferris at the Booth Showhouse around five p.m. August first. I wonder if Ferris drove back to see her later that night. Did we ever check that?"

"I don't think we did," said Wayne. "I'll find out. Anything else?"

"Just boring old police work. I've got the deputies calling the list of the frat boys. Dory is arranging to go to dinner with Evangeline Bontemps. I've asked her to pry the contents of the will out of the lawyer."

"You do good work," Wayne said and rang off. Ben allowed himself a brief flare of satisfaction.

LATER, DEPUTY ROB Fuller knocked on Ben's half-open office door.

"Come on in, Rob."

"I found somebody," He sounded excited. "Allan Curtiss was in Sigma Chi in college. After he graduated he started a landscaping business. It's called Curtiss and Daughters. Al Curtiss and his daughter, Janie, did one of the outdoor areas on the Booth Showhouse project."

"Good job." Ben stood up and clapped the young deputy on the shoulder.

"Can I go talk to him, boss? I'm dying to get out of this office and do some real investigating."

I know just how he feels.

"Go ahead and pay a visit to Mr. Curtiss. See what he remembers about the suicide or murder of Ryan Gentry. See if he was in Rosedale or at the Booth Showhouse when Tom Ferris died."

Rob's face split in big grin. "Thanks, Sheriff."

TWO HOURS LATER, Deputy George Phelps and Dory both appeared at Ben's door.

"I think we got our guy," George said. The excitement was palpable in the demeanor of Ben's normally phlegmatic deputy. "His name is Henry Covington. He was in the Sigma Chi fraternity and he's an investigator for Osbourne, Townsend, Phillips and Coniglio—the law firm located in the same building where Ms. Bontemps has her office." George's eyes were practically dancing.

"I checked his record," Dory went on. "The man's got quite the sheet. He's been in for simple assault, aggravated assault, attempted murder and carrying without a permit. Here's the most interesting part: all the charges were dropped. The man's like butter. Nothing sticks."

"Terrific work, you two." Ben stood up, shook Deputy George's hand and patted Dory on her shoulder. "I wish there was a way to get more info on Covington without alerting him to our interest."

"I have an idea," Dory jumped in, even more animated than usual. "I know a little about Henry Covington. He used to date a woman I know. Her name's Randee Scofield. She's a biker chick, and before Henry got respectable, he rode with the bikers. She turned him in for a beating that put her in the hospital."

"Woman, you're amazing," Ben told her. "I'd like to interview Randee with you," he added wistfully, "but I know Captain Paula wouldn't approve." He had just emailed Captain Paula his report, telling her about going through the list of fraternity men. She had reminded him that until they had a suspect under arrest, he wasn't to interview anyone. Her prohibition was foremost on his mind.

"You just leave this to me, Sheriff. I have an idea of how to get the down and dirty on Mr. Henry Covington," Dory said.

BEN WALKED TO the conference room and surveyed the murder board. The top of the left hand column was labeled "Suspects," the wide middle column, "Time Line," and the column to the right, "Alibied Out".

Dory had originally put the names of July Powell, Fred Powell, Miranda Stackhouse, Bethany Cooper and Dan Cooper in the Suspects column. Since then, Dory had moved Miranda, July and Fred's names to the inactive column. Ben moved Bethany Cooper and her husband out of active consideration.

Then he picked up the grease marker and wrote Allan Curtiss and Henry Covington's names in the "Suspects" column. He felt a distinct sense of satisfaction. He looked at the time. It was 5:40.

Deputy George Phelps was busy hunting down the rest of the frat boys. Dory was downloading pictures and background on their new suspects. Detective Nichols would find out if Tom Ferris went to see Bethany Cooper the night before he died and if so, what transpired. Deputy Rob Fuller was checking on Al Curtiss, the head of the landscaping firm. Perhaps taking Mae and Matthew out for ice cream might just help get him back into Mae's good graces, he thought.

As he was leaving the office, he felt a little guilty about poor George Phelps still slaving away. He turned the knob of the door very quietly.

"Sheriff?" his deputy called.

"What?"

"You aren't leaving, are you?"

"I have an errand to do. I'll be back in an hour or so, unless something comes up." *Like Mae forgiving me and inviting me to stay over.* "Call me if you come up with anything. And when Rob gets back, have him start looking for Covington and Curtiss on the CCTV tapes. Dory left pictures of both those guys on her desk."

Deputy Phelps gave him the look of a martyred bloodhound.

Chapter Twenty-One

Detective Wayne Nichols

WAYNE NICHOLS HAD just opened his refrigerator door to pull out a cold beer when his cellphone rang. Dory's picture showed on the screen.

"Hey. What's up?"

"What's up is that you need to pick me up on your Harley in two hours. I'm meeting Evangeline for dinner and then you're taking me to a biker bar."

Wayne hesitated, wondering if this was work related. "Are you asking me out on a date, Miss Dory?"

"Nitwit." She sounded exasperated. "Not sure if Ben reached you earlier, but we found a man on the list named Henry Covington. He was in Sigma Chi fifteen years ago and he has a sheet. He was at the frat house when Ryan Gentry fell to his death and in town when Tom Ferris was killed. He's been arrested for assault, aggravated assault, attempted murder, and other sordid matters."

"Excellent. I know that guy. His nickname is the Hench. But what evidence, other than being in the right place at the right time, do we have?" Wayne sat down and took a long pull on his cold beer.

"None. That's what we're going to get tonight. I happen to know Henry Covington's old girlfriend, a biker chick named Randee. He beat her up until she'd had enough. She may know whether he was involved in the Ferris murder. So, come get me in about an hour. Wear leather."

Wayne sat back on his couch and finished his beer. He stripped off his work clothes and stepped into the shower. Once clean and dressed in faded jeans and a sleeveless T-shirt with a Harley emblem, he went out to his garage and took a look at his hog. He hadn't had time to ride her at all recently. Although dusty, she was a beauty—a newer model Road King Classic with twin cams. He'd named her Francine and had her customized with flames all along the gas tanks on both sides. He pulled into Dory's driveway an hour later, having given the beauteous Francine a thorough wash.

It was too hot for the full leather jacket, so he wore a tack button vest over his blue cotton T-shirt. Leather chaps with brass trim covered his blue jeans and black riding boots protected his feet. He'd grabbed his helmet and one for Dory.

Dory lived in a part of town with small, brightly colored houses. Hers was lavender with dark gray trim. The window flower boxes overflowed with purple petunias and lime-green foliage that cascaded down the siding. It was a trim one story cottage with a separate garage. Wayne was standing on the threshold, fist poised to knock when Dory opened the door.

She gave him an up and down look and he returned the favor, grinning. She wore the traditional ladies Drifter leather jacket, tight black leather pants and black gloves. Her boots came up above her knees. A brilliant shade of orangey red lipstick and earrings that fell practically to her shoulders completed the ensemble.

"Looking good, woman," Wayne said with a chuckle, "What bar are we going to?"

"It's called the Gilkey Lake Tavern, out of town about thirty miles east."

Wayne nodded and walked back toward his bike. He swung on. Dory followed suit and he turned to say, "Ready?"

After she fastened her helmet and nodded, they spun out of her driveway.

It was nearly dark when they arrived. The bar was a ramshackle wooden affair with a low porch that ran along the entire front of the building. The porch had a biker's railing and Wayne saw almost a dozen hogs. Music poured out as a couple came outside. The detective and Dory stepped on to the porch, nodded to the couple, and opened the door to the establishment. A live band was playing "Highway to Hell."

Taking a seat at the bar, they ordered two draft beers and clinked their glasses together. Dory laid her hand on Wayne's thigh and smiled seductively. He ignored her with some difficulty. She leaned forward and he put his head close to hear what she said over the music.

"See the chick with the long blonde hair sitting at the end of the bar?"

He nodded. The woman was too thin; the planes of her face angled sharply. She had a scar on her neck that looked like an old cigarette burn, and smaller scars around her left eye. Her hair was long and had been bleached so many times it looked like straw. She wore full leathers and was drinking shots with a big guy with a shaved head.

"That's Randee. Signal me when she gets up to go to the ladies.'"

Wayne nodded. The band took a break and a young girl walked up to the lead singer. She must have requested "Born to be Wild" because they started the next set with that number. The girl went out on the floor and began to dance alone to the music. Whoever was running the lights switched to a red spotlight. Her hair was long and spun out in a wide spiral as she danced.

Dory hit Wayne in the thigh, almost crotch high. He winced, frowned at her and directed his gaze quickly back at the blonde. A guy sitting next to them at the bar had been observing the interchange and laughed.

One more song and Randee Scofield got up, walking in the direction of the ladies'. After Wayne signaled Dory with his eyes, she rose and followed.

While Dory was gone, Wayne struck up a conversation with the guy on the next barstool. He was a slim black man, wearing a baseball cap and jeans. The letters on the cap read Tennessee Smokies, a good minor league team. There were a couple of other men in chinos and polo shirts. Clearly this was not exclusively a biker bar or everyone would have worn biker apparel.

"Is Henry around tonight?" Wayne asked.

"Covington? No, he cleared when Randee and Spike came in."

"Yeah," Wayne said, "I heard they were history. Supposedly, she turned him in to the cops."

"Against the code for a biker's woman to turn him in," the man said. "Surprised she's still around to talk about it. The only reason is that she's the mother of his son."

Wayne frowned. "It's that hard core around here?"

"Sometimes," the man said, drumming his fingers on the bar and bopping in time to the music.

Dory walked up behind Wayne and hooked her arm around his neck. "We're leaving," she said.

"I'm having another beer," Wayne responded, roughly throwing off Dory's arm. His nostrils flared.

Dory's eyes narrowed. Her pupils contracted. "You'll be having that beer in my bed," she said loudly, "or not at all."

The guy in the baseball cap laughed and said, "Baby, if your old man's not up for it, I'd be happy to ditch this place with you."

Wayne's chin jutted out and he reached for the man's upper

arm. He was breathing heavily. Dory put her hand on Wayne's wrist. She turned to the other man.

"Dial the testosterone down, gentlemen." Turning to the slim black man she said, "This one's enough trouble. You don't even look potty trained yet." Dory lifted an eloquent eyebrow.

"Let's go," Wayne said in a guttural voice.

They walked from the bar into the hot summer night, the sound of the band trailing behind them.

"Very convincing," Dory said.

Wayne nodded and mounted up. Dory put on her helmet and swung onto the bike behind him. They screamed out of the parking lot and down country roads. The moon came out from behind some streaky clouds. Dory tightened her arms around his waist. Wayne leaned into the corners and Dory gripped him with her thighs. The woman knew how to ride.

WHEN THEY GOT to Dory's house, she said, "Come on in."

Once they were inside, Wayne looked around. Dory's house was decorated with vintage furniture. Even her kitchen cupboards seemed to have come from an older house. She opened the fridge and pulled out two beers.

"So, which way to the bedroom?" Wayne asked, amused. "I thought I wasn't having any more beer unless it was in your bed." He looked down at her with a little quirk to his mouth.

"I do think you're fine, Wayne, but we both like our jobs too much to risk it. Besides," she said, putting one hand on her hip, "you couldn't handle a real woman like me. Do you want to hear what Miss Randee had to say?"

"Sure."

"She said Henry works for the Osbourne, Townsend, Phillips and Coniglio law practice, specifically for Greg Townsend."

"What the hell? Greg Townsend, the attorney? He's the guy who's up for Assistant Attorney General of the Criminal Division. Did Randee say what Henry does for Greg?"

"She says he does Greg's dirty work for him." Dory shrugged, pursing her lips in distaste. "That's why they call him Hench. He's Townsend's henchman. Plus, Townsend's office is in the building where Evangeline Bontemps has her office. She told the sheriff that Tom kept looking out into the parking lot like he was scared when he was meeting with her."

"You said Randee and Henry were an item once, right?"

"For almost ten years. She has a kid by him."

"Then, against the code, she turns him in for abuse. Was he found guilty for assault?"

"No. Randee says Henry never pays the price—not for any of his crimes."

"I'm sorry, Dory," Wayne frowned, "but I just don't see it. Greg Townsend's in law enforcement. He's a straight arrow. He's in line for the Attorney General's job. Sounds to me like Randee Scofield's still trying to make Henry pay for what he did to her."

Dory shook her head. "He should pay for what he did to Randee. But I have a feeling he's got a lot of things to answer for, and Greg Townsend does too."

Chapter Twenty-Two

—

Mae December

BEN STRETCHED LUXURIOUSLY in her bed, yawned and gave her a big smile. "Good morning, gorgeous girl."

"Sssshh. Good morning," Mae whispered. "Please get dressed, and don't wake Matthew."

"Oh, okay." He hopped out of bed and dressed quickly, while Mae enjoyed the view.

"Are you ogling me from your bed, Miss December?" He bent down and gave her a quick kiss. "That's not going to get me out of here any faster, you know."

"I know." She smiled up at him. "Why don't you go downstairs and let the dogs out. I'll be down in a minute."

"So I don't get to watch you get dressed? Not fair."

She giggled. "No. Please, before your mini-me wakes up, get out of here!"

"I'm going, I'm going." Ben looked back from her doorway. "I think he's already downstairs, though."

Mae closed her eyes, envisioning her kitchen at the mercy of an unsupervised four-year-old. She got out of bed, grabbed underwear, shorts, and a tank-top from the drawers of her antique dresser and scurried into her bathroom to dress. She heard a delighted squeal from Matthew downstairs. His father must be tossing him in the air already.

When she was decent, Mae went downstairs. Her house was empty of men, boys, dogs, and puppies. The back door stood partway open, so she poured herself a cup of coffee before peeking out. Matthew and Ben were standing with their backs to her, apparently taking a potty-break with the dogs.

When Mae and Ben first started dating, Mae had talked to her sister, July, about Matthew.

"Do you have any advice about little kids for me, Jules? I'm dating a single dad now."

"Well, let's see. Little girls like to scream for no apparent reason, and little boys like to whack things with sticks. Oh, and they love to pee outside."

"That's it?"

July laughed. "Yes, that's the sum total of my maternal wisdom about little kids. And if you can get them to eat and sleep on a regular basis, everybody's happier."

Mae looked out her kitchen window and laughed at the pant-less little boy and his daddy, thinking big boys love to pee outside too. Matthew and Ben concluded their business and walked back toward her.

"Good morning, Matthew. How're you today?" He smiled up at her.

"I left my T-Rex underpants upstairs."

"I can see that. Could you go put them on for breakfast, please?"

Matthew frowned. "My mommy makes me wear pants at the table too."

She looked at Ben, who was unsuccessfully stifling a laugh. "I think that's a good rule, don't you?" She gave Ben an imploring look. *You're the dad, help me out here.*

"Yes, that's a good rule. Go on, pants before pancakes," Ben grinned.

"Yay pancakes!" Matthew sped back into the house on chubby little legs, slamming the door behind him.

After Matthew came back downstairs, clad only in his dinosaur underpants, he handed her his extremely wet Pull-Ups from the night before and wolfed down a stack of pancakes the size of his head. Ben told him it was time to go to school.

"But I want to stay here, Daddy." He looked like he was about to cry. "I don't want to go to school today."

"Your mommy's going to pick you up from school this afternoon. You want to see her, right?"

"Mommy can pick me up here," he pointed out, with impeccable four-year-old logic. "She knows where Miss Mae lives."

"That's true, she does. But it's a school day. You need to get dressed, sport. I'll help you pack your things."

Matthew threw his fork down and glared at his father. "I want to play with the puppies," he shouted.

The light of battle began to gleam in Ben's eye. "Don't yell at me, young man. Get your butt upstairs right now!" Matthew remained seated. "I'm going to start counting now, and by the time I get to four, you better be on the stairs." No action from the little rebel. Mae stood and began to clear the table; she was trying not to giggle.

"One." The two Bradleys locked eyes. "Two …" Matthew inched one bottom cheek off his chair. "Three!" Ben roared, and Matthew broke for the stairs. Mae laughed and Ben followed his little man out of the kitchen.

They left within the hour after each gave her a kiss and a hug. Matthew clung to her for an extra beat.

"Can I come back and see the puppies again, Miss Mae?"

"Of course, thanks for being such a good boy while you were here. Good-bye."

She watched them drive away, and then collapsed on the couch. "Good Lord, how does July do it with three of them?"

Chapter Twenty-Three

—

Mae December

Mae hadn't talked to her mother in a few days, so she took care of a few quick house and dog chores and then carried her cellphone and a glass of raspberry iced tea out to her screened porch. Although it had been rainy and cool this August—for middle Tennessee, anyway—it was already eighty degrees out and very muggy. She turned on the ceiling fan and took a seat. After a refreshing gulp of tea, she called her mother's home phone.

"Suzanne speaking."

"Good morning, Mama, it's me."

"I'm glad you called me, Mae. I'm really worried about your sister. I took the kids out to the lake house yesterday, and July's not in a good place right now."

"I know she's not," Mae said. "She dropped both her dogs off here night before last. She was only here about ten minutes, but she was in tears. She got into it with Ben too, about him having her house searched."

Suzanne sighed. "I hope she's not headed toward a major

depression of some sort. Can I come over there? I'd rather not discuss all this on the phone."

"Sure, Mama, you can meet the Tater. Just give me an hour to get my house put back together first. Matthew was here all weekend, so I'm a little disorganized."

"The Tater? Is that what you named your new puppy?"

"December's Sweet Potato is her full name. She's so cute. You're going to love her."

"I'll pick up some barbecue for us for lunch on the way over. See you in an hour or so."

"Sounds good." Mae pressed the 'end call' button on her cellphone and went upstairs to change out of her grungy shorts and tank-top. In the back of her closet, she found a short denim skirt and sleeveless brown blouse. It was time to do laundry. She was officially out of clean clothes.

She took her full hamper down the hall to the spare bedroom and stripped the sheets from Matthew's bed. Mae had made extensive changes to the floor plan on the main floor of her historic farmhouse, removing all the non-supporting walls and converting a parlor into an art studio. She'd also divided what had been an office into a laundry room and powder room.

A hundred years ago, when her house was built, big families were the norm. When she and Noah bought the house, they joked that they would have to plan on lots of kids to fill all of the five original bedrooms. The first change they made to the house was to turn the two bedrooms on the front of the house into one large room with a walk-in closet, but it was still a four-bedroom house. She smiled, thinking that at least this bedroom would have a little one in it now and then. She put Matty's sheets in the hamper, remade the bed with clean sheets, and took her laundry downstairs.

The Tater was in her crate in the kitchen. Mae put the overflowing laundry basket on the counter and released the puppy. Picking her up, she put her in the hamper on top of the sheets and carried her into the laundry room. Both of July's puppies were in the bed of their mother, Tallulah. Tallulah herself was nowhere to be seen.

"C'mon Soot, Ricky, let's go outside." She liberated the Tater from the hamper and carried her out the back door with the two older puppies in tow. All three of the pups sniffed around and got treats as soon as they went potty. Mae stood there enjoying the cuteness for a few minutes, then took them all back inside.

An hour later, her mother showed up with a bag of delicious-smelling barbecue and the puppy ran right over to her, looking up with a twitching nose. "You must be the Tater," Suzanne said with a laugh. "You're super-cute, but this food's not for you." The tiny corgi tilted her head and blinked her eyes. "Look at you," Mae's mother cooed, bending down. "You sure know how to work it."

Mae poured sweet tea into tall glasses with ice and put plates, forks and napkins on her kitchen table. "Thanks for bringing the 'cue, Mama. It smells great. Do you want me to toast the buns?"

Suzanne was cradling the Tater close to her face. "Yes, please. Should I put her back in her crate?"

"Yeah, she's far from potty-trained."

Suzanne set the little corgi in her crate and latched the door. She looked around. "Where are the rest of the dogs?" She asked.

"I've got Soot and Ricky gated into the laundry room. My other three are tired of puppies. They're hiding in my art studio. I just closed the door, so they could have some peace."

Suzanne washed her hands and took the buns out of the toaster. Seating herself at the table, Mae's mother piled the pork on her bun, added sauce and topped it with coleslaw and the top of the bun. She took a huge bite and Mae sighed, wishing she could eat like her mother and still stay thin. Mae fixed herself an open-face version of the same sandwich with less barbeque.

"So I had a long talk with your sister yesterday. I spent the afternoon out there with her and the kids. Mae, I think her marriage is in trouble."

"Really? I know she's upset, but I thought it had more to do with finding Tommy like she did. It must have been so traumatic."

Suzanne smiled at her younger daughter. "Who do you turn to when you're upset?"

"Ben, I guess, or you and Daddy. And Tammy."

"Uh-huh. And you and Ben have been together for three months now?"

Mae put her fork down and nodded at her mother. "I see what you're getting at. She's not turning to Fred."

"Right, she's pushing him away. It sounds like he doesn't trust her, and she's angry about it. Are you done with your lunch?"

At Mae's nod, Suzanne stood and cleared the plates. She set them down in the sink. "Could we take our tea out to the screened porch?"

"Sure, Mama."

The two women carried their glasses out to the porch and made themselves comfortable.

"July shared something with me," Mama said. Her voice was very quiet and she was looking down at her clenched hands. "She didn't say I couldn't tell you …. Do you remember when she and Fred were newlyweds, and she was trying to get pregnant?"

"I remember it took a little while. And then after she got pregnant she was so nervous about miscarrying—she acted like she was made of glass. Why?"

Her mother pursed her lips. "Well, apparently your poor sister got pregnant the first time she had sex. Tommy disappeared before she even missed a period, but after six weeks she miscarried and lost the baby."

"I can't believe July never told me that." Mae looked at her mother with a frown. "Do you think she ever told Fred?"

"She says not. And now she's afraid to. She knows that Fred's already upset about her relationship with Tommy."

"Oh, that's not good."

Suzanne nodded her agreement. "Your sister's not talking to her husband and she's holed up at the lake house with the kids. And your boyfriend is investigating Fred for Tommy's murder."

"Well shit, Mama. If I ever want to get rid of these two extra puppies, I'll have to do something to get July back home."

Suzanne gave a surprised snort of laughter. "Don't curse in front of me, young lady. But you're right. Six dogs in the house might be too much for even you."

Chapter Twenty-Four

Mae December

AFTER HER MOTHER left, Mae called Fred's cellphone and it went straight to voicemail. She tried his office and got his secretary. She identified herself as his sister-in-law and was told, "Mr. Powell is out of the office today. He wasn't feeling very well. Can I give him a message when he returns?"

"No, thank you, I'll try the house phone."

There was no answer at the house either, just July's voice on the answering machine, so she decided to go check on Fred. A flash of inspiration made her decide to take the porgi pups with her. She rounded up Soot and Ricky, their food, beds and leashes and took everything out to her car. Matthew's car seat was still latched into the backseat of her Explorer. Ben must have forgotten it, since he had a car seat for Matty in his truck. Katie would need it when she picked Matthew up this afternoon. Luckily, Mae knew where the pre-school was; her niece Olivia had gone there too.

Mae put the pups and their gear in the back of the Explorer and drove into Rosedale's historic downtown. After she parked and extricated the car seat, she carried it into the nursery school. The administrator's office was right inside the door. A woman with shoulder-length brown hair and glasses looked up from her computer monitor.

"Can I help you?"

"I'm just dropping off a car seat for Matthew Bradley. Should I leave it with you?"

She shook her head. "You need to sign in." She indicated a ledger on the desk. "Then you'll have to put it outside his classroom door. He's in the rainbow class at the end of the hall." She handed Mae a pen and resumed typing on her keyboard.

Mae printed her name, filled in the date, time, and reason for her visit, and then signed her name. Hoisting the car seat, she took it down the hall. The top half of the last Dutch door on the left was open and had a large rainbow decal on the wall next to it. Mae set the heavy car seat on the floor and peeked into the classroom.

"Hi, Miss Mae!" Matthew shouted. "We're having snack time. Do you want some of my fruit snacks?"

"Hi, Matthew, no thanks. I'm just dropping off your car seat." She looked at Matthew's teacher. "I'm leaving it right out here for his mom, okay?"

"That's fine. I'm Miss Jena." She walked over with an outstretched hand. Matthew darted in front of his teacher and looked up at Mae through the top half of the door.

"That's Miss Mae. I sleeped over at her house while my mommy was gone. So did my daddy." Mae winced. Miss Jena put her hand down on Mathew's head.

"I'm Mae, Ben's girlfriend. I kept Matty this weekend." She opened the bottom half of the door to give Matthew a quick hug. "Bye, Matty. I've got to get going. Bye, Miss Jena." Matty's teacher gave her an insincere smile, and Mae made a speedy escape.

IT WAS LATE afternoon by the time she reached her sister's house and found Fred sitting on the wide stone steps by the front door. He was wearing running shorts and a faded Vanderbilt T-shirt. He looked up from his coffee cup when Mae came up the walkway with the two exuberant puppies on their leashes.

"Hi Mae." He put the cup down, then got up and gave her a hug. He smelled like stale sweat and cigarette smoke. She looked up at him with concern.

"I thought you quit smoking years ago, Fred. Are you all right?"

He shook his head. "C'mon in." He took the leash handles from her and opened the carved wooden door. "I'll put these two rascals out back."

Mae patted his shoulder. "I'll grab the rest of their stuff from the car and come in. We need to talk."

MAE LEFT TWO hours later with her head in a whirl. Things were even worse between Fred and July than she had feared. As soon as Mae got home and the Tater had been attended to, she called her mother.

"Hi. I just spent the last two hours talking to Fred."

"What'd you learn?"

"He's a mess. I took the puppies to him, and his eyes got all red watching them play in the backyard. He told me he hasn't slept or eaten much since July left. He's smoking again, too."

Suzanne was quiet for a moment and Mae heard a sigh.

"I don't know why he doesn't just go to the lake house and talk to her."

"I suggested that, but he feels like that would just make her angry. He really doesn't want to fight with her in front of the kids. I fixed him some scrambled eggs while I was there and he ate them, but he looks terrible. I'm worried about him being there alone. It was so sad, Mama. He said he doesn't think July ever really loved him."

"What?"

"Yes. He said that Tommy was a ghost in their marriage even

when he was alive. Now that he's dead, Fred thinks she'll never get closure. He's making it sound like July's going to ask for a divorce."

"I'll invite him over for dinner soon. Your father's getting back from his fishing trip tomorrow night. We'll try to cheer Fred up. What do you think we can do to get your sister to come home?"

"She'll probably come for Tommy's funeral, but she still might not be talking to Fred. I'm going to call Sandi Townsend. She might be able to persuade July better than I can."

"Your sister's pretty hard-headed, but that might work. Thanks, sweetie."

"You're welcome, Mama. Talk to you later."

The rest of the evening Mae thought hard about her sister. By the time she took her dogs outside for a potty-break before bed, she had decided there was only one thing that would help. If July wanted to save her marriage, it was time for her to say good-bye to Tommy Ferris once and for all.

Chapter Twenty-Five

——

Sheriff Ben Bradley

THE SHERIFF BUZZED Dory and asked her to come to his office.

"You wanted me, boss?" she stood in his doorway.

"I don't think you've told me yet what happened when you and Miss Bontemps went to dinner. From the look on your face, I'm guessing it went well." She nodded, smiling. "What did you learn from your new friend?"

"Well, Sheriff, you know I believe you have to give if you wish to receive. I shared what Bethany Cooper told us." She held up her hand as he opened his mouth to speak. "Before you start objecting, you need to know that it was no surprise to her. She didn't tell me specifics, but Tom Ferris told her that Bethany was his stepsister, and he left something to both Miranda and Bethany in his will. And he left July something too." Dory sat down in the chair across from his desk and stretched, arching her back. "We had a delicious dinner with several alcoholic beverages, by the way."

"I wish we knew the specifics, but well done. What about

Bontemps' secretary? Does she type up the wills?"

"As a matter of fact, she doesn't. Evangeline has a software program that basically does the whole thing automatically. She just fills in the information the client gives her. It's all on her computer and password-protected."

"Excellent work, Investigator Clarkson," Ben said, grinning. "I'd like to get a warrant to search Henry Covington's house and car. Can you get started on that?"

Dory pursed her lips but nodded and returned to her desk.

BEN DECIDED TO make another effort to reach Nellie Franz, the housekeeper of the Sigma Chi house. His previous calls had been unsuccessful. This time, he got a hit.

"Hello," said a weary, high-pitched voice.

"Hello, is this Nellie Franz?"

"If you're looking for money I'm not giving you any. I'm old, I'm sick, and I don't share."

Knowing he had only moments before she hung up the phone, Ben said, "It's Sheriff Ben Bradley calling from Rosedale, Tennessee. I would like to ask you some questions about the death of Ryan Gentry."

'That's a long time back, young man," she snapped. "The case was closed."

"It links with a murder that was committed a few days ago involving the shooting death of Tom Ferris."

"Oh dear." Her voice softened.

"Ms. Franz, may I come and meet with you? I've talked with Detective Pascoe and he said you might know something that could help us." Ben wanted to flatter the old woman. It often opened doors—and mouths.

"All right. My address is 1489 Pimpernel, in Muley. How long before you get here?"

"Thank you very much. I can get to your house in about an hour."

Relieved, Ben typed the address into his GPS and thought about how to conduct the interview. It was unlikely to give him anything, but he wanted to cover every possibility.

Nellie Franz' place was quite a ways out of town. A small, rusty trailer stood surrounded by enormous old willows that leaned over the slowly collapsing dwelling. Green lichen spotted the tin roof. He knocked, and a tiny, stick-thin woman appeared in the metal doorway. Her white hair was fine and fell to her shoulders. A heavily spotted apron was tied around her middle, and on her feet were white, rolled-down socks and orthopedic shoes.

"I'll see a badge, Lawman," she said.

"Yes Ma'am." Sheriff Bradley pulled out his sheriff's star and identification.

"Let's sit at the table," she said, pointing to a decrepit picnic table. It was green with mold, almost hidden under the willows. Ben hadn't seen it in the shadows. Incongruously, it had a tiny vase of red wildflowers sitting on it. "I won't have the law inside my house."

"I understand," Sheriff Bradley said. They walked to the table and Ben sat, feeling it creak beneath his weight. "I hope I don't break your table, Ma'am." When she looked at him, her eyes were sharp. He added, "As I told you on the phone, we're looking into the Ryan Gentry case again."

"Didn't kill himself, did he?"

"We don't think so," the sheriff said. "Do you have any idea what was going on that would make one of the other young men in the fraternity want to hurt Ryan?"

"The old detective, Pascoe, asked me already. Told him what I'll tell you. I was cleaning the third floor, mopping the hall. When I heard the hullabaloo outside, I walked downstairs to see what was happening. Once I saw the cops, I went back upstairs. My bucket had been moved."

"Why did you think someone moved your bucket?" Sheriff Bradley asked.

"Thought they were cleaning up something."

"Probably right. The question is, why?"

"I'd finished mopping the floor in Ryan and Tommy's room about an hour earlier. I waxed it too. It would have been shiny, slippery like. If there was a scuffle between Ryan and another guy and the floor got messed up, there would have been marks in the wax."

"You're one smart cookie," the sheriff told her. Nellie Franz preened. "Do you have any idea why there would've been a fight?"

"I don't know anything for sure, but a couple of times when I cleaned Henry and Greg's room there was a lot of money lying around—too much money for kids. I always wondered about it."

Ben nodded. "We think whoever killed Ryan probably killed Tom Ferris too. We're hoping to make an arrest soon. If we arrest Henry Covington, would you be willing to testify to seeing large amounts of cash in his room?"

She looked at him for a space of time. "I'm Shawnee," she said calmly. Ben waited, intrigued. "I'll agree to nothing until I consult my elders."

Elders? The woman was ancient. It didn't seem likely that there would be older Shawnee Indians still alive in Tennessee.

"After you've done that, if you're willing to testify, call me." Sheriff Bradley handed her a card. Unsure if he had convinced her to testify, he said, "You know it's not right that a person gets away with murder ... twice." He looked straight into her eyes. She stared back, unblinking; then she nodded.

She reached into her apron pocket and pulled out a little corncob pipe and a tobacco pouch. "I'm going to smoke a while," she said and smiled at him for the first time. "Care to sit and smoke with me?"

"I'd enjoy that some other time." He relaxed, smiling back at her. "I'm on my way to another interview right now. I need to do some convincing to get Ryan's case reopened. Thank you very much, Ms. Franz. You've been more helpful than you know."

Ben turned and walked back to his car, wondering what the old lady lived on and hoping she had enough to eat. He entered the address for Mrs. Trula Godfrey, the housemother for Sigma Chi in the late nineties, into his GPS. The house was in Jefferson City. Once on the main road, he dialed PD Pascoe.

"Hello." The old man's voice was quiet.

"Hello, Detective. It's Ben Bradley. I just met with Nellie Franz, the housekeeper for Sigma Chi. I'm on my way now to see Trula Godfrey, the housemother. After that I'd like to get ahold of several things from the Gentry evidence box. Where are the old evidence boxes kept?"

"Before I retired, I worked out of the Jefferson City post. We were the jurisdiction for crimes that took place at Southeast Tennessee State, but evidence for cases more than ten years old is transferred to off-site storage in Nashville. What did you learn from Nellie Franz?"

"She told me Covington's room had a lot of cash lying around, more than college kids should've had. Henry had the room next door to Ryan and Tom Ferris, so maybe there's a connection. She's uneasy about the law, but I think she'll testify to seeing the money in the room if it comes to trial."

"So what's next?"

"I'm going to talk with Trula Godfrey, and then I'm going to try to get ahold of Ryan Gentry's computer."

"Keep me apprised. I have a doctor's appointment. Need to get going but thanks for the call."

BEN LOCATED THE suburban neighborhood where Mrs. Godfrey lived. Her suburb consisted of small ranch houses, most about thirty years old and crowded with overgrown shrubbery. Trula Godfrey's house was built of yellowish brick. Her driveway had been paved, but weeds grew through the asphalt. Ben parked and walked up to the door.

A woman around sixty came to the screen door, chubby with white hair and glasses. It was already hot, and there was no sound of an air conditioner. She was wearing a house coat, faded from a hundred washings.

"Hello?" she said, smiling up at him. It was obvious she was delighted to have company, any company.

"I'm Sheriff Ben Bradley of Rose County. Are you Trula Godfrey?"

"I am. Please come in, Sheriff," she said, opening the screen door wider. "Have a seat. I'll get us something to drink."

Ben heard her fussing around in the kitchen. The living room had way too much furniture. His knees were mashed against her dark coffee table.

"Now what can I help you with, Sheriff?" Mrs. Godfrey asked, handing him his lemonade. "Does that need more sugar?"

"No, thank you. I'm here because we're looking into the Ryan Gentry case again."

"Oh." Mrs. Gentry's face grew pink and she put a hand on her cheek.

"I wonder what you remember from that day."

"I wish I *didn't* remember," she said softly. "It was awful. Ryan Gentry was a nice boy, very responsible. He was the treasurer for Sigma Chi."

"Were you surprised he killed himself?"

"Very. But he did come to see me once to complain about the fraternity hazing. He said it had gotten out of hand. The leader of the hazing was a kid named Henry Covington. He'd broken a pledge's hand."

"What else do you remember about Covington?"

"After Ryan's report, I looked into his background. He'd been raised by a single mother and was there on a football scholarship. His father was not in the picture. I was a little bit afraid of him, to tell you the truth, but I called him into my office. I tried to scare him by saying the pledge with the broken hand might sue, but Henry wasn't fazed. His roommate was Greg Townsend, who was pre-law, and he said Greg and his family would protect him."

"Do you think Henry might have been involved in Ryan's death in any way?"

"I hope not," she said. There was a note of sadness in her voice. "After the pledge incident I called the coach of the football team. I told him Henry needed a father figure and urged him to take the boy under his wing. Henry wasn't really college material. Greg had to help him a lot with his classes and the football players had tutors or he wouldn't have made it. After Ryan died, I finished out the year and then retired. My husband was sick, and I needed to take care of him. May I get you some more lemonade, Sheriff?" she asked.

"No thank you, Mrs. Godfrey. You've been very helpful. And your lemonade just hit the spot. I need to get going now, but I appreciate your seeing me."

ONCE BACK IN the car, Ben had plenty of driving time to think about the motive for both killings. As a football player, Covington could have been shaving the point spread on games. That would have explained all the money in their rooms. Ryan Gentry was the treasurer for the fraternity and might have seen some big money being laundered through the account. If Ryan had gone to either Henry or Greg asking questions about the money, he'd signed his own death warrant.

When Tom Ferris returned to college the day Ryan died, Covington or Townsend must have been apprehensive that he knew something and told him to leave town. Ben didn't know why Tom Ferris returned to Rosedale so many years later, but he was obviously spotted when he went to meet with his attorney. If Covington or Townsend saw him, they must have assumed Ferris could still finger them for the Ryan Gentry killing and decided to shut him up forever. Ben needed to get Gentry's case reopened, or at least get Ryan's computer. Because, as of now, he had zero evidence to support his theory.

Chapter Twenty-Six

———

Sheriff Ben Bradley

THE NASHVILLE POLICE precinct where Captain Paula worked was located in a light-orange brick building. A stone planter that ran all along the front was filled with fading yellow day lilies. Ben walked through the large glass door and checked the list of office numbers, noting that Captain Paula was in Room 8-A. He went to the front desk, where a weary sergeant looked down at him from a raised seat.

"I'm Ben Bradley, Sheriff of Rosedale County. I'd like to speak to Captain Paula Crawley. Is she in?"

The sergeant didn't respond, just pushed a button on the phone.

"Cap'n, there's a Sheriff Bradley here, wants to speak to you." Turning back to Ben he said, "She'll be out in about fifteen."

Sheriff Bradley sat in one of the oak chairs along the wall along with three other men. He pulled a small pad of paper from his breast pocket and jotted down several points he wanted to make to Captain Paula. He decided not to discuss his suspicions about Townsend, since he was an attorney, but just focus on Covington.

When Captain Paula appeared, he was surprised. Ben had expected a fifty-something battle axe. The woman walking toward him was young, probably not even forty. She was less than five and a half feet tall and had dark gray eyes. She seemed preoccupied. Although her hair was cut close to her head, it suited her—complementing her heart-shaped face and emphasizing her eyes.

"Hello," he said, standing up and holding out his hand. "I'm Ben Bradley."

"Hello." Her small hand grasped his firmly. "Follow me."

She led him to her office. "Have a seat. I don't have long, but I appreciate your taking the trouble to give me a report in person. How's the investigation coming along?"

"We have a theory that links Tom Ferris' murder to Ryan Gentry's death at Southeast Tennessee State fifteen years ago. Are you familiar with that case?"

She nodded, holding his eyes with hers, hardly blinking.

"I believe Henry Covington was involved in fixing the spread on college football games as a student. It's likely that he needed somewhere to put the money he received from the gambling. He could have used the fraternity account. Ryan Gentry was the Treasurer for the Sigma Chi house. If he saw a large deposit and questioned Henry about it, it would have been a motive for what I think was murder, not suicide."

"Okay," she said.

"We like Covington for the Gentry murder and for the Ferris killing. He was in the frat house when Ryan was killed. He now lives and works for a legal firm in Rosedale. Tom Ferris went to see his attorney, Evangeline Bontemps, the day he was killed. She thought he'd seen something or someone on his way into her office—said he looked resigned, as if something he had feared for a long time was about to happen. I think Covington saw Ferris and decided to get rid of him, believing Ferris could link him to the Gentry death."

"Okay, hold it right there." She held up her hand. "I admit the theory of the crime is ingenious. However, you're pretty light on evidence to support this theory.

"I'm aware of that. I'm here because I'd like to see what was kept from the Gentry case. If I can find some supporting evidence, I can use it to get a warrant to search Covington's apartment. "

"Getting a search warrant is your problem, not mine." Her voice was calm but unsympathetic. Her eyes never wavered.

"It is." The sheriff stayed composed. "However, if you'd be willing to reopen the Gentry case, I think the judge in Rosedale would grant a search warrant for Covington's place. I've talked to Detective Pascoe and he told me Gentry's computer should still be in the evidence locker in old case storage here. Forensic computer work has progressed enormously in the last fifteen years. A forensic analysis could determine if there were any large deposits recorded in the fraternity account and if they were made in cash."

He thought he had made his case well, but there was no way to know how Captain Paula was reacting. The woman's expression was completely deadpan.

"So, that old coot Pascoe is still chewing on the Gentry case, is he?" She shook her head.

Ben nodded.

"Most of the officers here think he's a nutcase," she said, as steely eyed as ever. "Frankly, I don't. Five years ago when I started working here, I reviewed all the cold cases from the last twenty years. Pascoe made sure I included the Gentry case in my review. He always thought Gentry's suicide was dubious. No suicide note, no pattern of depression, and according to everyone quoted in the case file, Ryan was a well-adjusted young man."

"Do you think we have enough to reopen?" the sheriff asked.

"No, and neither do you or you wouldn't have come all this way to make your pitch in person," she said with a faint smile. "I won't reopen the case, but I'll give you the computer. We often share old case information among detectives. I can justify this on the basis that you're looking into a closed case which might have been mishandled. Another set of eyes is often helpful. I'll get somebody to take you over to off-site storage."

Captain Paula led Ben through the halls and down into the basement. The officer sitting behind a metal screen looked up when they walked in.

"Captain," he said, nodding respectfully.

"Jim, I need somebody to take Sheriff Bradley to off-site storage. He wants to take a look at case number 169325D." Ben was not particularly surprised she knew the case number by heart; she was that kind of woman.

"Right," the officer said laconically. I've got Deputy Gomez working in the back." He buzzed Gomez with his intercom and a good-looking young Hispanic woman appeared. She had honey-colored skin, dark melting eyes and a uniform that did nothing to disguise her abundant curves.

"Deputy, this is Sheriff Bradley. I'd like you to take him over to off-site and get him the computer from the old Ryan Gentry case."

"Yes, sir," Gomez said. Clearly Captain Paula preferred being called 'sir,' even by her own staff.

Sheriff Bradley thanked Captain Paula and followed the deputy out to a state police vehicle. An hour later, Ben had Ryan's computer in a box, along with one other item he thought might be helpful in making his case—Ryan Gentry's belt.

On the way back to Rosedale, Ben called the office. Deputy Phelps answered the phone.

"George, why are you still on the phones? Where's Dory?"

"She's in the interrogation room with Detective Nichols. They're talking to Henry Covington."

"Damn it! I told them to wait to talk to him until after we got that search warrant." White hot anger flashed in Ben's chest. "Get Wayne and Dory out of there and into my office now. I want to talk to both of them. Put them on speaker."

A couple minutes later, he heard Wayne and Dory's voices.

"Hey," Detective Nichols said.

"What the hell were you two thinking?" Ben felt a rush of adrenaline race through his body. His nostrils flared and he hit the steering wheel with the flat of his hand. "You've just tipped off our prime suspect. Couldn't you have waited one damn day for me to get the search warrant?"

"Hang on," Nichols said and Ben heard his detective say something to Dory. Then her voice came on the line.

"We already got the warrant, boss. Fuller's at Covington's place now, looking for the murder weapon."

Ben sighed, partly in relief and partly in exasperation. "Why the hell didn't you call me? What evidence did you use to convince the judge? Seeing as there wasn't *any*, it must have been a tough sell."

"I told her we had an eye witness who could identify him." Dory's voice sounded unsure, apologetic.

"Oh you did, did you? I take it you were talking about Mrs. Laurel Anderson. If Fuller doesn't find something incriminating in Covington's apartment, the defense attorney is going to make mincemeat out of poor little Mrs. Anderson. I can hear it now. 'The only witness the prosecution could produce was an eighty-three-year-old lady who is short-sighted and saw *someone* leaving the Booth Showhouse by the side door at dusk.' If this guy, who's already killed twice, gets off again, it's going to be you who tosses and turns at night, Dory Clarkson."

"I'm truly sorry, sir." Dory sounded chastened.

"I trust you at least remembered we can't keep him more than forty-eight hours without arresting him? What time did you bring him in? Has he asked for his attorney?"

"Wayne and Deputy Fuller picked him up after lunch. I clocked him in at one thirty-four p.m. We're going to put him in a line-up tomorrow morning. We got lucky on the attorney issue; his lawyer's out of town."

"You best kneel down and pray Mrs. Anderson identifies him. Who else were you going to have in the line-up?"

"Lester and Dean are in the drunk tank; they're both about Henry's size."

"Keep your fingers crossed that Deputy Fuller finds the gun. Even if Mrs. Anderson is certain about identification—which I think is a long shot—without the weapon we have nothing."

"Yes sir," Dory said.

Ben hung up, still raging.

Chapter Twenty-Seven

Detective Wayne Nichols

A SUMMER THUNDERSTORM was crashing down when Detective Nichols ran into the sheriff's office the morning of August 8th. Once inside, he dripped across the tile floor to his office. As he passed the line-up room, he saw Dory ushering three men inside. One was Henry Covington; the other two were from the usual parade of miscreants. Dory had managed to get all three men to dress in identical T-shirts and jeans. He watched as she hung numbered signs around their necks.

Detective Nichols opened the door to the line-up room and signaled for Dory to see him when she was finished. She walked into his office a few minutes later.

"Did Deputy Fuller find anything in Covington's apartment?" he asked.

"No gun that matched," Dory said gloomily. "The boss is going to have a hissy. Covington had three pistols and four rifles, all registered. We sent them to the lab, but Rob said he doubted they had been recently fired. No cordite smell. Rob did find a box of the ammo of the kind used to kill Ferris, but of course that's common." Dory looked positively depressed.

The sheriff walked into his detective's office. He frowned at both his detective and his office manager and asked what Deputy Fuller had found at Covington's place.

"We got nothing," Dory said and Ben's mouth quirked in a tight line.

Deputy Phelps knocked on the door frame. "Mrs. Anderson is here for the perp walk," he said.

Sheriff Bradley and Detective Nichols walked out into the waiting room to greet her.

"Good morning, Mrs. Anderson, thank you so much for coming down to the station," Ben said. "We have a line-up of suspects in the room we'd like you to take a look at."

Mrs. Anderson was dressed in a white cotton blouse and navy blue skirt. Her hair was white and curly, baby fine. Her skin was lined, but her pink cheeks still looked soft.

"I've seen line-ups in detective stories on TV," she said, smiling. "I never thought I would be the one to point a trembling finger and say, 'That's him.'"

"I certainly hope you can identify the man for us," the sheriff said and she took his arm. He led her to the one-way view screening room.

"Can they see me?" she asked, sounding a bit fearful.

"No, they can't. Don't worry. We're not going to release them until after you're safely back at home. I don't want to risk my star witness," the sheriff reassured her with a grin.

Mrs. Anderson took her time looking at the men standing in line. Detective Nichols switched on the small mike, "Turn left." Two of the suspects turned left, and one turned right. Wayne rolled his eyes. Under his breath he murmured, "Your other left, idiot."

"Take your time, Mrs. Anderson," Sheriff Bradley said, soothingly.

"Turn right," Detective Nichols told them. They did so and both Ben and Wayne looked intently at Mrs. Anderson. "Face front," the detective told the three men.

"Do any of them look like the man you saw come out of the Booth Showhouse on August second?" the sheriff asked.

"I think number two. The one in the middle?" Her voice was uncertain, and she seemed to be asking for confirmation. "But I couldn't swear to it, I'm sorry."

"That's okay," Ben said. "You did very well. Thank you again for coming.

Detective Nichols watched from the window as the sheriff escorted her out of the building to her car, standing beside it until she pulled out of the parking lot.

"All of you, in the conference room. Now," the sheriff yelled when he came back inside the building. Once they were assembled he said, "Mrs. Anderson pointed to Covington in the line-up, but said she couldn't swear it was him. Do any of you have anything I don't already know?" he asked, glowering. "Somebody better have something."

Deputy George Phelps raised his hand. "I do, sir. After I got through the list of the fraternity brothers, I reviewed the CCTV footage, like you said. At four thirty-six p.m. on the day Tom Ferris was shot, the Final Touch florist brought in their arrangements. The camera shows them unloading the van in the parking lot. Two young women brought in the flowers. A man walked up to them and must have offered to help, because he picked up the largest arrangement and brought it inside. The flowers were so tall, nobody saw his face."

"*You* are a jewel," the sheriff told him. He turned another frown on Dory, Detective Nichols, and Deputy Rob Fuller. "So, while the rest of you were disobeying orders, writing requests for court orders based on nothing but *conjecture* or coming up empty, George here got our guy. Please tell me it was Covington who carried the flowers inside the Booth Showhouse."

Deputy Phelps blushed and nodded.

"You're certain you recognized Covington?" Wayne asked, intently.

"It was him." George was beaming. "He got out of his car and I ran the plate. It was his vehicle."

"Did you see him leave the Booth Showhouse after that?"

"No, there's nothing on the tape showing him leaving. He must have left by way of the side door and was most likely the guy Mrs. Anderson saw."

"All right, excellent. We're back on track. And I got Captain Paula to give me Ryan Gentry's computer and one other item— Ryan Gentry's belt. Detective Pascoe thought he was thrown from the window by somebody who lifted him by his belt."

After the buzz of questions died down, Wayne said, "I'll get the belt to Emma Peters and have her check it for fingerprints and DNA. Obviously we'd expect Ryan's fingerprints to be on it, but if Henry Covington's prints or DNA are on that belt, we have him cold for that killing."

"Do we have someone in town who could get into that computer?" Deputy Rob Fuller asked.

"The Mont Blanc Police Department has a forensic IT guy who comes by every couple of weeks. He rotates there from the Nashville post. I'll try both places," Dory said. Turning to Ben she asked, "Sheriff, do you want me to retract my request for the court order and apologize to the judge?"

"No," Ben said. "Thanks to Deputy George here, it looks like we're on the verge of solving the Ferris case. When we started this one, I told Detective Nichols what we had was a new case on top of an old case—like two sleeping dogs. It appears we've stirred up the dogs." He smiled.

"Don't get cocky yet," Wayne said. "We don't know what, if anything, the lab will give us on the belt. Without that, we're back at square one with the Ryan Gentry case."

"What's your theory for that one?" Dory asked.

"I think it might've involved fixing college football games," Ben said. Several pairs of eyebrows went up. "I met with Nellie Franz, the housekeeper for Sigma Chi. She told me there was an awful lot of money sitting around in Henry Covington's room. Way more than young kids should've had."

"Was Covington on the football team?" Wayne asked.

"He sure was. Played tight end."

"Okay. How does that involve Ryan Gentry?"

"Ryan Gentry was the treasurer for the fraternity. I think Townsend may have laundered some large deposits through the Sigma Chi account. Thus, the need for the IT guy." Ben stopped talking and narrowed his eyes at Dory.

"I'm on it, boss," she said, and darted from the room.

THE SHERIFF AND Detective Nichols were walking into the interrogation room when Deputy Phelps appeared with Covington in cuffs. He shot them a questioning look. Ben nodded, indicating he could join them for the interrogation. Deputy Phelps turned on the audio equipment and sat down. Henry Covington was dressed in jeans and a faded blue shirt with a button-down collar. His light brown hair was disheveled and he needed a shave. His gray eyes regarded them with wariness. Detective Nichols indicated a chair across from Ben.

"Sit down, Mr. Covington."

The sheriff spoke first, announcing the names of everyone present for the audio capture system. "Sheriff Bradley, Detective Nichols, and Deputy George Phelps present to interview Henry Covington on August eighth about his involvement in the death of Tom Ferris. Covington, you were informed of your rights when you were brought in yesterday, correct?"

"Yes," Henry said with a nod.

"Say it aloud that you've been Mirandized," Detective Nichols insisted.

"I've been informed of my rights, okay?" Covington glared. He sounded sulky, aggrieved.

"You've been identified as leaving the Booth Showhouse five minutes after Tom Ferris was shot to death," the sheriff said. "We have you on tape coming into the house helping the florist bring in the arrangements. And we have you exiting the house through the French doors on the side. You turned around and closed the shutter dogs. We've sent those prints to the state lab."

"We've got you, Covington," Detective Nichols said bluntly. "You shot Ferris in the back. We're assembling evidence showing that this wasn't your first murder. You killed another fraternity brother of yours at Sigma Chi fifteen years ago."

Covington's face blanched slightly. For the first time, he started to look uneasy.

"You've got squat," he replied, recovering quickly. "You haven't got any real evidence or you would've already arrested me rather than just hauling me in here. I want my lawyer. I already asked for him yesterday. I'm not saying anything more until he gets here."

"Okay, who is it?" the sheriff asked.

"Rod Coniglio, with the Townsend practice. Here's his number." Covington handed the sheriff a small white business card.

"Premeditated murder carries an automatic life sentence in Tennessee, unless there's some extenuating circumstance," Sheriff Bradley's voice trailed off. Henry Covington didn't say a word.

"You better start talking, Henry." Detective Nichols got up and began to pace the small room. Standing behind Covington, he leaned forward and said, "You didn't shoot Ferris on your own initiative. Somebody told you to shoot him. If you want to get a reduced sentence and get paroled before your son's on Social Security, you need to tell us who told you to kill him."

Covington shook his head and started to stand up. Detective Nichols grabbed him by the shoulder and pushed him back into his chair, hard.

"You sit your ass down," he said, eyes snapping. "We're not done here yet."

They heard a tapping and the sheriff tilted his head toward

the door. Both Detective Nichols and Deputy Phelps rose and followed him out of the room.

Dory was standing in the hall. "His lawyer's on his way," she said.

"Let's wait in my office." Ben led the two men down the hall. Deputy Phelps sat in the chair, the detective leaned against the wall, and Ben paced until they heard the buzzer indicating Rod Coniglio's arrival.

"Show him to the interrogation room, Dory," the sheriff said over the intercom. "Meet him back there please, Wayne. Let me know what happens. You're dismissed." The sheriff nodded at Deputy Phelps.

Detective Nichols opened the door and gestured for the man to precede them into the room. He was expensively dressed in a silver-gray custom-made suit, white shirt, and purple silk tie.

Pausing at the threshold, he asked Detective Nichols, "Why are you holding my client? What's he been charged with?"

"We have evidence he shot Tom Ferris in the back and killed him."

"What evidence? Do you have the murder weapon?"

"We have definitive proof that he was in the Booth Showhouse at the time of the murder."

"So, you have opportunity. That's it?" Coniglio waggled his eyebrows, looking amused. He sat down next to Henry and put his hand on his client's shoulder. "You don't have means? You don't have a motive?"

"Your partner Townsend ordered the killing." Detective Nichols spit out the damning words. His eyes bored into Rod Coniglio's. The attorney shook his head, gave Wayne Nichols a supercilious smile, and looked at Henry.

"Whatever you think you may have on my client or on Townsend comes under the heading of privileged communication. We're leaving." He and Henry Covington stood up and both men turned to leave.

Detective Nichols stepped back and watched them go.

The smooth son-of-a-bitch was right. All they had was circumstantial evidence. Without the murder weapon they didn't even have enough to make an arrest. He slammed his hand on the conference room table.

They had already searched Covington's condo and his car and came up empty. He could have disposed of the gun, but Wayne thought he wasn't the type. All the guns he had were registered and in a special locked cabinet at his place. They were obviously Henry's prized possessions.

He buzzed Ben and they agreed to have Deputy Phelps follow Covington and his attorney. He hoped they could find evidence on Covington and Townsend's involvement. He wondered if they'd played their hand too soon.

Chapter Twenty-Eight

—

Sheriff Ben Bradley

"Dory," the sheriff called out as he and Detective Nichols walked toward the front office.

"Yes, Sheriff?"

"We've got to find that murder weapon. I've just had an idea. Does Henry Covington have a hunting cabin?"

"He might. I'll see what I can find."

"Do it now." The sheriff's voice was low. "When Rob searched Covington's apartment he found every gun he'd had since his first twenty-two rifle. I'm betting he's still got the murder weapon, but he's going to get rid of it now that he knows we're on to him. We have to find it before he does."

Sheriff Bradley and Detective Nichols had their heads together and were deep in conversation when Dory walked back into Ben's office half an hour later. Both men perked up, looking at her eagerly.

"Good call, boss. Henry owns a hunting cabin up on Pinhook Hill, close to the summit. I found a map. Just coordinates, latitude and longitude. There's a lot of logging roads up there.

It's going to be tough to find at night." Dory waited for his answer.

"Deputy Fuller," the sheriff called.

"Sheriff?"

"Come in here, Rob." When everyone was assembled, the sheriff said, "We're going to keep following Henry. We need to have at least two cars on him. Deputy Phelps took the patrol car. He just called in. At the moment, Covington is at the Townsend firm on Main Street. George is going to stay on him until I tell him otherwise."

"He'll spot the patrol car, boss," Deputy Rob said.

"I know, I want him to. Once Henry leaves the office, he's going to try to ditch him. Rob, I want you in an unmarked car. You'll take over as lead once he spots George."

"He might go to Randee Scofield's place," Detective Nichols said.

"Agreed. If he goes to see Randee, let us know by police radio. Dory, I want you to call her. See if she's ever been to the hunting cabin and if you can, get directions."

"We're betting he'll head out of town after dark on Old Hickory Boulevard going north," the detective said. "Once he's past the entrance to White's Creek State Park, he has to enter that whole spider's web of logging roads to reach his hunting cabin."

"What vehicles are we watching for?" Deputy Fuller asked. "He was driving a 2011 white Lincoln town car at the Booth Showhouse."

Wayne Nichols looked at his notes. "He'll probably drive his truck up north. It's a white 1996 Ford F-250 four-wheel drive. It might have a camo wrap. Dory will get you the license numbers."

"On it," Dory said.

"After you take over following Covington, Rob, I'm going to have George switch vehicles and drive up to White's Creek," Ben said. "It's the closest little town on the road to Pinhook

Mountain. Dory, give him the map, will you? Once Covington turns off the main road, you and George will veer off, call us and find a place to park. He'll spot you if you stay with him once he enters the fire roads."

When he knew Ben had finished speaking, Wayne said, "Rob, it's possible you and George might be in the car for ten to twelve hours. Stay concealed. I don't want him spooked. Keep in touch with us by radio. This man is armed and dangerous. Watch yourselves," he added.

"Ten to twelve hours?" Deputy Fuller sounded dismayed. "What if George has to pee?"

"Just take an empty bottle. Don't leave the damn car," the sheriff snapped. George had abandoned his post at a suspect's house during their previous murder case because he had to pee.

"I figure we've got about two hours to get a precise location on that hunting cabin. Wayne, you and I are going to be waiting for Covington when he arrives. What ideas do you two have to get the address?"

"I can call the township. Probably they have a plat map they can fax over," Dory said.

"Good idea. Wayne?"

"He might have listed the address on a hunting license. I'll check the DNR records. And I think they're required to have a house number on a post, in case of fire. I'll get the number."

"Good. While you two do that, I'm going to make a call." Once Wayne and Dory departed, Ben dialed Mae's phone. He didn't catch her on either line or her cell and was only able to leave a message. "Mae, it's me. Listen, we're closing in on Tom Ferris' killer. Wayne and I are going on stakeout to catch him in the area north of the Pinhook State Park. We may be gone a day or two before he shows up. I don't want you to worry if you haven't heard from me."

Dory stuck her head in his door. "In case it didn't dawn on you, Sheriff, if Rob and George are following Covington, and

I have to leave the office to meet with Randee, who's supposed to be on duty? I've been telling you for months we don't have enough help around here." This was not the first time Dory had urged Ben to add more staff, but this time he had no argument. She was absolutely right.

"Okay. I'll call John over at the Rosedale PD and ask him to send two floaters over for the next week. Whoever he sends, I want one on phones to release you. I'll put the other one on patrol to cover George and Rob's usual routes. Will that do it?"

"No, it won't. Rob's taking the detective exam in three weeks and if he passes, we're going to be short a deputy. Plus, I have ambitions beyond running your office."

Ben tried to contain his frustration. By allowing Dory to take Evangeline Bontemps to dinner and go with Wayne to the biker bar, he had given her way too many ideas.

"How am I supposed to get any experience if you have me chained to the desk?"

"Seriously, Dory, 'chained to the desk'? You make it sound like a torture chamber. Just tell me what you want."

"I want you to take a look at the applications I've been collecting for deputies. Here's the folder." She plopped it on his desk. "While you're going through those, I'll call John's office at Mont Blanc and get a time you can talk with him to request the floaters. We're going to need them here by five today."

"Okay. I'm also going to call Captain Paula, give her an update and see if the deputy who took me to off-site storage might be interested in working for us."

"Okay, what's his name? I'll do some background."

"*Her* name is Cameron Gomez."

"Well, well, well, good for you Bradley. We could use some more estrogen around here. I suppose she's cute too."

Ben nodded, grinning. "I'm taken, but she would give Wayne and Rob some hope."

"I just hope she's enough of a bad ass to control you guys."

Ben sighed. Things in his office were getting more complicated by the day.

With the address for Covington's hunting cabin obtained from the plat map office in hand, Sheriff Bradley and Detective Nichols left the office at five o'clock, leaving Dory to brief the two floaters, Ned Thompson and Jackie Forte. Jackie would be on phones; Ned would cover the usual patrol routes. To Ben's surprise, when he called Cameron Gomez, she was very interested in applying for the deputy position. She said she'd have to tell Captain Paula, though, who might not be too pleased. Ben left a voice message for the captain telling her their plan for the evening, relieved she was unavailable to comment on his probably foolhardy venture.

Deputy Phelps called in several times over the next two hours. He followed Covington when he left the law offices on Main Street. Henry stopped at a local biker bar and Randee met him there. An hour later, Randee rode out on her bike, heading in the direction of her house. George said he'd then followed Covington to his place. As Henry opened the door to his townhouse, Phelps said he peeled out of the parking lot ostentatiously and returned to the station.

"Why did you make a production of leaving Covington's apartment?" Ben asked.

"I wanted him to think we were done for the night."

"Good thinking, George," Ben said, wondering if there might be more to Deputy Phelps than he had thought.

By SUNDOWN THE sheriff and his detective were already past the entrance to Pinhook State Park, heading up to White's Creek. They were a good hour or so ahead of Covington. Around eight, Deputy Fuller called to say that Henry had left his place, switched cars, and was headed north on Old Hickory. Rob said following Henry's camo-covered Ford truck was going to be a piece of cake.

"I've gotta hand it to you, Sheriff," Wayne said. "You called this one right down the line."

"Yeah. So far, so good. Now if he does what I expect, he'll get to the cabin and take the gun out, intending to hide or bury it. When he walks out of the cabin with the gun, we'll jump him."

"Can't we break into the cabin?" Wayne said with a grin. The detective loved pushing the envelope.

"No. We don't have a warrant. I'm hoping a window will be open. If he comes in and meets two armed lawmen, he'll hand over the gun. If that doesn't work, we'll watch from the undergrowth until we can get inside. The cover is pretty dense up there."

The sheriff asked the dispatcher on the police radio to give him the weather report for Pinhook Mountain. A few minutes later he had his forecast. A line of thunderstorms was moving in.

"Well, my luck is officially over." He felt a tinge of foreboding.

Wayne Nichols nodded. He had heard the forecast too. Soon after that, the radio buzzed with static. It was hard to hear Deputy Fuller's voice.

"Say again," the sheriff said, with a sinking feeling.

"Suspect not alone. Accompanied. Repeat, suspect is accompanied."

Sheriff Bradley and his detective looked at each other. Wayne Nichols pulled out his gun and twirled the bullet chamber.

Chapter Twenty-Nine

—

Detective Wayne Nichols

SHERIFF BRADLEY WAS driving, but even with the coordinates and a fire post number, he got turned around a dozen times on the fire roads. The rain started. They were both swearing at the vehicle; its tires continually slipped in the clay. The gears clashed as they clawed their way up the mountain. The sheriff was ready to park and look for Covington's place on foot when they finally spotted a little log cabin, almost completely hidden in the brush.

The car came to a stop, and Detective Nichols rolled down his window. The scent of old tar permeated the moist air. The cabin's timbers had been oiled with creosote.

They lost another half hour covering their car with branches and making their way through the rough underbrush that led to the cabin. Every door and window was locked tight. The sheriff's plan to have a lone Covington confront two armed representatives of the law was falling apart.

The whole forest smelled like rain-washed pine. Every now and then lightning hit someplace higher up on Pinhook

Mountain, followed by thunder so close it startled them. It was totally dark when the lights of Covington's car finally came bumping up the washboard road, its headlights striking through the trees. He turned off the car and ran cursing into the cabin. Someone followed him—impossible to tell who it was or even if it was male or female. The lights came on inside, and it was like watching a drive-in movie from the bushes.

They saw two men. One was definitely Covington; Detective Nichols didn't recognize the second. When they pulled off their overcoats, he saw holsters. Both men were packing. Covington sat down on a decrepit brown couch and the other man went to the small, round-shouldered fridge and pulled out two beers. The rain turned cold during the hour that Wayne and Ben watched them. Ben texted his deputies, telling them to move their location closer.

Finally, Covington stood up. He walked toward the rear of the cabin, moved aside a dirty sheet that served as a bedroom door and disappeared into a back room. When he came out, he said something to his companion and started putting his wet coat back on.

Ben pushed aside the underbrush separating him from Wayne and said, "He's going to come outside now. I'll follow him. You stay here and keep an eye on number two in the house."

Wayne nodded. The screen door squeaked open and then slammed shut. Covington pulled out a flashlight, which jumped around with his long stride. He crashed through the underbrush. When lightning hit close by, Wayne could see both the sheriff and Covington. He turned back to see what was happening in the cabin.

The second man was opening doors and drawers. He flipped up the cushions on the couch and put them back again. He looked under chairs and in the kitchen cupboards. As the man moved into the bedrooms, Wayne made his way around to the back of the house, trying to see into the high windows.

Suddenly the suspect opened a window. The sash lurched up and Wayne flattened himself against the exterior wall. A branch snapped under his weight and the man swore and came out on the back porch, breathing heavily. He was holding a gun, braced in a shooter's position. When he stepped off the porch into the wet underbrush, Wayne crept closer, panther quiet. When the man turned back to go into the cabin, Wayne rushed forward, stuck his gun into his ribs and said, "Drop your weapon. Put your hands in the air, slowly."

The man did, and Wayne grabbed both his arms, snapping them into handcuffs. He pushed him back into the cabin.

"Who are you?" he asked.

"You're making a big mistake," the man said.

"I don't think so." Wayne hit the man in the side of the head with his gun and made a satisfied sound as his captive grunted and fell to the floor. He unlocked the cuffs and attached the man's right wrist to the small leg of the old refrigerator before running back out into the storm. Hearing the sounds of men fighting, he raced in the direction of the noise. Then he heard a shot.

In a flash of lightning he could see two men grappling on a footbridge. It was Ben and Covington. They were high above the river. Covington was holding a gun in the air and Ben was trying to get it from him. Covington's back was against the railing of the bridge. Wayne ran toward them; he was breathing hard. Covington saw him coming and pointed the gun in his direction. The detective saw the sudden flash of a silver pistol and felt a searing white heat. He fell to the ground, struggling to breathe. The shot had knocked the wind out of him. A piercing pain ran up his leg; he felt along it carefully. When he pulled his hand away, it was sticky with blood. There was a coppery smell.

Through the brush he could see the two men. They were still fighting, but the scene slowed way down. Ben lurched in the air, grabbing for the pistol just as Covington threw it. It made a slow motion high arc. There was a long terrible moment before Wayne Nichols heard the splash from far below. Sheriff Ben Bradley howled in rage. Covington wrenched himself from Ben's grip and crashed away through the wet brush.

Wayne managed to yell out, "I got the other guy. He's in cuffs in the cabin," before the sheriff disappeared, roaring down the mountain after Covington.

Detective Nichols dialed the deputies. "George, get up here. I've been hit."

Moments later, Wayne heard George lumbering through the brush. He yelled, guiding George to the place where he'd been downed. He was lying in the wet leaves when George's flashlight hit his face.

"Go to the cabin and get the guy that's handcuffed to the refrigerator. Put him in the back of your patrol car. I think I can make it to your vehicle."

His leg hurt like hell, and he left a blood trail behind him, but he got to the car and pulled himself into the front passenger seat. When George appeared, he said, "Where's the suspect?"

"I didn't see him. Sorry, Detective, he got away."

"Damn it, George, how did that happen?"

"He must have removed the leg of the old fridge you cuffed him to. Cabin was empty when I got there."

"Better get me to the ER," Wayne said, gloomily. He glanced at his watch; it was almost one-thirty in the morning.

Chapter Thirty

Sheriff Ben Bradley

THE NEXT MORNING Ben drove into the office in a fog. He had gotten what seemed like only minutes of sleep since the Pinhook fiasco. Scenes from the night before kept roiling around in his brain. He had managed to wrestle Covington to the ground and get the cuffs on him before Deputy Fuller appeared with a huge police flashlight.

"Hey, boss," Deputy Fuller said as he yanked Covington to his feet. "Detective Nichols was hit, did you know?"

"No. Is it bad?"

"He says it's just a scratch, but I guess he's bleeding pretty heavily."

The sheriff shook his head, sick with rage. His fists were tight, fingernails biting into his palms. His supposedly foolproof plan had crashed and burned. They reached the police car and Deputy Fuller pushed Covington's head down, forcing him into the backseat and cuffing him to the bar. Wayne was in the front passenger seat of the deputy's car with George Phelps at the wheel.

"Where's the other suspect?" Ben asked Rob.

"Ran away before George got to him," the young deputy answered.

The sheriff sat down heavily in the driver's seat, totally spent. He had risked everything on this crazy notion that he and Wayne would be waiting snug and dry when Covington arrived at his hunting camp. The two of them, with guns drawn, would easily make him relinquish the murder weapon. The presence of the other man and the crashing storm had destroyed their advantage. Now the gun would never be recovered. It was deep in the clay, somewhere at the bottom of the Pinhook River.

Sheriff Ben Bradley and Deputy Fuller arrested Henry at two in the morning, read him his rights and put him in a cell. Then they'd gone wearily home.

"Call my lawyer," was the only thing Covington said, through gritted teeth.

As soon as the ADA's office opened the next morning, Sheriff Ben Bradley called the Prosecutor. He got lucky and was put right through to Terry Arnold.

"We arrested Henry Covington for the murder of Thomas John Ferris around two this morning."

"Okay. Why call me, Sheriff Ben? You know the drill. I'll wait for your report."

"You'll have the report in an hour, but this case has garnered a lot of publicity already and I wanted to run over the evidence with you to be sure you would try it. It's not cut and dried."

"Fine, make it short."

"First off, Covington had opportunity. He was in the house at the time of the Ferris murder. We've got CCTV tape that shows him there. Two other women were in the house. They've both been eliminated as suspects." He thought for a moment about Mrs. Anderson, wanting to spare her from testifying if possible, but then added, "We have an eye witness who saw him leaving the house immediately after the murder."

"Go on."

"Second, we have motive. We believe Covington killed Ferris to conceal a murder he committed fifteen years ago. That case was misclassified as a suicide of a fraternity brother of Henry Covington's named Ryan Gentry. At that time, Covington threatened Tom Ferris—who was Gentry's roommate—and told him to leave town. Probably thought Ferris could identify him as Ryan's killer.

"Third, there's means. The bullet that killed Ferris was a Winchester one fifty-eight grain semi-wad cutter hollow point. We retrieved it from the body. Covington tried to dispose of the gun that killed Ferris, injuring my detective in a shoot-out last night up in the Pinhook."

"Where's the gun now?"

"The bottom of the Pinhook River," the sheriff admitted. "It was the murder weapon, though, I got a good look at it. It was a Beretta Tomcat thirty thirty-two. I looked up the caliber this morning, and it was thirty-two ACP. That's the kind that uses one fifty-eight grain semi-wad cutter hollow points. And why would Covington have been so hell bent on throwing it in the river if it wasn't the murder weapon?" Ben exhaled slowly, hoping to God the DA's office would think they had enough evidence to indict.

"Can't you just get him to confess? That would make my job a lot easier."

Ben felt his whole body begin to relax. The ADA sounded like he was on board.

"Not without violating every rule of the Geneva Convention. And while I'm tempted, Captain Paula from Nashville would have my ass."

"Get your report to me and I'll talk to the district attorney. If he agrees to try the case, the perp will need to come before the Judge. I'll request remand. His defense attorney will ask that he be released on the basis that you don't have the murder weapon, blah, blah, blah. Since it's a capital crime, we'll need to assemble a grand jury. Man, it's just not my day." His weary voice trailed off and there was a click.

At the end of a long afternoon of tying up loose ends, the sheriff got a call from Hadley Johns in the lab. When they finished talking, euphoria raced through him like a shot of hard liquor. Their first check of the shutter dogs for fingerprints at the Booth Showhouse had turned up pieces so fragmentary and minimal, the system gave them nothing. Johns had forwarded the data to the state lab, where they had new equipment that could take partial fingerprints and stitch them together like a piece quilt. The result was a match to Henry Covington. The gun was at the bottom of the river, but the fingerprints were conclusive. They had the bastard in the house at the time of the Ferris murder, and now tiny Mrs. Anderson wouldn't have to be torn to shreds by a defense attorney.

The sheriff called everyone and said it was time to celebrate. Dory ordered pizza. His two deputies, George and Rob, left to go to the liquor store. Detective Nichols lumbered through the door just as the deputies returned.

"Hey, man, how're you feeling?" Ben asked, noting Nichols' limp and the white dressing on his upper arm.

"I've had worse."

Ben turned to the deputies. "Beer?" he asked, throwing up his hands. "That's all you got? I've got some real stuff in my desk. I'll get it."

He returned shortly after with a half empty bottle of Jim Beam, poured some in paper cups and passed them around.

"Here's to my team; I salute you all." The sheriff held his glass up in the air. "Dory, you're officially included in briefing meetings from now on."

"What about me questioning suspects?" she asked, walking over to Wayne. Dory looked up at him and winked. "Seems like you needed my help to get Covington."

"Hey, hold on. What about me?" Deputy Rob Fuller asked. "I've been the one studying for the detective exam and I'm set to take it in a few months. Dory has no training at this," he insisted, running hands through his hair and pinching his lips together.

"Time out, guys," Ben said. "I'm going to have to give this some thought. However, right now we're in the enviable position of having Tom Ferris' killer in a cell. I'm in the mood to party with my pretty lady. The Ferris funeral is tomorrow morning. It's at All Saints Episcopal on First Street at nine a.m., if any of you can make it." Ben took a huge bite of pizza.

AN HOUR OR so later the group broke up. Deputy George Phelps sauntered out, saying he and his wife were headed to his mother's place for a family reunion. Deputy Rob Fuller said he had a date. When Ben closed the office door behind him, the only people still drinking were his detective and Dory. On his way to Mae's, the sheriff called Detective Pascoe. The old man didn't answer, so Ben left a message.

"We arrested the bastard," was all he said.

Chapter Thirty-One

Detective Wayne Nichols

Despite the pain in his leg, Detective Nichols had joined the office party in full swing, enjoying the flush of victory, even though he sensed the case was far from over. Once everyone else left, Wayne and Dory were alone in the office.

Wayne was grabbing his jacket from the rack when Dory said, "There's something about this case that's still eating you, isn't there?"

"There is." Wayne shrugged his shoulders, shaking off whatever still bothered him. "Maybe I'm just having a hard time letting it go." He put on his jacket but stayed put.

Dory finished her drink but lingered, picking up the pizza boxes and napkins.

"It's nothing," the detective said, shaking his head. "I'm out of here."

"Wait." Dory put a hand on his arm. "It's something personal, isn't it? Sit down a minute, Wayne."

"No, it's nothing." Wayne stood by Dory's desk looking out the window of the office, but he didn't leave. He felt his leg muscles tighten, as if he was getting ready to run. His shoulders were tight. He had the sensation of things moving too fast to process.

"You can tell me." Her voice was almost a whisper. "They say confession is good for the soul, you know."

Finally Wayne sighed deeply and said, "When I was a teenager, I was in foster care in the UP. I ran away when I was seventeen. There was a younger kid there, about ten years old. We weren't brothers, but he was the only family I ever had." This case, with Bethany Cooper and Miranda both wanting to cherish Tom Ferris as a brother, brought the kid back. "Truth is, I've always felt guilty about leaving him." He bit his lip. He felt frozen to the spot. He was staring at the walls, but not seeing. As if talking to himself, he continued, "I told him when he got a little older, he could come and live with me, but it never happened." He felt the wall of ice he had built around the past start to crack.

Dory touched his arm. "I can see why this case was a gut-wrencher. You're such a private guy, Wayne, sometimes I forget that there's a human side of you. You're a detective, so of course you need answers, but you're human too."

"I want you to keep this to yourself, Dory Clarkson." Wayne's voice was full of menace. "No one else can know. It was hard enough for me to tell you."

He swallowed hard. He felt like he had opened a vein by talking about his past. He feared the wound would never heal, now that he had shared it with another person. He avoided eye contact with her, looking at the floor.

"When I give my word, I keep it."

"If I ever find out you told anyone, you'll be very sorry."

Dory rested her arm on his. There was a long silence before she said, "I'm hitting the town with my new girlfriend, Evangeline Bontemps, tonight. Would you like to come with us?"

Wayne shook his head, dragging his palms down his pant leg, wiping off sweat.

"Was it that hard to tell another person a little bit about yourself?"

Wayne grabbed her upper arm and then just as suddenly released it. His hands trembled. Without another word he hobbled to the exit, slamming the door behind him.

DRIVING TO HIS apartment, Wayne picked up his phone. He pushed the letter "L" on his Contacts button. Lucy Ingram's phone number popped up, along with an image of her winsome face. He didn't push the 'send' button.

When he had seen her at the ER the night before, all the months since their break-up seemed to vanish. His profuse bleeding got him to the front of the triage line. A nurse recorded his blood pressure, which was elevated, and took his temperature. Dr. Lucy Ingram came into the cubicle a few minutes later.

"What have you let yourself in for this time, Detective?" she asked. She cut away his pant leg and said something to the nurse that he didn't catch. Wayne felt anxious when the nurse returned with a long, silver-bladed instrument.

"This is going to hurt," Lucy said, but her eyes were warm.

She was right. Once she removed the bullet and tended to the wound, Lucy bandaged his leg, cleansed the scrape on his arm, and put on a dressing.

"Looks like you're going to live. I figured you would. You're too tough to die. Come see me some time, Wayne, but not at the hospital." Still slim as a reed, she slipped out through the drapes.

WHEN WAYNE NICHOLS reached his apartment after the impromptu party at the office, he grabbed a beer and looked around. He had a sense of the past colliding with the present. He was breathing in short bursts, the back of his throat ached, and his chest was so heavy he wondered if he was having a heart attack. Telling Dory about the foster brother he left behind brought to the surface the pain that always rode beneath his skin. Had it really been that hard telling Dory he felt guilty about leaving his young brother? Would it really be so hard to tell Lucy?

He and Lucy had stopped dating a few months before the Ruby Mead Allison case began the previous spring. On one of their last dates, they had gone horseback riding. She was in the lead on the trail. Her long brown hair streamed behind her in the sunshine. When they stopped in a meadow, she set out a blanket and food. He could still feel her lips on his as she bent to kiss him where he lay in the tall grass. She smelled like lemons.

He groaned, remembering the pain in her face the night they broke up. He heard her say, "It's not enough anymore Wayne. You want to know everything about me, but you won't tell me anything about yourself. I want to really know you, down deep. I want all your stories." He hadn't been able to share anything with her then.

"You're an idiot," he told himself. "Man up." He dialed Lucy's number.

She wasn't home and for a moment, he almost hung up. Then he took a deep breath and left her a message.

"Lucy, it's Wayne. If you're still interested, I'm ready." He walked to his bedroom and sat down on his bed. Then he stood up and opened the safe he had installed in the wall. He pulled out a St. Anthony's medal and draped it around his neck. Its metallic coolness helped a bit. He lay down on his bed and tried to close off his mind.

When after midnight the phone rang, he reached for it automatically, barking out, "Nichols."

"It's Lucy."

"I need to see you." His hand clasped the medal.

There was a pause and an indrawn breath. "I want to see

you, too, Wayne, but only if you want a relationship, a real relationship, not just a roll in the hay. When you're ready, come over." She clicked off.

He sat up, putting his feet on the cool wooden floors. The air conditioner hummed. This was harder than anything he had ever done. Feeling like he was going to his hanging, he walked naked into the shower and let the hot water steam on his back and shoulders. Half an hour later, he was on his way to Lucy's house on Little Chapel Road.

As HE DROVE into Lucy's driveway, all the memories came flooding back. She was the smartest, sexiest woman he had ever been with. He turned off the car and sat there for a few minutes. Lucy's porch light was on. She came to the front door and opened it, looking out, silhouetted by the light. She was wearing green hospital scrubs; she'd obviously just finished her shift. He felt his leg. It still ached, but the swelling was going down.

Lucy didn't walk off the porch toward him, and he didn't get out of his car. They looked at each other across the distance as the moon came out from under the clouds. Lucy crossed her arms in front of her chest, hugging herself. He turned off the car, his fingers sweaty on the key. As he opened the car door, he realized he was trembling.

You've got to do this, he told himself as he got out of the car and headed straight for her door. When he reached the porch, he took her in his arms and murmured, "It's you I've wanted all along. Nobody else, just you."

She took his hand and led him into the house. Neither of them spoke as Lucy took him into her bedroom. He sat on the edge of her bed as she pulled her scrubs off. She sat down and started unbuttoning his shirt. When she saw his St. Anthony's medal, she gasped. Her fingers touched her parted lips.

Her voice both shaky and soft, she said, "In all the times we slept together, I never saw this."

When they were both naked, lying side by side, Wayne leaned over and kissed her passionately. He ran his hand up her body to touch her breast.

"I want you," he whispered, his voice raw.

Lucy sat up in bed and said, "Not yet, my friend. You have things to tell me. Begin at the beginning." She touched the medal around his neck.

He felt the wall of gray ice sliding, breaking in chunks and falling away.

"The medal belonged to my foster mother," he said. He took a deep, shaky breath and groaned quietly as the words poured out of him like water over a broken dam. He told her about the fear and rage he felt when he listened to his foster father beat his wife. The sick thud of his fists hitting her. The anger he felt when his foster mother showed him the bruises. His frantic departure when he realized there was no other way to keep from killing his foster father. The tears on the face of his little brother as he pleaded, "Don't go." The mist that took him that morning. When he was finished, he stopped, panting as though he had just run a race.

Lucy got out of bed, walked to the kitchen and padded back, carrying two drinks, ice clinking. "Go on," she said, and he did.

"I went back there three years later," he told her, again seeing the dingy ranch house on the gravel road. "It was getting dark by the time I found the house. His pick-up truck was parked in the yard. Broken whiskey bottles were everywhere. I opened the screen door and called her name—Jocelyn. She came into the living room and cried out. She didn't recognize me." He stopped, breathing hard.

"It's Wayne," I told her. "Wayne Nichols. She screamed, 'You're too goddamn late. I always thought you would save me, but you never came. I had to end it myself. I stuck the pig with a knife.'

"I felt cold all over and I nearly fell against the wall. I asked her if he was dead. She said she didn't know. We walked out to the pick-up and opened the door to the truck. His body fell out onto the gravel. He was still warm, but when I touched his neck to feel a pulse, there was none. He was dead. The smell of his blood made me sick."

Wayne took a long hard swallow of the whiskey, feeling it stabilize his nausea.

"Shhhh," Lucy said. "Enough. That's enough for tonight." She laid her long trim body on top of him, feeling his shuddering breaths. He was cold, almost in shock. She waited until he warmed and started breathing slowly. Her compassion enveloped him. Blanketed with her care, he felt something in his core melt.

Later Lucy moved off him and sat up on the edge of the bed. She reached for the soft, extra-large T-shirt she slept in and pulled it over her head. The rain had cooled the air, banishing the heat of the summer night. When she slid back under the sheets, Wayne sat up. "I have to say the rest," he told her.

"It can wait," she said, her voice warm and slow. She reached for him.

"No. It has to be now. If I don't say it now, I never will." He was shuddering.

Lucy sat up beside him and hugged her bent knees.

"I asked Jocelyn about my brother. 'I found his body a week ago,' she told me. 'Was there an accident?' I asked her. 'No, he'd done it,' she shouted. 'It took me weeks to find the boy. He'd buried him without even wrapping him in a blanket. Not even his blanket. That's why I stabbed him.' She was shaking so hard her lips were blue. I realized then that she was still holding a long butcher knife in her hands.

"I'd been shadowing a detective and I asked her if there was any evidence that her husband had killed the boy. May God forgive me for asking her that question. I disgusted myself. Asking her for evidence. She knew!"

Wayne took a deep, raggedy breath. The story dragged itself into the present, tearing and ripping, like a wolf chewing off its foot to escape a trap. Lucy didn't move; she hardly breathed.

"We dragged the man's corpse to the place where she found my brother's body. We laid them side by side in the dark, under the shadows of the trees. 'We need to inform the police,' I told her.

"'I'll kill you first,' she screamed. I knew she meant it. She was so little, standing furious next to me. I held her arms tight to her sides. 'It's okay. I'll help you,' I said. 'Let me have the knife.' She gave it to me. We got a shovel and buried them. At dawn we drove his truck to a nearby gravel pit and sunk it. 'You need to leave here and never come back," I told her. I gave her the keys to my truck. She hugged me and said good-bye.

"I cleaned myself up and waited two days. Then I walked over to the neighbors' farm. I said I had come back to see Jocelyn and the family but they had cleared out, all three of them." Wayne was exhausted, enervated. He lay back on the bed, choked with harsh sobs.

"Lucy, I've lived a lie. I'm a counterfeit detective who never got justice for the only person I ever really called family. My little brother lies in a nameless grave."

"It's over now," Lucy said and kissed him, gently tasting his lips with her tongue.

"It will never be over," he murmured, but he took the peace she offered. The pain in his leg had lessened. They made love with a ferocity that surpassed anything he'd felt before. He had to have her, the clean warmth of her; the pure hard release.

Chapter Thirty-Two

July Powell

A T LEAST IT'S *not raining this morning.* July was outside, sitting at the picnic table, still wearing a robe over her pajamas. The kids were sitting with her, wearing their bathing suits, the remains of breakfast in front of them. The nine-year-old identical twin boys were thin and lanky in their red swim trunks, tan with sprays of freckles on noses and shoulders. With their shirts off, they were easier to tell apart—Parker had a mole on his left shoulder and Nathan was slightly more muscular. Olivia was paler, having inherited her father's blond hair, blue eyes, and milky complexion. Her arms and legs were starting to thin out, but she still had an endearing chubbiness to her torso. *Six years old already. That baby fat won't last much longer.*

Nate asked, "Can I take the kayak out by myself?"

"If you wear your life-jacket and stay in sight of our dock you can." She held her hand up to forestall the inevitable whine from Parker. "You get a turn after Nate. But all three of you need to carry your cereal bowls into the kitchen and make your beds before you get near the water."

"Amberleigh never has to make her bed," Olivia informed her mother, "or clear dishes."

"I'm your mother, not Amberleigh's," July replied. "The chores we do in our family may not be the same as the family of your best friend." All three of her children regarded her with wide eyes. "Seriously, get a move on."

She stood up and grabbed the milk carton, cereal box, and her cup of coffee. "Nate, bring your bowl in to the sink, please."

She picked up her cellphone, which was ringing on the counter. Seeing her husband's picture on the screen, she pressed the ignore button and put the milk and cereal away. Pouring herself another cup of coffee, she took it and her phone into the bedroom. Sitting on her bed, she looked out the window at the sparkling water in the cove and felt like she was going to cry. She could hear the kids clanking around in the kitchen, followed by muffled thumps that hopefully indicated bed-making.

After sending Fred a quick text to let him know she and the kids were fine, July blew her nose and put on what she thought of as her 'mom bathing suit.' It was a modest tankini with a matching cover-up. She smeared sunscreen everywhere she could reach. Her hair was a mess, but she didn't care. She found a ball cap on Fred's side of the closet and pulled her ponytail through it, then went outside to make sure no one drowned today.

AFTER LUNCH, AGAIN served al fresco, the skies clouded up again, so she shepherded the kids inside for another movie. Then July went upstairs to call her closest friend, Sandi Townsend, who lived down the street from her in Rosedale.

Sandi answered on the first ring. "July, where are you? I haven't seen you or the kids. I went for a run this morning and saw Fred sitting on your front steps. He looked awful.

Is everything okay with you guys?" Sandi could carry a conversation all by herself.

"I'm at the lake house with the kids, and honestly things aren't great. Do you have a minute to talk?"

"I'm just leaving to take my kids to the doctor's office. I missed some immunizations for them, and they have to get them before school starts. Can I call you back?"

"That's fine. Call me when you're alone."

"I'll call you as soon as I can. Do you want me to check on Fred tonight?"

"No, Sandi, don't. He's hardly a child. I'm sure he's fine." July clenched her fists until the nails bit into her palms. "I'll talk to you later. Bye."

July watched *Finding Nemo* with her kids in the basement, laughing at the movie the way she always did. Then she broke her own rule and ordered pizza for dinner without making a salad to go with it. The kids were thrilled.

"Yay, no yucky green stuff," Livy exclaimed, then chowed down four pieces of pizza.

"What's for dessert?" Parker asked. "Can we go out for ice cream?" July didn't answer right away.

"Please, Mommy, please?" They all chimed in.

"Oh, why not?" July asked the rhetorical question. In the stampede for the door, Parker knocked his sister into the side of the refrigerator and kept on going. July pulled her daughter to her feet.

"Are you okay, sweetie?"

Olivia's forehead had a rapidly purpling welt. She blinked her eyes and started to sway.

"I don't think so, Mommy." Her six-year-old collapsed on the kitchen floor.

After telling the boys to get into the car, July picked Olivia up, grabbed her purse and car keys and ran out the door.

Chapter Thirty-Three

July Powell

JULY LAID HER daughter's limp body in the front passenger seat of her Suburban and buckled the seat belt across her little chest and shoulders. Nate and Parker were already in the third-row seat in back.

"Why does Livy get to sit up there, and not in her booster?" Nate whined.

"Because we're taking her to the hospital. I think she has a concussion." July spoke calmly in the startled silence that followed those words. "I always tell you two not to be so rough with your little sister, and now look what's happened." She closed the passenger door and went around to get into the driver's seat.

"Stupid! Now we can't get ice cream," was the first thing she heard after she closed the door. "It's not my fault, Mom. Parker pushed her, not me."

Parker started to cry. "I'm sorry! I didn't mean to hurt her."

Dear God, help me. July started the car and put it in gear. She decided to ignore the boys rather than scream at them about their selfishness. That wouldn't do any good right now. Olivia's eyes fluttered, and July heard her murmur, then she threw up all over herself.

"Livy, can you hear me, honey?" Her daughter looked at July with wide eyes.

"Where am I?"

"We're in the car sweetheart. You hit your head. We're going to the hospital right now, as fast as we can." Tears squirted from Olivia's eyes and she swiped the vomit from her chin.

"I don't want to go to the hospital," she wailed. "I want to go home. I want my daddy!"

July saw blue lights flashing in her rearview mirror. She looked at her speedometer and realized she was going eighty miles an hour. She slowed down, put her turn-signal on and eased off onto the shoulder of the road. Putting her window down, she waited for the officer to come to her window.

"Ma'am, do you know how fast you were going back there?" The Highway Patrolman was a gray-haired man with a strong jaw. He bent down to the window and peered into the interior of the car with a suspicious glare.

"I know I was going too fast, Officer." July gestured at her sobbing six-year-old. "I think she's concussed. I'm trying to get her to the hospital." She looked back at her sons, wide-eyed and, for once, silent, in the back of the vehicle. "I've got my boys with me too, as you can see."

The patrolman rubbed his jaw. "All right then. I'm Lieutenant Whyte. Do you want to follow me, or shall we load y'all into my car?"

"Your car!" The boys chorused. Lieutenant Whyte looked at July.

"Up to you, Ma'am."

"I'm July Powell. Olivia and I will follow you, but Nathan and Parker can ride in your car, if that's okay with you." The boys scrambled out and slammed the door behind them.

"Is there anyone you'd like me to call to meet us at Good Shepherd?"

"My husband, Fred Powell." She gave him Fred's cellphone number.

"Will do, you just keep up with me. I'll get you there."

He walked away before July could thank him. She watched him usher the boys into his car, then climb in and take off with a spray of gravel. Pulling out right behind him, July glanced over at Olivia.

"Hang on, Livy. Your daddy's going to meet us there."

Olivia was pale and trembling. Her nose was running and her shirt was soaked with vomit. She nodded wordlessly. July put the accelerator to the floor.

JULY WAS IN the exam room with her daughter, trying to keep her awake. She had texted her mother and Mae, promising to update them when she knew more. The police had contacted Fred, and she hoped that her parents would come and pick up the boys soon.

The twins were out in the waiting area. The ride in a patrol car had been the highlight of their summer, but after all the excitement they'd faded fast. Last time she had checked on them in the gray plastic chairs of the ER waiting area, they were almost asleep.

Olivia had been examined by the triage nurse, who said, "I don't like the look of her pupils." She had left them in the room and gone to call Dr. Selfridge, the on-call Pediatric Resident. He'd ordered a CT, and they were waiting for results. Olivia's eyes were fluttering, closing again. She looked tiny in the ER cot, dressed in a hospital gown with her normally buoyant hair matted to her head. July had cleaned her up as best she could, but the little girl still smelled faintly of vomit. The bump on her forehead was swollen and purple.

"You've got to keep your eyes open, honey," July reminded her softly. She picked up her daughter's limp hand.

"I can't stay awake anymore, Mommy, I'm so tired."

"Yes you can." Fred Powell stood in the doorway. "Can I come in, or is this a girl's only room?"

"You can come in, Daddy." Olivia gave him a solemn look. "But Nate and Parker are *not* allowed."

Fred walked to the other side of the cot from July, pulled a chair over and sat down. He took Olivia's hand and rubbed it.

Looking over at July, he said, "Do you need a break?"

"I'll go check on the boys." July stood up.

"They're fine. Your parents took them to the cafeteria."

"Mama and Daddy got here?"

He nodded, his expression somber. "I was at their house when the officer called. They followed me. They offered to take Nate and Parker home with them. Then we can stay with Livy if they admit her."

July stretched and rolled her head from side to side. "I'm … glad you're here, Fred. She's been asking for you." She looked into his light blue eyes. "And we need to talk, but it doesn't have to be right now. I'll go track down my parents and tell them to take the boys and go."

Fred smiled. "You know they're not leaving without seeing her, right?"

"I know."

After July located the rest of the family in the cafeteria and her parents had kissed Olivia and left with the boys in tow, Dr. Selfridge stuck his head in the door.

"The CT scan looks good. I think you can take this brave little lady on home."

Fred crossed himself. "Oh, thank God. Did you hear that, Livy? You can sleep in your own bed tonight."

"Not exactly," the doctor said. "She does have a concussion. You can let her sleep for twenty minutes out of every hour, but you'll have to do that for the next twenty four hours. If she starts to vomit again or loses consciousness, you should call 911."

July and her husband both looked at him in dismay.

"You'll have to take turns and set an alarm so you don't all sleep too long. The good news is, there's no sign of a skull fracture."

Skull fracture? July felt sick. Fred's normally pale complexion had faded to ash.

"Should we take her to the lake house, or back home to Rosedale?" Fred asked.

"Rosedale. She'll be closer to Vanderbilt Children's Hospital if anything goes wrong. The nurse will be in with some paperwork for you. Good-bye, Miss Olivia."

Livy gave him a half-hearted smile and a little wave.

Chapter Thirty-Four

—

Mae December

IT WAS AUGUST 10th, the day of Tommy's memorial service. Mae hurried from her car into the All Saint's Church and found a seat in the back. To her surprise—given how long Tommy had been away from town—the congregation filled the church. She didn't see her parents or July. *With Olivia's accident, they couldn't make it.* She had heard that Olivia had made it through the night just fine. Miranda and her husband were in the front row, and Dan and Bethany Cooper turned their heads to look when the door opened to admit Ben, Tammy, and Patrick. The three of them slid in next to Mae just as the organist began to play. The man in an expensive suit in front of her looked back and nodded at Ben, who stiffened beside her.

"What's Townsend doing here?" Ben whispered in her ear.

"Greg was in Tommy's fraternity. I guess he's paying his respects. Shh …."

The minister walked into the sanctuary and paused beside the casket. The organist played softly while he stood staring down at the closed casket that contained the body of Tommy Ferris, the man her sister had once loved. The Reverend Father Joseph Brice ascended to the altar and began to speak.

"I normally think of death as a blessed homecoming." His voice was soft, yet it carried to every corner of the old stone church. Light flooded through the stained glass windows, casting shadows of reds and blues across his thin face. "But Thomas John Ferris was taken from us too soon. On the verge of reconnecting with his family, he was struck down."

Miranda sobbed loudly from the front pew. The smell of lilies floated through the warm air. Ben took Mae's hand and squeezed it as the tears began to roll down her face. She looked over at Tammy, whose face was buried in Patrick's shoulder.

"At times like this, the love of our Heavenly Father can seem out of reach," Father Brice continued, "but we won't know the strength of the anchor until we're tested by the storm."

All the women and several of the men in the church were crying openly now. Reverend Brice took a deep breath. "I know, deep in my heart, that we'll be reunited with Tom one day, and that he's at peace now. Let us pray."

"Do you want to go to the cemetery?" Ben asked Mae.

They were standing by her car in the sunny parking lot after the conclusion of the emotionally draining service. Patrick and Tammy had already left, and Mae and Ben were watching as the rest of the mourners filed out. Miranda emerged, supported by her husband. Bethany Cooper went over to her with her hands outstretched, but Miranda and her husband walked right past and climbed into a waiting limousine.

"I think that's just for the family," Mae answered.

"Well, then the Coopers should be in that limo with Miranda."

"Why? Miranda was the only family Tommy had left," Mae replied in confusion.

"Bethany's Miranda's half-sister." Ben put his arm around her shoulders. "You look wrung out. Let's go get a coffee and I'll explain."

Chapter Thirty-Five

Mae December

AFTER HAVING COFFEE with Ben, Mae made the short drive to her sister's house. She still wished that Ben had not kept the information about Bethany Cooper from her. Sometimes it was hard being involved with a sheriff. She knew his duty was to the job and the citizens of Rose County, but it wasn't easy when she felt cut off from part of his life. Ben asked her to keep quiet about Bethany, but it was especially problematic keeping information about this case from July, given her history with Tommy. And it was very hard to keep Ben in the dark about what July had shared.

On the drive, Mae thought about her role in the family as the loyal little sister. Since she was a toddler, July and her parents—especially her mother—had been in charge of her life, protecting her and gently telling her what to do. Getting engaged to Noah had helped her separate her life from theirs, but after he died, she was devastated. Her mother and sister quickly moved back to their places as older, wiser guardian angels. Keeping secrets from her family went against everything Mae believed in. *I'm at a crossroads here.* She took in a deep, shaky breath.

Driving into July and Fred's neighborhood, she crossed her fingers that Olivia was okay and that July and Fred had reconciled. Her sister's Suburban was in the parking court in front of their large, Georgian style home. One of the three garage doors was open, and Fred's navy blue Mercedes was parked at an odd angle inside. Everything was quiet.

Three newspapers lay at the end of the cobblestone driveway. Mae parked her car and walked back to the street to pick up the newspapers—two waterlogged and one dry. She checked the mailbox and added the substantial pile of mail to the top of the dry newspaper. Carrying the two wet papers in her other hand, she walked through the open garage door and set everything down on the counter.

She threw the soggy papers into the nearby trashcan and began to whittle down the stack of mail, throwing away flyers and obvious junk. Halfway through the pile, she came to an ivory envelope bearing July's name, handwritten in blue ink. There was no return address, but the initials T.J.F. were written on the top-left corner of the envelope. It was postmarked in Rosedale. Mae laid the envelope aside to give to July. After quickly sorting through the rest of the mail, she carried everything inside.

The kitchen was empty. "July?" Mae called out. "Fred? Anybody home?"

Her brother-in-law walked around the corner and put his finger to his lips. "Ssshh. July's asleep."

Fred wore running shorts and an inside out white T-shirt. His white-blond hair stood on end. He yawned, rubbing the back of his neck.

"You can just set that mail over by the coffeemaker. Thanks for bringing it in. Are you here to check on Livy?"

"July texted me that Livy was being seen in the E.R. I talked to Mama early this morning. So it was a concussion?"

"Yes, it was. I was over at your parents' for dinner and a state trooper called my cellphone to tell me that he was escorting July and the kids to Good Shepherd Hospital."

"Is she going to be all right?"

Fred walked over and gave her a quick hug. "She'll be fine, but we can only let her sleep for twenty minutes an hour for twenty four hours after she bumped her head. July and I are taking turns sleeping ourselves." He closed his eyes for a second, and then went on. "Olivia's in the den if you want to see her." Fred motioned to the state-of-the-art coffeemaker. "I'm going to fix myself a cappuccino. Can I make you one?"

"No, thanks. Ben and I got coffees right after Tommy's funeral, so I don't need any more caffeine."

Fred shook his head. "I forgot all about that funeral. Did your parents make it?"

"I didn't see them. It was packed, though. Half the town was there."

"They took Nate and Parker home with them last night. I guess they couldn't find a sitter today." He busied himself at the coffee machine, filling the reservoir with bottled water and putting beans in the grinder. With his back to Mae, he said, "I know they were planning to attend." Pausing to look over his shoulder, he added, "Was he really so great?"

"What do you mean?"

"Tom Ferris. Was he really this amazing guy, or is it just that people were fascinated by his disappearance and murder?"

Mae pulled one of the barstools out and sat down at the counter. *Poor Fred. How do I answer that?* She rubbed her temples.

"I was very young when he disappeared, you know. He was nice to me, though. He never treated me like an annoying kid-sister. I had a little bit of a crush on him back then. But who knows what kind of man he would have been? As it is, he's the guy who left my sister when she …."

Fred turned around. "She told me, Mae. She told me everything last night, about the pregnancy, the miscarriage—

all of it. What I don't understand is why she's pined for him all these years."

Mae started to protest, but Fred held up his hand. "She did. She kept the key to that damned house all this time. His class ring is in the drawer of her bedside table. Shouldn't she be furious at him?"

She took a deep breath. "I was mainly confused when he disappeared, but I've been furious ever since I learned about the pregnancy. July's an enigma to me in some ways. I have never quite understood what makes her tick."

Fred nodded. "She's a puzzle to me too, a lot of the time. But since this happened, I'm determined to spend the time to understand my wife."

"Good for you, Fred. Maybe, after things settle down around here, you can ask July about her feelings for Tom Ferris. It might help you both."

Fred finished making his coffee and picked up the mug. "I need to go wake Livy again. Do you want to come with me?"

"Yes, and I can sit with her awhile if you need to shower or anything." She wrinkled her nose. "You know I love you, man, but you've smelled better."

He laughed. "It's been a rough one. I'm not sure when I had my last shower. And thanks, Mae. I love you, too." Fred squeezed Mae's hand.

Chapter Thirty-Six

Sheriff Ben Bradley

ON THE MORNING of August 10th, the sheriff finished his report to the prosecutor and had Dory fax it over. Covington had been in the holding cell for forty hours. He rubbed his eyes. He stood up, sat back down, then he stood up again, this time walking out to Dory's desk.

"Any luck getting info on the three guys on the football kicker squad?"

Dory was wearing dark red this morning. Ben wondered what that might say about her mood.

"I have all three of their names," Dory said, her voice clipped and efficient. "Rob's talking to one of them on the phone now. I've placed calls to the other two. Hopefully we'll hear back shortly. The prosecutor has to file the charges pretty soon."

"I don't need you to remind me of that," Ben snapped.

"Sorreee." Dory rolled her eyes. "No need to get your undies in a bunch."

Rob poked his head in to say he'd just finished talking to the field goal kicker. "Guy's name is Charlie Armor. He lives in

Nashville. I asked him to come in. He'll be here at one o'clock."

Ben turned on his heel and left the reception area. He called Detective Nichols again.

"Nichols." Wayne sounded as if he'd just woken up.

"Sorry to keep bugging you, Wayne. We just got ahold of the kicker, name's Charlie Armor; he's coming in at one. Could we meet before that? I really need your help." Ben hated how desperate he sounded.

"Okay, I'll be in at noon."

When Wayne came in, he was pale and limping.

"Are you feeling okay?" Ben asked.

"I'm fine," Wayne said in the gruff tone that Ben knew meant he wanted the subject dropped. He and Ben discussed their strategy for over an hour and decided to make the conversation with Armor a casual one. Ben would conduct the interview. Wayne would observe from the two-way mirror.

At one point Dory knocked on his office door and when Ben yelled, "Come in," she brought in sandwiches and fresh coffee. Ben heaved a sigh of relief. He hadn't eaten in what seemed like days. He felt renewed appreciation for Dory.

Dory buzzed the intercom a few minutes later saying Mr. Charlie Armor had arrived.

Both Sheriff Bradley and Detective Nichols walked out to the front office to meet the former player. Armor was muscle heavy, with thinning hair and dark eyes.

"Mr. Armor, thank you for coming in. I really appreciate your making yourself available," the sheriff said. "If you haven't eaten lunch, we have sandwiches and coffee."

"I've eaten," Armor said, looking at them warily.

The sheriff showed him to the interview room. Once they were seated he said, "We're not taping this interview, and as you see, I'm alone here. If this were an official interrogation, we would be taping and two of us would be present. Anything you say will go no further; you have my word on that."

Armor nodded, but still looked suspicious. "What's this about?"

"The 1998 Bowl Game between Southeast Tennessee and Florida State."

Armor inhaled sharply.

"Just after that game, one of the guys in the Sigma Chi fraternity died. At the time it was thought that he killed himself by jumping out the window of the frat house. His name was Ryan Gentry. Do you remember that?"

"Yes," Armor responded, looking down at the table.

"It turns out that it was murder, not suicide." Ben waited, but Armor didn't say anything. "We think Gentry's murder had to do with him discovering some golden handshake money that came to Henry Covington and possibly Greg Townsend to shave the point spread on the bowl game. Do you know anything about that?"

Armor didn't respond right away. Ben waited. Finally, Armor sighed and said, "If I tell you what I know, are you going to prosecute?"

"Unlikely, but tell me what you know first," Ben said, "Were you offered a bribe to miss that last field goal kick?"

"I was offered ten thousand, but I turned it down," Armor said. "Naturally, I got blamed for missing the field goal, but it wasn't my fault. The guy who set the football did it wrong. I didn't put it all together until later, but that's what happened."

"So you didn't take the money?"

"No, never saw a dime of it then or later. I thought they might pay me after the game because of the missed goal, but that didn't happen."

"Then you didn't commit a crime. Truth is, we don't really care about the money or that game. If you know the other player involved in the kick, you can tell him we aren't going after him either." Armor was leaning back now and starting to look more relaxed. "The guy we want is the person who killed Ryan Gentry. We think it was Henry Covington."

"I wouldn't be surprised, but I don't know it for a fact. There were lots of rumors after Ryan died—rumors that Covington and possibly Greg Townsend were involved."

"Do you know anything that would implicate Townsend? We have a lot of evidence against Covington, mostly circumstantial, but we think it's enough to nail him. Townsend is the guy who probably masterminded the whole thing and we haven't got a thing on him."

"About two weeks before the bowl game, a big time gambler from Las Vegas met with Townsend, Covington and me. I never got the guy's name but he was the one who offered me the ten K. I was offended and walked out."

"Would you testify to Covington and Townsend being at the meeting?"

"I sure would," Armor said. "I always thought both those guys were bent."

WHEN ARMOR LEFT, Ben called the ADA again. He put the phone on speaker so Wayne could hear the conversation.

"It's Sheriff Bradley. I'm calling to let you know that we have some new evidence that links Covington to the Gentry killing." He told him that Armor was prepared to testify that Covington and Townsend were at the meeting with the Las Vegas gambler.

"You still haven't got anything but a circumstantial case," Terry said. "You haven't got any evidence. Covington could have turned down the golden handshake just the same as Armor did. Nor can you prove that somebody in that frat house killed Gentry to keep him from talking about the money. During your crazy trip up to Pinhook, you managed to lose the murder weapon. You're going to have to let Covington loose."

"What the hell? You're the prosecuting attorney, Terry. You're supposed to be on my side here. We've got plenty of evidence to nail Covington for the Ferris murder at least. We've gone all over that. He was in the house at the time of the murder.

We've got his fingerprints on the shutter dogs. I don't get this. Is somebody higher up telling you to let this one go?"

The prosecutor sighed. "Sorry man. All I've been told to tell you is that since you don't have the murder weapon, you have to release Henry Covington."

Ben stared down at his empty hands. He rubbed the heel of his palm against his sternum. His chest ached and he felt cold inside.

Wayne put a hand on his shoulder.

Chapter Thirty-Seven

———

Sheriff Ben Bradley

O N AUGUST 11TH, Sheriff Bradley and Dory stood in the basement of the sheriff's office building hovering over Captain Paula's IT expert, Mark Schneider, who was seated in front of the ancient computer. After several abortive conversations the previous day with Terry Arnold the prosecutor—who still insisted that Henry Covington be released—Ben realized he needed specialized help with the old computer. He had to obtain proof of the bribe Covington and probably Townsend had accepted to change the point spread on the old football game. After the requisite begging and groveling, he was given access to Captain Paula's whiz kid.

Mark Schneider was a skinny, nerdy looking youngster with spiky black hair and black-rimmed glasses. He reminded Ben of a punk version of Clark Kent, only without the muscles. He had three silver studs sticking out of his left ear, and a tattoo on the back of his neck. The head of a dragon stuck up out of his T-shirt. Mark's fingers were flying over the computer. The language emerging from his mouth became increasingly more profane until he took a deep breath, turned around, and threw up his hands.

"My decryption software doesn't seem to be working on this relic, and I can't do this with you two watching me," he frowned. "So unless you can come up with Ryan Gentry's password, you need to leave."

"Did you try Sigma Chi?" Ben asked.

"Seriously, dude? It was the first phrase I tried. So, I repeat, unless you can come up with Ryan's password …." He looked daggers at them.

Ben and Dory exited the basement.

"Do you think July might have any ideas?" Dory asked as they climbed the stairs. "You told me she visited Tom Ferris often at school before his disappearance. She probably got to know his fraternity brothers pretty well. If so, she might remember something about Ryan and what he might use for a password."

Ben clapped her on the shoulder, "You're brilliant. I'll call and ask her."

He dialed July's cellphone on their way up the stairs. "July, it's Ben," he said cautiously, knowing he was far from her favorite person at the moment.

"What do you want?" *Sounds like she's still mad.*

"We think we got the guy who killed Tom Ferris. We're trying to get into Ryan Gentry's old computer. We have a forensic IT guy here, but he needs Ryan's password. Mae said you used to visit Tom at his college whenever you could, so I thought you might have gotten to know Ryan enough to give us some idea of his likes and dislikes—we're trying to figure out his password."

"I don't really have time for this, Ben. Olivia had a concussion, and Fred and I have had to keep waking her up. We're exhausted."

"Is Livy okay?"

"I think so. It was a booger keeping her awake." July stifled a yawn. "But her CT scan was fine. She'll be all right in a few days."

"That's good. Can you remember anything about Ryan that might help?" he asked quietly. "Any ideas are welcome. I've got to get into that computer."

"I thought Ryan committed suicide. Didn't he?" July's voice sounded calmer and suddenly sad.

"Doesn't look like it. We think the same guy killed both Ryan and Tom Ferris."

There was a long silence. At last July said, "Well, then you have to get him. The only thing I remember about Ryan is that he loved *The Hobbit*, the book by Tolkien. Does that help?"

"You know," Ben said, "I think it might." He said good-bye, trying to remember the names of the Hobbit, the Wizard, the names of all the dwarves and the dragon in that wonderful story. He walked back downstairs murmuring, "Bilbo Baggins, Gandalf, Balin, Dwalin, Fili, Kili, Ori, Nori …." and told Mark that Ryan's favorite book was Tolkien's masterpiece.

"Piece of cake then," Mark said, grinning. He pulled up his T-shirt in the back and Ben and Dory were greeted by a large fire breathing reptile. "The password's got to be Smaug." He typed the dragon's name into the computer. The screen opened. "Okay, now what are we looking for?"

"We need to see if there are any unusual deposits in November or December prior to the 1998 Bowl Championship game that year. The final game was between Southeast Tennessee and Florida State. We were favored to win and we went down twenty-one to twenty."

"I'm on it," Mark said, turning his head and looking pointedly at the stairs.

"And we're leaving. Thanks, man."

HALF AN HOUR later Mark came upstairs with a flash drive. He stuck it in Dory's printer. Mark had isolated all the deposits for the Sigma Chi account that year. A typed list with dates spit out of the printer. Most deposits were made in August/September and were payments for room, board, and dues for the inhabitants of the frat house. There were several deposits in October; late payments for room and board. In November, however, there were two deposits of $10,000 each, made on the same day.

"Anything else?" he asked with a cocky smirk.

"You're da Man," Dory told him. Ben shook his hand.

"You puny little crime fighters call me if you need my superhero skills for anything else." Mark strode out looking supremely self-satisfied.

"You can practically see that boy's Superman cape." Dory grinned.

Ben called Wayne, who was still at home recovering.

"How are you feeling?"

"Stiff and sore."

"It's going to take a while," Ben told him. "I called to give you some good news. The IT guy Captain Paula sent over got into the Sigma Chi records and found two ten-thousand dollar deposits the month before Ryan Gentry died."

No reply from Ben's detective. He continued.

"I tried to get the financial records from '99 to see if any more payments were made into that account after Ryan died. The old records, all nice and tidy in boxes labeled by year, were in the basement of the frat house. I got the current fraternity president to go down and check it out. He found everything except the boxes for '98, '99 and 2000. Those are missing. I called Mrs. Trula Godfrey and found out that Greg Townsend graciously stepped forward and offered to assume the treasurer role after Ryan died. He conveniently *lost* the records for those years."

"If you can't find the records, do you want to focus on getting Greg Townsend for conspiracy to commit Ryan Gentry's murder?"

"I looked it up again last night. You can't get someone for conspiracy after ten years."

"Damn, guess we'll have to concentrate on Townsend's role in the Ferris murder then." Detective Nichols' voice was rough with frustration.

"That's going to be tough. We can't exactly commandeer a computer from Townsend's law firm and hack into it to see if Henry Covington got an extra payment from them on or about August second for the Ferris killing." The sheriff sighed.

"Didn't we get Henry's financials from his bank?"

"Of course, but there's no sign of a big deposit. The payment was probably made in cash. Or Covington has another account under a different name."

"I think it's time that you paid Mr. Townsend an unofficial visit, boss," Wayne said. "I'll follow up with the other two players, but my gut feeling is that they won't have anything else to add. I'm thinking you need to put pressure on Greg Townsend and try to scare him into giving something away."

"You read my mind, buddy. One thing's still bothering me, though. That second man in the car with Covington when we all went up to Pinhook, the guy who escaped? You said he was searching the cabin. What do you think he was looking for?"

"If Greg Townsend paid Covington in cash for the hit on Ferris, maybe the money was hidden in the cabin. I don't think he found it, though. He was looking pretty frustrated before he heard me under the window and we had our little scuffle."

"When do you think you'll be back in the office?"

"I'll be in later." He hesitated. "Ben, something's happened in my personal life and I'm going to need a leave of absence for six months to take care of business."

Ben was stunned. He didn't know his detective even had a personal life. "Is it because of the gunshot wounds?" he asked, a stab of remorse hitting his gut.

"Hell no, it's something else. I'm going to stay on board until this case is tied up. Don't worry about that."

The sheriff drank the last of his cold coffee, knowing he was drinking too much of the stuff lately. He ran a jerky hand through his hair and pinched the skin at his throat. "We'll talk when you get here," he said.

Chapter Thirty-Eight

July Powell

A FTER TALKING TO the sheriff about Ryan, July put her phone down. She'd slept soundly for the first time since Olivia's concussion and was back to feeling somewhat human. *Time to give Fred a break.* She went into their master bath. It was huge, with a marble tile floor, a tub with curved legs standing in front of a frosted glass window, a separate shower, and two raised marble sinks. A sparkly chandelier dangled from the ceiling, casting prisms of light around the opulent room. She gave her hair a quick comb, brushed her teeth, and hurried out to the kitchen.

Fred was nowhere to be seen. She filled a plastic pitcher with water and went out her back door to check on the dogs. Soot was sleeping in his favorite spot—on a patch of creeping jenny under the bird-feeder. Ricky, who Mae had originally named Eric the Red, was on top of the stone retaining wall that delineated the back boundary of the lush landscape. The pup tilted his head when he saw her, jumped down and ran over. She set the water pitcher down and picked him up.

"I missed you, Ricky." She kissed him on the top of his reddish-gold head and stood there holding him for a minute. Soot uncurled his small black body and stretched in the sunshine. She put the pup down, filled the water bowl on the top step and called him over. She made much of Soot, too, petting him and talking to both of the porgis. The sun was warm on her back. The landscapers must have come recently, because the air smelled of freshly cut grass. It was good to be home.

With both dogs at her heels, July took the empty pitcher back inside. She scooped dry dog food out of the bin, watched them eat, and then scooted Soot and Ricky back outside. At the sound of Olivia laughing in the den, she smiled. Fred had to be back there with her. Her daughter must be feeling better. She hoped her headache was gone.

A towering stack of mail and newspapers caught her eye. July went over and began to sort through the accumulation. Bills, magazines, and catalogs, the usual. When her sister walked into the kitchen, she gave July a strange look.

"Hi Mae, didn't know you were here."

"Yeah, I was here yesterday too, but you were asleep. I just arrived—brought the puppy over to cheer Livy up. And I wanted to make sure you saw this; it looks important." Mae took a thick envelope out of the pile. Her name was written on it—her maiden name. Three initials stood in place of the return address. July froze. She recognized the handwriting; it was Tommy's. With shaking hands, she tore it open, unfolded it, and began to read.

July stood at the counter with tears rolling down her face. Finally she looked at Mae and smiled, wet cheeks shining.

"He *did* write me a letter, like he said." She waved two pieces of stationary at Mae. "God, he must have mailed this on the day he died."

"It's from Tommy?" Mae asked. "What does it say?"

July looked around. "Is Fred with Livy?"

"Yes," Mae said, "they're playing with the puppy. It seems like Livy's feeling better today. He's got her laughing back there."

"Good. Let's go outside and sit on the patio. You can help me figure out what to do."

"Do you want me to read it, July?" Mae asked.

July bit her lip. "There're some parts that are very … private. And his handwriting was atrocious. I'll just read two sections to you." She unfolded the letter and laid the first page face down on the glass-topped patio table.

"The first page is the personal part. He says how much he always loved me," July started to cry, "and then he says I needed to understand why he left. He figured out that his old roommate Ryan Gentry was killed because he knew that Henry and Greg were up to something involving a lot of money. He says he was afraid that if he talked or stuck around, I'd be in danger. If he broke off contact with me, then they would assume I knew nothing."

Mae gasped. "That's why he disappeared! He was protecting you."

July nodded. "There's a couple of words that I can't decipher here, see? Right after Greg's name." She showed Mae the handwritten sheet.

"I can't tell what that says, either," Mae told her, after she looked at it. "I think it's a name or maybe a title. Never mind."

July cleared her throat. Flipping to the third sheet of paper, she started reading:

> Bethany Cooper convinced me that Wade Rawlins was her father. She told me he signed a Declaration of Paternity form. There are a few places in the house where documents could be hidden: the attic above my old room, the safe in Wade's study, or the compartment under his desk chair. You remember, July, I told you about Wade showing me the secret compartment under the chair seat.

I'm writing this letter to you sitting in my car outside of the mansion. I saw Henry when I walked into Evangeline's office, and I know he saw me. It's time for me to stop running away. I don't have long to live, sweetheart, about another six months. I have cancer. Henry is going to come after me; I know that. I'm going to the police after I look for the Declaration of Paternity. This time I'm not running. Once Henry is in custody, I know you will be safe.

July was crying so hard by then, Mae could hardly understand her.

"He said if he didn't have a chance to find those papers, he needed me to look for them. For Bethany's sake. His last words were that he would always love me." July's tears were falling on the letter.

"How was he able to mail it before he went into the house?" Mae said.

"There's a postbox right there," July answered. "I guess he had planned to send me the letter all along, because he was prepared with stationery and a stamp."

Mae looked at her sister with compassion. "He couldn't run forever, July. He did a very brave thing. He came home. So we need to finish this for him, don't we?"

The glass-topped wrought-iron table where they sat was shaded by a huge oak tree. Ricky was curled in Mae's lap, and Soot was draped across July's feet. July pulled a tissue from her pocket and wiped her nose. They heard noises inside the house and the voices of their parents.

"We better go in, July," Mae said. "But we have to get to the mansion as soon as possible, and we need to give this letter to Ben."

Her sister nodded. "Put it in your purse. I'll check with Miranda, but we'll probably need to wait until after hours. They finally opened the mansion officially yesterday, and tours are going on every day right now from ten to five."

Chapter Thirty-Nine

———

Mae December

MAE AND JULY walked back into the house. Their parents had arrived. Suzanne looked up and saw July's face. She walked over and hugged her.

Nate and Parker were taking turns "watching" their little sister and hounding their grandfather to take them back to the lake house. The Tater was sniffing around the kitchen floor, so Mae picked her up.

"Please, Papa? We didn't get to stay very long, and I left my backpack out there. Now that Livy's better, can't you take us back?" Nate pleaded.

July was still in her pajamas. She pre-empted her father, who looked like he was about to give in.

"That's *enough*, Nathan Frederick Powell! You and your brother need to stop pestering your Papa about this. Go outside and play with your dogs, or ride your bikes and give the adults some peace."

Parker came running through the kitchen and skidded to a halt, seeing Mae and eying the Tater acquisitively. "Can I hold her?" he asked. Mae looked at her sister.

"That's fine, Parker. Just take her out in the backyard—careful, don't drop her. Soot and Ricky will be happy to see her. Nate, go with them." The boys started to leave.

Olivia sent up a wail of protest from the nearby sofa, where she was ensconced with her grandmother. "But I want the puppy. Mommy, don't let him take her outside."

Suzanne December sighed, got up from the sofa and walked into the kitchen. She smiled at Mae, took the Tater out of Parker's hands and raised her eyebrows at her husband.

"Don, would you take the boys outside for a minute? Maybe the three of you can toss a ball around." Her husband laughed, cocked his handsome head of thick, graying blond hair, and regarded Suzanne with affection.

"Why didn't I think of that?"

"After Livy sees the puppy for a few minutes, I'll bring her out to you boys," Suzanne said.

Fred downed the rest of his coffee, put the mug in the sink and kissed July on top of her head. "I don't know how your sister handles all this," he told Mae with a smile. "She deserves a lot of credit for managing these little varmints so well, that's for sure. I've got to go into the office. Bye girls." He swatted July's butt, winked at Mae and went out the door.

"So … Fred and I made up, in case you couldn't tell." July laughed. "We're both running on fumes, but I feel better about our marriage than I have in months, maybe years."

"Well, that's great. But we need to take care of some things." Mae took Tommy's letter out of her purse. "Are you going to tell Fred about this?"

July shook her head. "I don't want to drag him through any more issues related to Tommy."

The doorbell rang. July raised her eyes heavenward, as if to say, *What now?* "Could you go answer the door, Mae?" she asked. "I'm going to run and get out of my pajamas."

"Go on, I'll get it."

A dark-haired little girl stood on the front porch. Her hair was braided to one side, hanging down over her left shoulder, and her green eyes were wide and heavily lashed. Mae was enchanted.

"Can I, I mean may I visit Olivia?" she asked.

"Yes, you may. Please come in." Mae held the door open wide for the small, Disney-esque child. "I'm Olivia's Aunt Mae. Who're you?"

"I'm Amberleigh Townsend." She gave Mae a shy smile. "Is Livy in her room?"

"No, honey. She's in the kitchen. Go ahead, I'm sure she'll be glad to see you."

Amberleigh scampered off, and Mae went to find her sister. July was standing in her room in shorts and a bra when Mae walked in.

"There's nothing clean to wear," July said. "I took most of my stuff to the lake house."

"Just throw on *something,* July. It doesn't matter what you wear right now. Get a move on, girl."

July pulled open her bottom dresser drawer and dug down. She pulled out an Ole Miss T-shirt. Frowning, she pulled it over her ponytailed head. "Okay, let me fix my hair and I'm ready. My cellphone's out in the kitchen. If you go get it, I'll call Miranda."

Mae went back to the kitchen, where Olivia and Amberleigh were sitting under the table with the Tater. They were giggling and the puppy was obviously enjoying their company. Mae located July's cellphone on the counter near the prep-sink. She picked it up and started scrolling through her sister's contacts, looking for Miranda's number.

"Look, Aunt Mae. Amberleigh gave me a present." Olivia crawled out from under the kitchen table. She held out her hand. "It's a best friends' ring. Isn't it pretty? Mommy has one just like it."

A man's class ring lay in her niece's outstretched hand. Mae picked it up. The heavy ring had a large, black stone in a gold setting, with 'Sigma Chi-SETS' engraved around the stone.

July walked in with her hair clipped up in a pile atop her head. "Hello Amberleigh." She took her cellphone from Mae's hand and stopped, staring at the ring. "Where did that come from?"

"It's mine," Olivia informed her. "Amberleigh gave it to me."

July took the ring from her sister's hand. "Amberleigh, is this your father's ring?" She distractedly handed the phone back to Mae and took the ring over to the window, turning it to catch the light.

Amberleigh crawled out from under the table, followed by the Tater. "No, Ma'am. Daddy's wearing his ring. I found that one this summer in Daddy's box with his cufflinks, and Mommy said I could keep it." The little girl's forehead creased as she went on. "I gave it to Livy, 'cause she's my best friend."

July smiled at her. "That's fine, sweetie. You're a very good friend." She handed the ring to her daughter. "Don't lose this, Livy. Could you girls take the puppy outside, please, before she has an accident?"

"Okay, Mommy." Olivia looked down at the ring.

"On second thought, do you want me to keep it in my jewelry box for you so it doesn't get lost?" July asked.

Olivia nodded. "That's a good idea." She handed the ring to her mother, and she and her best friend dashed out with the Tater in hot pursuit.

"This ring has initials engraved inside it." July's dark eyes were wide. "Mae, I think this was Ryan Gentry's ring."

"July, we have Tommy's letter and now Ryan Gentry's ring. We have to tell Ben about this."

"I know we do, just give me a heads-up if I need to warn Sandi about anything, okay? Here, take the ring. Put it in your purse with the letter. You can give them to Ben."

"I will. When do you want to go to the mansion?"

"I'd like to go today, but it would be better to search for the

Declaration of Paternity after it closes. Miranda should be there too."

"You're right."

The two little girls ran back into the kitchen, shrieking. Olivia's face was ashen. "Nathan's playing with matches, Mommy. And Parker's getting sticks to build a big fire. They're being really bad!"

July sighed. "I'm sure Zana and Papa can handle it." She put her hand on Olivia's forehead. "Does your head hurt, sweetie?"

"Just a little bit."

"Okay, playtime's over." Both the girls began to protest, but July held up her hand. "Sorry, Livy needs to rest. Mae, would you walk Amberleigh home? I want to make sure Sandi's home. Sometimes she runs an errand while Amberleigh's over here."

"Sure, let me grab Tatie and put her in the car first. Could I just drop Amberleigh off on my way home?"

July gave a distracted nod. "In the back seat, remember. Thanks, Mae. I'll call you after I talk to Miranda. Say bye to Amberleigh, honey, and to Aunt Mae."

AMBERLEIGH HAD BEEN thrilled to sit in the back seat and hold the Tater—so excited that she forgot to tell Mae which house was hers until they passed the driveway. Mae had backed up and into the circular drive. She walked Olivia's friend to the door and passed her off to her mother without incident, leaving her Explorer running and the puppy inside. When she got back in the driver's seat she heard whining but she couldn't see the Tater. Mae got back out to look under her seat, spilling her purse in the process.

"Dammit!" The contents of her bag were strewn across the pavers. Ryan's ring rolled under her vehicle. She knelt down. Grabbing everything else and stuffing it back in her purse, she peered underneath, trying to see where the ring had landed. All she could see was a man's feet in black dress shoes. She stood up fast.

"Looking for something?" Greg Townsend enquired in a quiet voice.

"Y-yes," Mae stuttered. "I brought your daughter home. She came to see my niece, Olivia, and I just spilled my purse." The puppy emerged from under the driver's seat. "There you are, Tatie!" Mae set her purse on the seat and seized the Tater. She took a deep breath. "I'm Mae December, Mr. Townsend. I don't know if you remember me."

"July's sister, right? Call me Greg." He stepped around the front of the car toward her and then bent down. He stood back up and started to hand her the ring. "Is this what you dropped?" Glancing at her outstretched hand, he paused, then placed it on her palm. She quickly closed her fingers around the warm, heavy gold of the ring and stuffed it in her pocket.

His brow knitted in a frown. "Where'd you get that ring?" he demanded.

"From uh, my boyfriend, Sheriff Bradley," she babbled, in a panic. "Bye! I've got to go." Mae jumped in her still-running car and slammed the door. She hit the lock button, put the puppy on the passenger seat and reversed out of the drive as Greg Townsend stared after her.

MAE'S HEART WAS pounding and her breath was coming in short bursts. She pulled off onto a side street as soon as she was clear of the neighborhood. She parked for a few minutes and sat staring out the window, catching her breath. Hearing the soft whine of the Tater, Mae got herself together and drove towards Rosedale. July had just texted her that they would not be able to get into the Booth Mansion until tomorrow morning. *Guess I'll stop at the deli and grab a sandwich.* She parked in the back alley. Leaving the puppy asleep on the passenger seat with the windows cracked open, she locked the car and ran in. When she came out ten minutes later, there was a man leaning on her car. He straightened up and smiled at her.

"You're the sheriff's girlfriend, aren't you?" He took a step toward her. She didn't like the way he looked at her.

"Yes. I'm Ben's girlfriend. Do you need something?" She looked back at the door to the deli, but no one else was coming out. Suddenly the man grabbed her arm so hard that she dropped the bag with her sandwich in it.

He pulled her in tight so that her back was up against him. Twisting her arm behind her, he said, "Yes, I need something." Mae gasped, struggling to pull free.

"You give your boyfriend a message from me, sweetheart. Tell him Henry says to leave Greg's family alone, or next time you'll get more than a sore arm." He let her go, pushing her roughly away. By the time she turned around, he was walking around the corner. She heard an engine roar to life and picked up her sandwich bag. Climbing back into her car, she picked the Tater up and held her tight. Mae sat staring at nothing, petting the puppy's soft fur. Her lips and chin trembled as she held back a scream.

Chapter Forty

———

Sheriff Ben Bradley

BEN SAT STRAIGHT up in bed, his heart pounding. He looked over at Mae sleeping on her back next to him and tried to slow his breathing. He loved watching her sleep. She slept so deeply, the way his son did. Her thick, golden hair rioted all over her pillow, covering half her face. Mae's mouth fell open with a snort. He smiled. *She's even cute when she snores.*

Ben ran over the events of the previous days in his mind. There was something he'd forgotten to check on—something critical.

He got out of bed, careful not to wake Mae. She was so precious to him and he felt a flare of guilt that his job had taken her again into danger. She'd almost died during the Ruby Mead-Allison case and then yesterday Henry Covington had threatened her. He got dressed, picked up his shoes and quietly left the room. After checking on the dogs, he made sure the house was locked up tight and left.

Easing the patrol car down the driveway, Ben realized he was not comfortable leaving Mae in the house alone. During the day she would be fine, but nights were another matter. He called Tammy. Her sleepy voice answered.

"Hi Tammy, its Ben." He heard a quick indrawn breath. "Don't worry. Everything's okay, I just left Mae, and she's still sleeping." He could hear the shower running in the background and a man singing. "Did I get you out of the shower?"

"No," she gave a little laugh. "That's Patrick."

"He sure sounds happy this morning. Listen, I have a favor to ask. Could you and Patrick go over to Mae's and stay with her for a few nights if I can't be there? Like you did during the Mead-Allison case?"

"That won't be a problem. Did Mae tell you Patrick moved in with me?"

"Yes, she told me. I was glad to hear it. I've gotta go. Thanks, Tammy."

As Ben drove to Rosedale, past damp fields and yellowing tobacco crops, he was still probing his memory for the missing piece of the puzzle. He drove in and out of two cloudbursts on the short drive into town. *It's gonna be a steamy one today.*

Walking into the office, he remembered what it was. He'd never read the report from the lab on the fingerprints from Ryan Gentry's belt. If Covington's prints were on it, the assistant district attorney would have to prosecute him for Ryan's murder. They could stall on the Ferris case, but the Gentry case would be cut and dried. He would get PD Pascoe to go with him to visit the ADA in person if necessary.

He was well aware they would have a tough time getting Covington for premeditated murder for Ryan Gentry. But they could probably get him on Murder Two, which would result in ten to twelve years of jail time. Ben was sure Townsend had planned the Gentry murder in advance, even if only a day or two before. That should result in Murder One, but the rule that prohibited them from proving conspiracy because it had been more than ten years would bar that door. However, if the prints on the belt were Covington's, it would provide Ben with enough ammo to keep him locked up until the trial. It would also give him more time to get evidence on the slippery Greg Townsend.

The sheriff glanced at his watch; it was only 7:30. He opened the office door and saw Ned Thompson sitting at Dory's desk. Between Deputies George and Rob, Dory and their two floaters, Ned and Jackie Forte, they'd managed to cover the office 24/7 for the first time in living memory.

"Good morning, Ned," he said. He thought Ned looked tired. He was a big, slow-moving guy, with a bald head and hardly any eyebrows. At first, Ben thought he shaved his hair off, until Dory told him that Ned had alopecia, an autoimmune disease that causes hair loss all over the body.

"Morning, boss."

"Ned, could you call the lab and see if Emma Peters or Hadley Johns are in yet? Put them through if you rouse anybody." Ned nodded and Ben walked back to his office. His phone rang about an hour later.

"Sheriff, Emma Peters here. What did you need?"

"Did you ever check the fingerprints on Ryan Gentry's belt? Detective Nichols said he was taking it to the lab on the eighth."

"Sure did. I sent a report upstairs the next day. You should've gotten it on the ninth."

Ben gave an inward howl of frustration. Whoever had failed to give him that information was going to die. "Okay. Thanks. Other than the vic, did you get a match to anyone in the database?" He tried to keep his voice neutral.

"Sure did, a lowlife named Henry Covington."

The sheriff felt an enormous weight lift from his shoulders. "Thanks, Emma."

He looked through his inbox for the first time in several days, dismayed when he saw the Lab Report lying there. He had no one to blame but himself. He dialed Wayne.

"Nichols." His detective's voice sounded better than it had since the shooting.

"You can go pick up Covington again." Satisfaction permeated Ben's voice. "I have his fingerprints on Ryan Gentry's belt, and he threatened Mae yesterday."

He heard Wayne mutter, "If he hurt her, that son-of-a-bitch'll be sorry."

"He twisted her arm, and he's going to have years in jail to regret it. Take Deputy Fuller with you and go get Henry. When you bring him back here put him in a cell. Read him his rights, but take your own sweet time before you call his lawyer. I have a visit to pay to Mr. Greg Townsend."

"With pleasure, Boss," he heard before he ended the call.

The sheriff dialed PD Pascoe's number and told him about the fingerprint match to Covington on Ryan Gentry's belt. "You were right, Detective," Ben said. "It was murder. You called it from day one."

He heard Pascoe heave a sigh of relief.

"Thank you, Bradley. The cancer is winning, but that's a big weight off my mind."

"I'll be thinking about you," Ben said softly. "Good luck, and I'll call you when Covington goes to trial."

DORY GOT AN appointment for the sheriff with Attorney Greg Townsend at two that afternoon. At noon, Ben went home to change into his uniform. He'd go strapped too, he decided. He needed all the props he could get. He walked into the lavishly decorated reception area of the Osbourne, Townsend, Phillips and Coniglio law firm half an hour early. It was an impressive old building. The floor was marble and the reception desk was dark wood topped with granite. A young blonde woman with her hair in a sleek twist at the back of her neck raised her large gray eyes.

"Do you have an appointment?" she asked, unsmiling.

"Yes. I'm Sheriff Ben Bradley; Mr. Townsend's expecting me at two."

"Just a moment," she told him, checking her computer

screen. "Please be seated, and I'll let him know you're here." She looked at his uniform and added, "Sheriff."

Bradley sat down in a dark blue velvet chair and looked out at a sign across the street with a continuous temperature reading. It read 87 degrees. The receptionist was back in ten minutes saying, "I'll escort you in now."

The sheriff followed her through a maze of cubicles to the back of the building, where the offices were much larger and still had their original wide baseboards and moldings. The multi-panel dark oak doors were at least seven feet tall and over three feet wide. The original black iron door handles and lock sets were still in place. The girl opened the door and called into the office saying, "Sheriff Bradley is here to see you, sir."

Greg Townsend, attorney at law, walked out and said, "Please come in, Sheriff." He seemed calm and welcoming, almost jovial. Ben's limbs grew shaky and he wished he'd brought Wayne with him.

"Let's sit at the conference table," Townsend said. The table was fifteen feet long and as far as Ben could tell was made of solid mahogany under the thick glass cover. Upholstered gray chairs encircled the table. A sideboard held coffee and tea. Townsend sat at the head of the table; the sheriff took his place to Greg's right.

"What's the reason for the visit, Sheriff?" Greg tented his fingers and tipped his thumbs to his lips. His eyes were dark, expressionless.

The sheriff waited a moment, trying to get control of his emotions. This was the man who had ordered Covington to murder two young men. He bit his bottom lip and felt a righteous anger bloom in his belly.

"Mr. Townsend, as you see, I'm here by myself. In case you were concerned, I'm not wearing a wire. I could have had you brought down to the station for this conversation, but decided to have a private confidential talk instead." Ben paused, lowered his shoulders and continued, "I know it was you who told

Henry Covington to throw Ryan Gentry out the window of the Sigma Chi fraternity house on January third, fifteen years ago. I also know that you, Henry Covington, and Charlie Armor were offered bribes of ten thousand each to throw the big bowl game with Florida State that year. We've talked to Armor. He's willing to testify. Ryan Gentry must have cottoned to the scheme when he saw the money in the fraternity account." Ben took a breath and his eyes bored into Greg's.

Greg leaned back in his chair, his eyes hooded, expressionless. His hands were resting on the table now, but Ben could see that a mist was beginning to form on the glass under his fingers. Greg Townsend's hands were sweating.

"The statute of limitations for conspiracy to murder runs out after ten years," Townsend said.

Sheriff Bradley nodded and continued. His throat was tight, but he refused to let Greg get to him. "My guess is that Henry Covington told Tom Ferris to leave town because he thought Gentry might have confided in Ferris about the money. When Ferris returned to Rosedale, Covington spotted him at his attorney's office in your building and came to you. You ordered Covington to take him out. We know that Covington shot Ferris in the back with a Beretta Tomcat. We have the bullet from his gun."

"You can stop right there. I'm aware that you brought these unsupported allegations about Henry Covington to the DA's office." His voice was a monotone, but Ben could see controlled anger in his eyes. "They tossed out the case. If you think they'll listen to more off-the-wall allegations from you, especially ones about me, think again." Greg's eyes were flat, serpentine.

"Since we brought the original case to the prosecutor, more evidence—irrefutable evidence—has come to light." Greg looked like a fox who had just heard the distant baying of bloodhounds. "Ryan Gentry was lifted by the belt and thrown from his bedroom window. We have the belt. We have Covington's prints on it. He's being picked up again now. He had the bad judgment to strong-arm my girlfriend yesterday—warned her to tell me to leave you and your family alone. Regardless of your pull with the DA, they can't refuse to try Covington with that kind of evidence."

"If Henry did that, he acted alone. Nothing you've said implicates me."

"How much more money went through that fraternity account after the game, Townsend? I can't believe you'd risk so much for a mere ten thousand dollars. You're implicated all right."

Greg's legs were crossed and his knee was bouncing repetitively. For some reason, maybe the mention of money, his composure was cracking. Beads of sweat were visible on his forehead.

"Is it getting a little hot in here?" the sheriff asked. "If I take these new allegations about you to the district attorney, you'll never get the assistant district attorney position. Nobody in this town will touch you with a ten foot pole. You won't even be able to make any money chasing ambulances."

Greg's eyes were hard and flinty, and his face was turning red. He crossed his arms across his chest, tapping his fingers on his upper arms. "If you're stupid enough to bring these unsubstantiated charges against me, I'll see to it that you lose the next election, Bradley. You'll never serve in law enforcement again." He stood up and pointed to the door. "Get out."

"What're you going to say when Covington flips on you, Townsend? He isn't that smart, you know. You've always had to tell him what to do. With one second degree murder and one pre-meditated on his slate, he's facing life without parole. He can shorten his sentence considerably by giving you up. With Detective Nichols interrogating him, he's going to crack. He'll confess to the murders. He'll be on his knees begging in twenty-four hours."

"It won't happen," Greg said, but a vein was twitching on his forehead.

"I wouldn't be too sure," the sheriff said. "I have a feeling Covington told Ferris to leave town without your permission. It was a stupid move. Then you had to make him clean up the problem. Once Detective Nichols gets going on him—and he probably has fifty IQ points on Covington—he'll give you up. You aren't Henry's attorney. Your communications with him have never been privileged."

"Out, Sheriff." Greg Townsend's voice was cold and furious. He walked over to the door and swung it open. "And if you ever repeat any of these allegations to the DA's office, you'll be very sorry."

"I'm leaving, but I'll be back, Townsend. This isn't over." Ben turned and left, closing the conference room door quietly behind him.

Chapter Forty-One

![decorative divider]

Mae December

Mae opened her eyes and looked around her sunny bedroom. Ben was gone. She stretched, feeling the soreness in her arm and shoulder. Climbing out of her bed with great reluctance, she pulled on a T-shirt and jeans. She looked at her right arm and saw that it was bruised where Henry had grabbed her. Rotating her shoulders and cracking her neck, she went downstairs for some much-needed caffeine and puppy time.

After she took all four dogs outside, she fed and watered them. Then she poured herself a second cup of coffee. Her cellphone, charging on the counter, started to ring. Mae pulled the charger cord out of her phone and sat down at her kitchen table.

It was her sister. They were going to meet up this morning.

Mae told her about Henry Covington's threat the day before.

"I'm so sorry, Mae," July said. "Are you okay?"

There was a loud ruckus in the background. "I've got to go. I'll see you over there. Parker," she hollered, "stop right there!"

Mae laughed. "Good-bye."

Her phone rang again. Mae recognized her best friend's number.

"Hi Tammy."

"Good morning—did Ben tell you he asked Patrick and me to move in with you again, temporarily?"

"No. But that's fine. One of the suspects in Tommy's murder threatened me yesterday. Let me check which nights Ben is going to be here before you start packing."

"Are you all right by yourself until dinnertime? We can be out around six."

"I think Ben's coming back tonight. Anyway, I've got to get off the phone and get dressed. I need to go do something this morning at the Booth Mansion. Can I call you after that? Or I'll text you if I need you tonight."

"Sure thing, Mae-Mae. Stay out of trouble."

AFTER GETTING DRESSED, Mae had a little extra time before she needed to leave. She decided to put in a session training her new puppy. Mae whistled for Titan and carried little Tater back outside. Putting the puppy beside the older corgi, she started with the easiest command.

"Sit," she said, trying to keep her voice calm. Titan obediently sat. She walked over to little Tater, who was rolling in the grass, and put her in a sit position. Then she petted Titan and said he was a good boy. She gave Titan a treat and praised him extravagantly, making sure Tater saw it. After two more tries, Tater started watching Titan. Once more and she had it. Mae worked on "sit" several more minutes before she was confident the puppy knew the command.

"Let's try another one," she said. "Titan down." He lay down in the grass. "Tater, down." The puppy ran over to her. "No." She carried the pup back. "Tater down." This one took a little longer, but eventually Tater would go into a very brief "down" position before she couldn't stand it any longer and dashed over to Mae.

"Just one more, guys, and then we'll call it a day," she told them. Mae placed the two corgis side by side. "Stay," she said, making her voice strong and deep. Keeping her arm extended and her palm up, she turned and walked eight feet away. She looked back to see Titan where she had placed him. He was so still, he looked as if he was about to go to sleep.

She looked all around, "Tater?" she called. *Where is she*? Hearing a tiny yip, she looked down. Tater was practically on top of her foot. Her little face looked up expectantly, ears raised. Mae sighed.

"Okay, we'll try again tomorrow. Titan," she touched him with the toe of her shoe. "Wake up. We're going back inside."

MAE PULLED INTO the wet parking lot behind the Booth Mansion at nine. It had rained on and off all morning, but the skies were clearing. For an August morning in Tennessee, the air was remarkably cool. She looked around with interest at the finished landscape and the beautiful old home. Having been here at the "before" segment of the project, she noted a striking difference in the "after." Miranda was waiting for her, framed by the open back door that led into July's assigned space. July was standing beside her.

Mae walked toward them. "Hi, Miranda, hi, July."

Her sister was pale and wan. Miranda's elbows were pressed hard against her body, as if she wanted to appear as small as possible. This was clearly difficult for both of them. Miranda gave Mae a half-hearted smile, gesturing for her to come in. Mae went inside and Miranda closed the door behind her. The light from the transom window above the door hit the floor, making it gleam. Their footsteps echoed on the hard marble as they walked down the hall.

"July told me about the letter from Tommy," Miranda said. "Apparently he asked her to search for some papers of my dad's. We're going to look in the study."

Mae and July followed her into the wood-paneled, richly furnished room. Miranda indicated the ornate desk by the fireplace. "That's my father's desk. The designer for the study wanted to use the original furniture. But I went through it carefully years ago, before the house was ever rented. There aren't any papers of his left in here."

July unfolded the letter on the top of the desk and tapped the second page. "Tommy said there's a compartment in the base of the desk chair. Can you help me turn it over?"

Miranda grabbed the arms of the green leather club chair and leaned it back, while July and Mae each took hold of the bottom section, where the wheeled casters were. When the chair was upside down, July twisted the base counterclockwise. The bottom of the chair came off, and in the hollowed-out space there was a metal box. Miranda snatched it up and placed it on the desk. She stood staring down at the dented tin of the lid. "How did Tommy know about that when I didn't?" she murmured.

"Your dad showed it to him when he got that chair." July spoke in a soft voice. "Miranda, are you going to open it?"

She gave a barely perceptible nod, took a deep breath and unhooked the latch. Mae and July looked at each other and leaned forward to peek inside. There was a folded sheet of paper that Miranda lifted and set aside. Underneath the paper were bundles of cash wrapped in paper. Lots of them. Miranda's throat moved as she gulped. She cleared her throat.

Unfolding the paper, she scanned it quickly. Putting it back in the box, she closed the lid and latched it. She heaved a deep sigh. Looking up at Mae and July with unfocused eyes, she said, "I guess you already know that Bethany Cooper believes she and I share the same father. I wouldn't even consider it before, but there's a Declaration of Paternity in the box. Bethany was right." Miranda was quiet for a moment. She looked away and then continued, "Looks like I need to call Bethany and apologize." She picked up the box and walked down the hall.

"What are you going to do with the money?" July asked.

"I don't know yet," Miranda said. "I trust the two of you will keep quiet about it until I decide."

"We will," July said, after a brief hesitation. Mae didn't answer.

They followed Miranda out of the silent house.

Chapter Forty-Two

━━━

Detective Wayne Nichols

DETECTIVE NICHOLS WAS driving the patrol car. Deputy Rob Fuller was in the front passenger seat. Henry Covington sat handcuffed in the back seat. All three of them were quiet as they drove back to the office. The only sounds were the bulletins from the police radio.

"Put Covington in the interrogation room," the detective told Deputy Rob when they walked inside. He walked over to the sheriff, who was standing by Dory's desk. "The perp's going to want his lawyer."

"Let's try to get something out of him before Mr. Slick gets here," the sheriff said. "I'll come in with you."

"Mind if I listen, boss?" Dory asked.

"Okay, but outside the room." Ben sounded distracted.

The detective and the sheriff helped themselves to coffee, went into the conference room, and sat down. Deputy Rob Fuller raised his eyebrows at them in question. Detective Nichols shook his head. This time he wanted it to be just himself and the sheriff questioning Covington. Deputy Fuller clicked the taping equipment on and departed quietly.

"Detective Wayne Nichols and Sheriff Ben Bradley interviewing suspect Henry Covington, August twelfth, 2013, regarding the murders of Ryan Gentry and Tom Ferris. We read you your rights, Covington. Tell the audio you were Mirandized."

"I was read my rights," Covington said, sullen as usual. "I want my lawyer. I don't have anything to say until he gets here."

"Dory's calling him now," the sheriff said. "We're just having a friendly little chat here before he arrives. You've been charged with the felony murders of Ryan Gentry and Thomas Ferris. The District Attorney is coming by to speak with you and your lawyer later today."

"You're done for in the State of Tennessee, Henry," the detective said, his voice deliberately flat. "We have opportunity, motive, and means for both killings. You did them both, but we know you were following Greg Townsend's orders. Do yourself a favor, man. You can give us Greg as the ringleader and maybe see the light of day in twenty years instead of dying in Riverbend Maximum Security prison."

"I don't have anything to say," Henry reiterated.

"Henry, you've got to know that covering for Greg Townsend is pretty damn stupid at this point. The DA will bring you before the Grand Jury. They'll put you under oath and ask you about Greg's involvement."

Covington shook his head. "Wouldn't matter," he said.

"Why don't you tell Covington here what we've already got on Greg Townsend," Sheriff Bradley suggested, with a mean twist to his mouth.

The detective smiled and held up an additional finger with each point he enumerated. "First off, we have Charlie Armor from the football team, who's willing to testify that you, Greg Townsend, and he were offered money to fix the point spread on a bowl game while you were in college. He can finger you two as having received the offer. We have the Sigma Chi computer and the evidence that two separate ten thousand dollar payments showed up in the frat house bank account the day after the big game. We know that Ryan Gentry was the treasurer of the frat house. He knew what you two were up to, didn't he, Henry?"

"I've got nothing to say," Henry snapped.

"Don't be an idiot, Covington. In twenty years you'll only be fifty-five. You can still have a life, a beer, go up to Pinhook and do some hunting in the fall. You can see your son's children."

When the detective mentioned Henry's kid, he swallowed hard. *At least he cares about his son.* Wayne could use that to pry away the layers.

"We know the cash payment for the killing never made it up to Pinhook, Henry," the sheriff said. "Once we get our hands on it, we'll have Greg Townsend without your testimony and you'll have lost your chance to cut your sentence."

Henry just shook his head. Looking directly at Detective Nichols, he said, "You guys are barking up the wrong tree. Greg Townsend doesn't give me orders. Never has."

The detective looked at the sheriff, who gave a slight head shake.

"Excuse us just a moment," Wayne Nichols said, and the two of them left the room.

Dory and Deputy Rob Fuller were standing just outside the door.

"On Covington's cell records for the day of the murder was there a call to Townsend?" the sheriff asked Deputy Fuller.

"He called Townsend's law offices several times that day, but he works for them. His defense attorney will get that thrown out. He didn't call Townsend at his home or on his cell that evening or on the night of the Pinhook raid."

The sheriff nodded, his brow furrowed. He scratched his head.

"What about Greg's financials?" Wayne asked, looking at Dory.

"Clean as a whistle. He makes a bundle, but he doesn't even get a cup of coffee that doesn't go through the practice. All accounted for."

"Damn it," Wayne said. "What do you think Covington meant by saying Townsend doesn't operate on his own?"

The sheriff's eyes narrowed. "I don't know. Possibly it's just to send us on a wild goose chase, although I don't think he's that clever."

Deputy Rob Fuller went back into the interrogation room, turned off the audio capture and led the hand-cuffed Henry Covington to the jail.

ABOUT AN HOUR later, the sheriff appeared in the doorway of Wayne's office.

"Can we talk?" Ben asked.

"You're here, aren't you?" the detective said, sounding distracted. He was rifling through his papers, searching for something.

"Listen Wayne, I started looking into getting that Leave of Absence for you and like everything else, there's a form I have to fill out."

Wayne nodded. "I figured there would be."

"Because you work here and for John over at Mont Blanc, I have to get his signature on the form. He'd like to know why you want the time off. I need to be able to tell him something."

Detective Nichols hesitated. It was wrenching, telling people his private business.

The sheriff waited.

Wayne rubbed the back of his neck. He could feel a flush that crept across his cheeks.

"It involves a woman," he finally said, avoiding Ben's eyes.

"Always does," Ben said cheerfully. "Come on, man, you can tell me. It certainly can't be worse than what happened to me last spring when I found out I had a four-year-old kid I didn't know about." The sheriff took a deep breath and shook his head. "Everyone in the whole county knew about my private business."

Wayne looked up at Ben. "The woman is a fugitive from justice. She committed a murder. It was her husband—an abuser. She knifed him."

"She's in the wind?"

"For almost thirty years now." Nichols fought the urge to flee the room. His thoughts were muddied, panicky. His heartbeat was rapid. He swallowed.

"What's this woman to you?" Ben asked. "Were the two of you involved?"

Detective Nichols took a deep breath and let it go. "I was in foster care until I was seventeen. She was my foster mother."

"Why didn't she turn herself in at the time? In those cases the woman usually is exonerated or at least gets a token sentence."

Wayne tucked his arms into his sides and gritted his teeth.

"And why do you need to look into this now? I don't get it. Even if it's important, how the hell are you ever going to find her?"

"I think you've got enough to fill out your form," Wayne said. He beat a steady tattoo with his fingers on his old metal desk. He would never be ready to tell Ben Bradley about his role in covering up two murders and his guilt about leaving his little brother.

"Okay, okay. I get it," Ben said, raising his hands. "I'll put Pursuit of a Fugitive from Justice on the form." Both men were quiet for a space of time.

Detective Nichols cleared his throat and said, "With regard to Greg Townsend, Ben, maybe it's time to pat yourself on the back that we got Covington and move on. I'm leaving as soon as you get approval for my leave. I won't be here to help."

"It's crossed my mind," the sheriff admitted. "I'll talk to the ADA today and they can offer Covington a plea if he'll roll on Townsend, but my guess is that they won't even raise it. The conspiracy to murder Ryan Gentry is beyond the statute of limitations, and they sure don't want their fair-haired candidate for the assistant district attorney job investigated for the felony murder of Tom Ferris."

"Why don't you bump the Ferris conspiracy investigation upstairs?"

"What do you mean?" Ben asked.

"Turn the investigation into Townsend's involvement in Tom Ferris' murder over to Captain Paula. I called her, by the way. I've been updating her by email all along, per her instructions, but yesterday I spoke to her and asked for the leave."

Ben smacked Wayne on the shoulder. "There've been days I've thought about tossing the case upstairs. You're probably right, my friend."

Wayne gave a little shake of his head at the word "friend."

"C'mon, Wayne, you know I'm your friend," the sheriff said.

"I know you're a good man." Wayne Nichols forced himself to smile. He was relieved they had stepped back from the edge of the cliff of his old memories.

"I've got an idea for you, Wayne. Why don't you call Nashville and give any information you have on your foster mother to Mark Schneider, their computer wonder boy? Maybe he can give you a place to start looking—the woman's last known address or something."

"Thanks, I might do that."

Chapter Forty-Three

—

Sheriff Ben Bradley

Before leaving the office, Sheriff Bradley made a final phone call: to Detective Pascoe.

"Detective, it's Sheriff Bradley. How are you feeling?"

"Not so good, Bradley. Have you got the bastard?"

"He's back in custody now. Despite the evidence, the DA's office ordered his release a few days ago. We had him in the Booth Mansion at the time of Ferris murder. He was caught on camera and his prints were on the French doors. I was floundering around for something to link him to Ryan Gentry's case, but we just got a report that it was his fingerprints on Ryan's belt. This time it's going to stick."

"I had the belt looked at fifteen years ago, but they said it was just a smudge. Couldn't get anything."

"It was smudged, but this modern technology, man, it's impressive. Anyway, we've got him. He's still not rolling on Townsend, but it's only a matter of time now. There's a former girlfriend with a son. Seems to me he has some feelings for the kid. We'll press on that and see what happens. When he goes to court for the indictment, I'll let you know. And when this whole thing is tied up, I'll take you out for a beer."

Ben heard a long sigh. "Thank you, Ben. I'm not supposed to drink, but your news requires a celebration. I'm going to down a cold one here and now. It's a good feeling to have my last case solved, even if I didn't solve it." The old man's voice was full of regret.

"Actually, you put me on the right trail by giving me that list of the fraternity guys."

"Thank you," Pascoe's gruff voice softened.

"It's me that should thank you, Detective Pascoe. We could never have done it without your help."

BEN LEFT THE office after six, looking forward to seeing Mae and having a drink and a shower. Swinging by his place, he grabbed a clean uniform and a nice bottle of Merlot from the wine rack, pulled two steaks and a six-pack out of his refrigerator. Then he drove to Little Chapel Road. Coming up the driveway, he noticed that his girlfriend's car was not there. He took out the extra key he had to Mae's place, unlocked the door and went inside. While he was unloading, he heard her car drive up and park behind his.

"Hey," she called as she came in.

Her hair was windblown and her cheeks flushed. When he glanced briefly at her upper arm and saw the large bruise, he winced with guilt.

"Hey, yourself. Where've you been?"

"Just running some errands," she answered with a smile. "How was your day?"

"Good. We arrested Covington today. It'll stick this time, so I thought we'd celebrate." He gestured toward the wine.

"Sounds good," she said, reaching for him and giving him a kiss. "I'll start the grill. Why don't you hit the showers?"

"Need one, do I?" he asked, grinning. He nuzzled her neck.

"Maybe." She nuzzled him back, flicking her tongue against his neck. "You taste salty."

When he came out, clean with wet hair, he grabbed Mae and kissed her again. So much of his life was spent dealing with people who were liars, thieves, and violent offenders. Seeing Mae was like coming into a quiet meadow or standing beside a trickling river. She washed it all away.

Mae had cleared two drawers out for him to keep some clothes at her house. It was convenient on days like this. One of these days, he needed to talk with her about them moving in together. They had been a couple for months already and they were both in their thirties; it was time.

"Better?" he asked when he came into the kitchen.

"Much better." She smiled.

THEY WERE HAVING a second glass of wine on the couch when Mae said she had something to show him. He had his arm around her and she turned her face up to him. Her eyes looked almost black, and when she spoke her voice was strained.

"Must be something important." Ben ruffled her hair.

"Oh it is," she said. She stood up and went over to the hooks on the back porch, where she usually hung her jacket and her purse. She pulled out a couple of pieces of folded paper and something that caught the light. "I have a letter from Tommy Ferris to my sister." She held the letter out to him and he unfolded the pages.

Ben read the letter carefully. Mae sat down beside him again.

"What do you think this says, right here?" He indicated a scrawl after the word "Greg's."

"I don't know. July couldn't read it either." Mae shook her head.

"I need to ask your sister about this hiding place he mentions." Mae was looking away, but a flush of red crept up the side of her neck. "You and July already went to look there, didn't you?"

She gave a tiny nod. "And Miranda."

"Would you please look at me, Mae?" She turned to face him once more. "Did you find anything?"

"Yes." The red flush covered her cheeks now. "We did, but Miranda told us to keep quiet about it. July told her we would and I—"

"I'm *always* in second place to your family." He realized he was shouting and shook his head in disbelief. "In your blind loyalty to your sister, did you forget that this is a murder case? There might have been evidence we could use in that house, and now it's inadmissible."

"But Ben, what we found has nothing to do with Tommy's murder, and the letter should help with your case against Henry Covington, right?"

He took a deep breath, trying to control his anger. "It sure is the final nail in the coffin for Covington with the Gentry murder," he said. "And we have him for the Ferris murder too. Left his fingerprints on the shutter dogs. Unfortunately, we have nothing much that ties Greg Townsend to Tom's murder." He frowned.

"You don't, but I might," Mae whispered. She looked like she was holding something back from him.

"Then for God's sake, let me have it," Ben said, frustrated. "I thought I saw something catch the light when you pulled the letter out of your purse."

"Here it is," Mae said, holding out her hand and opening it slowly. In her palm she had a large, gold ring. "It's Ryan Gentry's ring. Amberleigh Townsend brought it over to give to Olivia as a best friend's present after her concussion. She said it was her father's."

"Well, it really doesn't help me. It's from the Gentry case, not the Ferris case. I can see about returning it to Ryan's family, though."

Mae's face relaxed. "Actually, that's a relief to me. All I

wanted to do was help you nail Henry Covington, anyway. He was Tommy's killer."

"We have him now, honey," Ben said. "When did July get this letter?"

"The letter was … in the mail, and the ring just showed up yesterday."

"Did you talk to anyone else about the letter or the ring?" She looked down for an instant.

"To Greg, but I didn't mean to."

"What the hell are you saying, you didn't mean to?" He jumped to his feet. "How is that even possible?"

Mae got off the couch. "If you give me a chance, I'll explain." She paused and he waited, trying to slow his breathing. "I took Amberleigh—Sandi and Greg's daughter—back to her house on my way home from July's. Amberleigh had been to see Olivia because they're best friends. I had the ring in my purse, but it fell out in the driveway and Greg saw it. He asked me where I got it. I didn't really know what to say, so I just drove off." She stopped talking and her shoulders slumped.

"How long after that did Henry threaten you, Mae?" He stared into her eyes and stepped closer.

"About half an hour. And after Henry twisted my arm, I didn't remember to give you the ring or the letter." Her eyes widened. "That's why he threatened me, and I'm just now putting this together …. What an idiot." She sat back down, rubbing her forehead.

"We think Townsend was the man behind Ryan's murder, but as of now I have nothing on Greg Townsend. Turns out we can't ever get Townsend for his involvement in the Ryan Gentry case. The statute of limitations on that one ran out five years ago. All we could get him on is for paying Covington to shoot Tom Ferris, but I have no proof."

"Did any money show up in Covington's bank account after Tommy died?"

"No luck. My guess is that Henry was paid in cash, probably

after he killed Tom, since they wouldn't have had any time before that to get enough money together."

"If you didn't find any money, maybe Henry killed Tommy on his own."

Using a carefully controlled tone of voice and beating down his rising irritation, Ben said, "Henry was acting on someone's orders." He began to pace in front of the couch. "Covington would have been paid on the day the assistant district attorney made me release him, August eighth. His attorney, who's from the Townsend practice by the way, took him over to the law offices when I released him. I had George follow him. Covington left their office just before six, and went to a bar where he met his old girlfriend for a drink. Then he drove to his apartment, changed cars, and headed up to Pinhook."

"So he knew you were closing in on him."

"Right. He decided to get rid of the murder weapon and stash the cash somewhere we wouldn't find it."

"But you told me you didn't find any cash when you searched the cabin."

"We didn't. The second guy—the one Wayne caught in the cabin—was searching for the money too, but he didn't find it, either. We have no idea who he is and he got away, so it's not likely he'll turn up and testify. Without the money, or some other evidence on Greg, I don't think the DA will indict him." Ben sighed.

"Well, maybe that's for the best."

Heat flushed through Ben's body. "What are you saying? Greg Townsend gave the orders that sent two young men to their premature deaths. I'm doing everything I can to get the bastard." Ben's fists were tight; his fingernails bit into his palms.

"But you just said you don't have any evidence of Greg's involvement. Isn't it enough that you have Henry Covington?"

"Why are you trying to discourage me from getting Townsend? He killed Tom Ferris just the same as if he pulled the trigger. And he must've sent Covington after you, as soon as he saw that ring. You were threatened. Don't you take that seriously?" Ben was raising his voice again.

"I do take it seriously—I've just been so worried about July. In the last ten days her old boyfriend died from a gunshot wound right in front of her, her marriage has been in trouble, and her little girl had a concussion. Sandi Townsend is her best friend." Mae took a deep breath. "Arresting Greg could destroy that family, and I'm not sure my sister can handle one more tragedy."

"You can't seriously think I would hold off on arresting Greg Townsend just to make July's life easier." Ben felt an iron band tightening around his head.

"No, you're missing the point. You don't seem to realize the situation I'm in with this, I want to help you, but I don't want anyone else to get hurt. Don't you see?"

"You're the one who's missing the point, Mae. My hands have been tied for most of this investigation because of my relationship with you and your family. I have a duty to the people of Rosedale. Sometimes people do get hurt when the truth comes out, but it's still my job to find it."

Ben paused. His chest was tight and there were spots in front of his eyes. Thoreau came into the room and went straight to Mae. The old dog leaned into her. They both stared at Ben, and Thoreau gave a little whine.

Ben rose to his feet. "I'm done with this conversation, and I might need a break from this relationship. You're supposed to be supportive, not interfere with my investigation. Where's your loyalty, Mae, to your sister or me?"

Ben stomped out through the kitchen, slamming the back door behind him. Mae's car was behind his, blocking him from leaving. He started up his truck and whipped it around, driving right through a flower bed. He drove home at a furious pace.

Even after everything they'd been through, Mae had taken July's side, not his. He would be damned if he told her another thing about his cases. No matter how he examined the conversation, Mae December was dead wrong.

Sitting in his truck outside his house, he banged his hands on the steering wheel again and again and groaned aloud. His body was sore all over. He rubbed his clenched jaw. This was worse than anything he had felt when Katie Hudson left him.

Chapter Forty-Four

—

Mae December

MAE DIDN'T SLEEP all night, consumed with guilt and fear that her relationship with Ben was shattered beyond repair. When she went down to the kitchen the next morning, she was still thinking about his face right before he left. *What have I done? How could I let this happen?* She sat down abruptly and punched her fists against her thighs. Her throat was sore. She sat at the table for a long time, hunched and miserable. She hated the thought of what Greg Townsend's arrest would do to Sandi and her kids, and maybe even to July, but Ben was right.

Finally the dogs' whining penetrated her fog. She got up slowly and pulled the Tater from her crate. Carrying the puppy, she called the other dogs to come out. They walked outside into the dew that was fast burning off as the sun rose higher. She took a deep breath. Had she lost him for good? She started to cry.

After taking a shower and getting dressed, all in slow motion, Mae knew she had to do something to get Ben to forgive her. It wouldn't do to merely apologize. She had to show him that she supported him. Ben needed something concrete on Greg. He had checked Henry's financials to no avail. If Greg, or someone at the law firm, had paid Henry to kill Tommy, there had to be a money trail. Hiring a paid killer would require a big payoff.

Once in her kitchen, Mae texted the word "Avalanche" to her best friend's cellphone. It was the code word she and Tammy had chosen for disaster. Tammy called her back immediately, sounding energetic and happy.

"Hi, Mae," she said.

"Ben has Henry Covington, the one who threatened me, in jail, so you two don't need to stay with me. But I do need your help." Mae went over the events of the previous evening with her best friend. "Do you have a clue what I could do to make it up to Ben?"

"No, I really don't," Tammy said, her breathy little voice was almost a whisper. "That's awful. Taking a break from a relationship usually means breaking up."

"I know." Mae heard Patrick's voice in the background.

"What's Patrick saying?"

"He says you could get new black underwear," Tammy giggled.

"Tell Patrick to get his mind out of his pants," Mae snapped. "If you have a better idea, call me back."

Sitting at the kitchen table, Mae went back over everything she and Ben had talked about last night. Covington had been paid in cash to kill Tommy Ferris. It was likely that he got the money from the Townsend law offices before he met his ex-girlfriend at a bar.

That had to be it: he gave the money to the ex. If only there was a record of that payment. She wondered if Ben had looked for any large withdrawals from the Townsend practice. If they could find a record of a big payout, that would certainly implicate Greg.

LATER THAT MORNING, Mae assembled all the checks she had

received in the last month for dog boarding and drove to the bank. As she walked in, she noticed a coffee urn and a plate of chocolate chip cookies. She helped herself, hoping sugar and caffeine would settle her nerves. A young black man was standing behind the counter. His name tag read, "My name is Mike. May I help you?"

"Good morning, Mike," Mae said. Still distraught over her argument with Ben, she forced herself to smile at the teller. "I have a deposit and then I hope you can help me with a question."

"Happy to." He took the deposit slip. "Did you want cash back, Miss December?" he asked, glancing at her name on the deposit slip.

"No thank you," she said. "Here's what I wanted to ask. If I were to take out a large sum of cash, say twenty-five thousand from my account, would the bank keep a record of that withdrawal?"

He glanced at the computer screen. "Miss December, I'm very sorry, but you don't have *quite* that much money in your account." He was keeping a remarkably straight face, seeing that her balance was only a few hundred dollars.

"I certainly don't." She nearly laughed. "I was just asking hypothetically."

"Since 9/11, the federal government requires that any bank giving a customer a sum of money over ten thousand dollars must fill out a Controlled Transaction Report. The form requires the person's name, identification, and employment information. They can't simply say they're retired, for example; they have to say where they were employed and the reason for the withdrawal."

"Does the form require the name of the person who will receive the cash, by any chance?" she asked, crossing her fingers behind her back for luck.

"It does. They have to list the beneficiary of the money."

"Perfect," she said. "And if I gave you a date the money was received and asked to see this form, could I?"

He shook his head, and looked at her as if she was simple-minded. "Certainly not. It's a confidential form filed with the federal government. The forms are kept in a central location with the Legal Services Division. The only way you could see them would be if you were in law enforcement and you had a subpoena for the records."

"You've been very helpful," she told him. "Is there any other way to find out if a person was in the bank on a particular day?"

"Not in Rosedale, but in the bigger banks, they usually have video surveillance of the tellers, in case there was a robbery."

"Great idea," she murmured to herself, trying to think of a way to find out where the Townsend firm banked. "Thanks again, Mike."

When she walked toward the door of the bank she turned around, recognizing that Mike's information could possibly salvage her relationship with the sheriff. She blew him a kiss. Mike looked startled but then made a motion with his hand, as if he to catch the kiss and put it on his cheek. He winked at her.

ON THE WAY back home, she called Dory from the car.

"How's Ben been today?" she asked, dreading the response. Ben hadn't called and she hadn't called him either. She knew he needed some time to cool off but at least she had something helpful. Now that she had the ammunition, she needed Dory's help to take the next step.

"The sheriff? The man is a grizzly bear. He stormed in this morning, practically fired the floaters instead of thanking them, sent Phelps and Fuller scurrying to go through the trash at a house that had been robbed. Since then he's been sulking in his office. Our new deputy, Miss Gomez, was going to come in for an orientation. You better believe I cancelled that right away. What's going on, honey?"

"We had a fight last night. He was really mad when he left."

"About the Ferris case?"

"Yes. July got a letter from Tom Ferris in the mail. Among other things, it said he believed Greg Townsend was involved in the Ryan Gentry murder."

"Wasn't the sheriff glad to get that piece of evidence?"

"Oh, Dory, I thought he would be. I gave him the letter. I should have given it to him sooner. But you know what my sister's been through. I said it might be for the best if they didn't arrest Greg because his wife and July are best friends."

Mae started tearing up. She gripped the steering wheel hard.

Dory took a deep breath. "Young lady, as they used to say on the Lucille Ball show, you've got some 'splainin to do."

"I know, I was just torn between July and Ben."

"And it sounds like you chose your sister," Dory said quietly.

"That's what Ben thinks too. But I want to help him close this case. If Greg really is behind all this, then he's responsible for Tommy's death and he shouldn't get away with it. July will understand that."

"Mae, I've known you and July since you were little bitty girls. Your sister is tough. And you have your mother's intuition—you've always been good at figuring things out. What's your plan?"

Mae got control of herself and said, "I'd like you to meet me for dinner. I found out something that could nail Greg Townsend."

Dory agreed, but said it needed to be a late one. They picked a place and time, 8:00 at O'Brien's.

Chapter Forty-Five

———

July Powell

MIRANDA CALLED AFTER breakfast and asked July to meet her at Tommy's grave. She said they needed to say a final good-bye to the man who had been so important to them. Bethany would be joining them.

I do need to say my good-byes, July thought, inhaling deeply. *Especially since I never made it to Tommy's funeral.*

"Are you still there, July?"

"Yes, sorry. First I have to line up a babysitter. What time are you and Bethany going to be there?"

"Noon, if that works for you."

"I'll be there."

July got directions to the cemetery plot from Miranda before they ended their call. Then she dialed Abby, her seventeen-year-old babysitter. Abby agreed to come at eleven o'clock and take the kids to the neighborhood pool; that would give July a little time to get ready.

After Abby came for the kids, July showered, dried her hair, applied makeup, and dressed carefully in a navy linen dress and heels. She put her wedding ring on and got her diamond stud earrings out of her jewelry box. She hesitated, but then grabbed Tommy's class ring from the bottom drawer and dropped it into her purse. Once her earrings were on, she stood in front of the full-length mirror.

"You can do this," she told her reflection before heading off to bid a final farewell to her first love.

Driving over to the cemetery, she heard her phone ring. Mae's number was on the screen. She started to press the ignore button, then reconsidered. *Mae probably understands what I'm feeling better than anyone else could.* She answered, and asked her sister to meet her at the cemetery at one o'clock.

"Sure, I need to tell you something, but we can talk then, good-bye." Mae hung up.

Miranda and Bethany were standing on either side of Tommy's headstone when July arrived. She got out of her car and walked over to join them. Both the women looked up, and the resemblance between them was clear.

"I don't know why I never noticed before, but you *do* look like sisters," July said.

"You probably missed the resemblance because I've got thirty pounds on her," Miranda pointed out, a little rueful smile lifting the corners of her mouth. "My only excuse for not accepting the truth was that I idolized my father. I should have believed you, Bethany. I'm so sorry."

"I forgive you, Miranda. I wish Tommy was with us today." Bethany smiled sadly. "He would have been happy to see us together."

July reached into her purse and pulled Tommy's ring out. She took a deep breath, and then handed it to Miranda. "I want you to have this. It was his class ring from college."

"Thank you, July, but I think Bethany should have it. At least I got to have a little brother for part of my life. She missed out on a lot because of my—I mean our—father." Miranda's eyes were reddening, and she sniffled. "Bethany just told me that Tommy planned to leave the house to me. I'm giving Bethany the money we found in the chair, and this ring, if you're sure you can part with it."

"I'm sure." July smiled at Bethany and Miranda through her own tears. "Thank you both for inviting me here today. I don't need his ring anymore, but I did need to say good-bye to Tommy, and it's good to know he has two sisters to remember him."

The three women embraced and cried together. After promising to keep in touch, Bethany left first; Miranda followed a few minutes later. July looked down at the fresh sod mounded over the grave and then up at the carved granite marker. The headstone read:

THOMAS JOHN FERRIS—1978-2013—FOREVER YOUNG.

"Are you all right, July?" Walking up beside her, Mae rested a hand on July's shoulder.

July nodded. "I'm okay." She turned to her sister and looked at her searchingly. "How did you do it, Mae? How did you get over Noah and say good-bye to your future with him?"

"I'm not sure," Mae responded after a pause. "I loved him so much, but it might have been easier for me than it's been for you—wondering all these years. At least with Noah I knew what happened and that he really was gone. Then I met Ben and he made me think I had another chance." She winced. "Well, anyway, that's what I need to talk to you about, if you're ready to go. We can sit in my car together and I'll fill you in."

July hugged her sister and then nodded. "Good-bye, Tommy." She kissed her hand and pressed it against the cold stone, bidding farewell to their young love, to the baby they never had. She looked at Mae and reached out her hand. "C'mon, I think I'm ready to leave."

As the two sisters walked toward the parking lot, hand in hand, July couldn't stop crying, but for the first time, the tears were a relief. She took a deep breath, thinking about Fred and her children, appreciating the life she had. *Everything turned out for the best for me after all, because of what he did for me.* She stopped and turned back to look at his grave.

"Thank you, Tommy, for protecting me long enough so that I could fall in love again and have a family."

Mae gave her hand a squeeze and two women walked away together.

Chapter Forty-Six

Mae December

BY EVENING MAE was feeling a little better. Talking with July had been a big help. After Mae told her sister about the conflict with Ben and the questions surrounding Greg Townsend, her sister had apologized. "I'm so sorry I put you in that position, Mae. You need to tell Ben everything. If Greg told Henry to commit those murders, then it's better for Sandi and her children to know the truth about him."

July even urged her to text Ben about what they'd found at the Booth Mansion, saying she was sure Miranda wouldn't mind, now that things were resolved with Bethany. Mae sent the text but Ben had yet to respond by the time she left her house to meet Dory at O'Brien's for their late dinner.

The Irish pub was small, with stone walls that were white-washed. You had to walk downstairs to get into the pub, but the owners had removed the whole ceiling of the back half of the basement and made it into an enormous skylight. Patrons stepped off the bottom step of a dark staircase into a room filled with the colors of the sunset.

"Hi Dory," Mae said when she saw the always impeccably groomed woman sitting in a booth. They ordered burgers and glasses of the house red. After taking a little time to eat, Mae told Dory her idea.

"Ben thinks that Townsend paid Henry to do the murder, right? I figured out something at the bank today that Ben might be able to use to tie Greg to that money, and I think I know where the money is, but I need your help. Do you know who Henry's former girlfriend is?"

Dory gave her a slow smile. "I sure do, sugar. Her name is Randee and I know just where she lives. Can't imagine why I didn't think of this. Of course, Henry must've given the money to Randee. They have a kid together. He knew we were closing in and so naturally would have dropped the cash off with her. Very smart, Miss December. If you want, I'll take you to her apartment right now."

After Dory told the pub to charge their dinners to the sheriff's office account, the two women walked out to the parking lot. Dory unlocked her car door and turned to Mae.

"Why don't you follow me in your car? It's not far from here."

Mae drove behind Dory's red Thunderbird for a few miles. Dory pulled into a rundown one-story apartment complex behind the Rosedale Market. The building looked like an old converted motel. She parked on the street, in front of unit 103. Mae pulled in behind her. Dory started up the walk; Mae locked her car and hurried to catch up.

"I'll let you know when to start talking," Dory murmured and pressed the doorbell. After a few minutes, a thin woman with fried blonde hair opened the door. She stared at Dory.

"What the hell do you want?"

"Randee, this is my friend Mae. Can we come in?"

Randee didn't say anything, but stood back and gave a terse nod. They followed her inside the small unit that just confirmed Mae's suspicion that the building used to be a motel. The room had the impersonal, shabby look of the kind of room you rented by the hour. The air reeked of mold and stale cigarettes. Randee waved her hand at the card table and folding chairs that sat under a light fixture with several burnt out bulbs. One bulb was still lit, and the three women sat under its dim glow.

"Go ahead, Mae," Dory said.

"Miss Randee, we've come to ask for your help. We need to know what happened to a large amount of money Henry Covington received recently. We think he might've given it to you."

"Don't know what you're talking about," Randee said, taking a drag on her cigarette.

"We know you and Covington were together for many years," Mae said, keeping her voice low and her smile gentle. "We know he's the father of your son and it seemed to us that he would have given you the money."

Randee shrugged her shoulders. "Henry and I were together; now we're not. Things change."

"What Mae's trying to say here," Dory interjected, "is that we *know* Henry gave you the money from the hit on Tom Ferris to use for your kid if he got caught. He must've known the sheriff was closing in on him."

"Like I said, I don't know what you're talking about," Randee said, tamping out her cigarette. She looked down at the overflowing ashtray. "I got nothing else to say."

"Here's the thing," Dory said, "You can't really brush this off, Randee. If you get caught with that much money, the law's going to take it. Henry's going away for a long time. I could help you keep that money because I'm about to be promoted to investigator. You have a kid to support on your own. You might as well do it in style."

Mae cast a horrified look at Dory. There was no way Dory could guarantee that Randee could keep that money.

Randee clenched her jaw and shook her head. "Your promotion doesn't mean shit to me, Dory Clarkson. Anyway, my boyfriend Spike took off with all my money three days ago, and I haven't seen him since. I got no reason to help you out."

Mae decided on another tack.

"Truth is, Randee, we really don't care about recovering the money. What we want to know is whether Henry was paid to kill Tom Ferris. Henry's probably going to get life for killing Ryan Gentry as it stands. It doesn't make it any worse for him if you tell us. In fact, it could help shorten his sentence if he was pressured into killing them."

There was a long silence. "It would help Henry if somebody paid him to do it?" Randee asked.

Both Mae and Dory nodded.

"Yes, he was paid to do it." Randee's voice was flat.

"Who paid him? Was it Greg Townsend?" Dory asked. "When we talked at the bar, you said Henry took care of things for Greg."

Randee shook her head. "Greg was just the errand boy. The last time I saw Henry—the day we met in the bar—he told me Greg takes his orders from the firm's senior partner, Senator Osbourne."

The silence thickened and no one spoke. The women looked at each other in dread, registering the powerful name.

"Did you say *Senator* Osbourne?" Dory's voice was sharp. Randee looked around nervously and nodded. Dory's eyebrows shot up to her hairline.

"Randee, are you saying that Greg Townsend wasn't involved?" Mae asked.

"I don't know for sure, but I think he only does what his uncle tells him to do. He's the go-between."

"Senator Osbourne is Greg's uncle?" Dory asked. "Oh, now I remember. The Senator is Greg's uncle on his mother's side. We may need to call the Feds in on this."

"I'm not saying another thing. I haven't got any damn money and I won't testify against Henry, Greg, or the senator. If I do, I'll be dead too, and my boy will be in foster care."

"The sheriff can protect you now," Mae told her.

"Nobody can protect me." Randee's eyes were bleak. "In or out of jail, they'll get to me. I don't even know why you're here, little Miss White Chick, but you're messing with things way above your station." She stopped talking abruptly. To Mae she looked like a cowering, injured animal. A sheen of sweat glistened on her cheeks and forehead.

The women heard a powerful car engine pull up outside Randee's apartment and the sound of car doors opening. Her eyes opened wide and she staggered to her feet, bumping against the table and sending the ashtray to the floor. "I've got to get out of here," she murmured, in a desperate voice. Mae reached out to touch Randee's shoulder and she flinched. She whimpered and ran her hands through her hair. Then she bolted toward the apartment door, almost running.

"Stop, Randee. Stop." She turned back. "We all know Senator Osbourne's a powerful man. We're going to need to get you to a safe place. Where's your son now?"

They heard a furious pounding on the door and a man's voice saying, "Open the door." Randee was white, swallowing convulsively.

"My son's with my parents in West Virginia," Randee said. She was sweating, holding herself tight, her arms clenched around her belly. "They've been keeping him for the last month."

The man continued pounding hard on the flimsy door. "Randee, open this damn door or I'll knock it down. You better not be talking to the cops."

"Do you think my boy's safe?" The terrified woman whimpered.

Mae glanced at Dory, who gave an almost imperceptible shake of her head. "I don't know, Randee, but the sheriff's my boyfriend; you can trust him to help you. Dory can take you to him now and he'll contact law enforcement in West Virginia. What's your son's name?"

"David Henry Covington," She replied. Saying his name

seemed to calm her a little. "My parents live on Blue Ridge Street in Chester."

"I'm going to call 911," Dory whispered to Mae. She took her cellphone out and Mae heard her say, "This is Dory Clarkson. We need help. Get somebody to 103 Chestnut. Somebody's about to break down this door. There are three women here. The intruders are armed."

The three women looked at each other and Dory held out her hand for Mae's. The intruder went to the window and they could hear him trying to open it.

"Damn it, Randee, open up or I'm going to smash this window."

"Go away!" Randee screamed.

Two very long minutes later they heard the sounds of swearing, car doors slamming and a screech of tires just before they heard sirens and the voice of a patrolman saying, "Open up. It's the police."

Dory answered the door and introduced herself. The patrolman asked if they were all okay, and when they nodded, said he needed some information. When the police officer started asking Randee questions, Mae pulled Dory aside and told her what she'd learned at the bank.

"Tell Ben that before this mess goes to trial, he needs to get a Controlled Transaction Report from the firm's bank. Henry will be listed as the payee and the senator's signature will be on the form as payer. Please tell him that the evidence is my apology for what I failed to do the last time we were together— support him as Sheriff of Rose County. Please also say that I choose him and always will. He'll know what I mean." Mae paused before adding, "I'm going to head over to Tammy and Patrick's and ask them to follow me home."

Dory pursed her lips. "Are you kidding? Not yet you aren't, Mae December. If something happened to you, your mother would have my hide. Not to mention what Sheriff Bradley would do to me. You need an escort. I'm going to call the office, see who's on duty and have them come over. George or Rob will take you home. I'll tell the sheriff about your part in this when the time is right." She flicked her hand at Mae. "As soon as the back-up arrives, you can go. I got this mess covered." She grinned and added, "Little White Chick."

Chapter Forty-Seven

―

Mae December

Six weeks after Ben contacted the FBI and they took over the case, Ben wandered into the kitchen at Mae's house with the TV remote in his hand. Mae was attempting to stuff a protesting Tater into her crate. Thoreau was following Ben as usual.

"Just bring the puppy with you," he said, smiling. "They said the news conference would air at six. It's about to start. She can sit on my lap." He scooped the puppy up with one hand. Mae followed him into the living room and sat beside Ben, with Thoreau on the floor at their feet. The Tater wriggled herself down in between Ben and Mae. Her entire five pound body relaxed. Laying her muzzle on Ben's leg, she gave a contented sigh. Her little ears that were usually erect relaxed in sleepy pleasure.

"Everybody comfortable?" Ben asked. He stroked the Tater's head. She practically purred.

"Yes, I'm comfortable." Mae laughed. "Tatie's *always* comfortable when she gets between us. It's hard to believe you were aggravated with me for getting another dog; you two have such a bond."

Ben clicked the power button on the remote and smiled at her. "I can't help that the Tater has good taste in men." He flipped through the stations until he got to the local news. "Here it is. See that guy on my right? That's the FBI agent I told you about, Agent Quintana. He's the one who agreed to take over the case once we got that transaction report from the bank. It proved that Tom Ferris' death was a contract killing and that the money for the hit came from the senator's campaign funds. Our only loose end was the second man up at the hunting cabin. Wayne never did figure out who he was."

"It's weird to see you give a press conference without Wayne," Mae said. "Have you heard from him at all?"

Ben pointed the remote at the TV and hit the pause button. "I haven't, but he texts Dory every once in a while. He won't be back until January or February. I hope we don't get another murder case before then." He leaned back, putting his arm around Mae's shoulders. "Of course, between you and Dory, any case we did get would probably get wrapped up pretty fast. So, do you want to see your man in action at this press conference or not?"

Mae leaned over and kissed his cheek. The Tater squeaked in protest. "Sorry I squeezed you, Tatie. Yes, please, start it back up."

Ben pressed play and turned up the volume. Agent Quintana spoke first, announcing that Senator Heathrow G. Osbourne would be indicted on October third in Federal Court, on charges of conspiracy to commit murder, misuse of campaign funds, and numerous corruption charges. After thanking local law enforcement for their hard work and asking the assembled reporters to hold their questions until the end of the press conference, he turned the microphone over to Ben.

"Thank you, Agent Quintana." Ben looked straight into the camera and gave his movie star smile. "I'm Ben Bradley,

Rose County Sheriff. I have a wonderful team of people who worked very hard alongside me on this case. I'd like to thank retired Detective PD Pascoe—the original investigator for the Ryan Gentry murder who put me on the right track to start with—and Captain Paula Crawley from Nashville. I'd also like to thank Wayne Nichols, our chief detective, who suffered a gunshot wound during this investigation and couldn't be here today. Many others were courageous enough to come forward with evidence, even though we were investigating dangerous and powerful people. My entire team deserves thanks for their professionalism and dedication. Dory Clarkson is especially to be commended for her role in the investigation." Ben paused with a wink. "And Mae, honey, once again, I couldn't have done it without you." He handed the microphone to a woman standing next to Agent Quintana, before walking off-camera.

He clicked the remote and shut the TV off, looking at Mae with raised eyebrows. "What'd you think?"

She gave him a big smile and another kiss. "Thanks for saying that. I'm glad you aren't mad at me anymore. And I think you're a shoo-in for re-election. The camera loves you."

"I love *you*, Mae December."

Mae gave him a serious look. "I love you too. I'm glad you accepted my apology. I should've given you the letter and the ring sooner. And I should've known my sister would be fine."

Ben nodded. "I know, so let's just agree that our loyalty to each other comes first and that we'll both be more open with information from now on. But I want you to know that your safety means everything to me. You took a big risk going to see Randee. I know you did it for me, but I couldn't stand it if anything bad happened to you."

"I didn't know what a risk it was then. I mean, who knew that Greg's uncle was involved, or that he was a senator? I'll try to be more careful, I promise. I'm just so glad you called the FBI in and they got Randee and her son into the Witness Security Program.

The Tater stood up, stretched, and relocated herself to the other side of Ben's lap. He set the remote on the cushion and turned to face Mae.

"Covington seemed like a total scumbag, but as soon as he knew Randee and his son were safe, he told us everything. He got a reduced sentence, but that's not why he did it." Ben rolled his shoulders back and tipped his head. "He cared about his kid. We can't charge Greg on anything from that long ago. Plus, it really sounds like Greg was pressured into the point shaving by his uncle, who was paying his tuition when he was a college student. I don't know what kind of fine or sentence he'll get, but it won't be much. Have you talked to your sister lately? I heard that Tom Ferris' will finished going through probate. Dory said he left July something amazing, but she wouldn't tell me what."

"Dory sure likes to give you a hard time," Mae laughed. "And 'amazing' is a good word for it."

"C'mon, December, spill it. Don't you give me a hard time too."

"He left her the car," she told him with a big smile. "The little red convertible he got from his parents all those years ago. He kept it in perfect condition this whole time and left it to July."

"Wow." Ben shook his head. "How does Fred feel about that? Is she going to keep it?"

"Absolutely. You know they have a three-car garage. She said she'll use it as a fun car, and Fred is happy to have her drive it. The two of them already used it for a date night. They seem really solid and happier than ever. It's great."

"Well it sounds like everything worked out well for Fred and July too. Enough about them," he smiled. "Do you want to take the dogs for a walk? It's beautiful outside."

"All four of them?" Mae asked. "The Tater's not very good on a leash yet."

"You know, I've got a better idea." Ben stood up. He took

Mae's hand and pulled her to her feet. "Let me take you out to dinner to celebrate."

AFTER ARRIVING HOME from a delicious meal at The Bistro and a little too much wine, Mae and Ben sat on her couch, necking like teenagers. Ben sat up, disentangling himself.

"What would you think about the two of us moving in together?" he asked, in a low, husky voice. "Every night could be like this."

Mae sat up too. "I'd love to live with you, Ben, but you'd have to sell your place and move in with me. I can't relocate my business. Katie might not be happy about this—"

"Katie Hudson's happiness stopped being my concern a long time ago," Ben cut her off. "And one of these days, we still need to talk a little more about my job and you helping with my cases. No tonight though, sweetheart. I'm prepared to list my house with a realtor tomorrow if that's your only objection to us living together." He aimed a long, slow smile at her.

She took a deep breath. "I'm thrilled with the thought of us living together, but I didn't move into this house with Noah before he put a ring on my finger," she raised her eyebrows and tilted her head to one side. "I love you, Ben Bradley, but I won't agree to live together without that commitment."

Ben gave a half-smile, shaking his head. "Trust me to fall in love with an old-fashioned girl."

"Why do I get the feeling you'd rather have it that way?" Mae murmured.

Ben took her into his arms.

Lyn Farquhar

Lisa Fitzsimmons

Lia Farrell is actually two people: the mother and daughter writing team of Lyn Farquhar and Lisa Fitzsimmons.

Lyn Farquhar taught herself to read when she was four years old and honed her storytelling abilities by reading to her little sister, Susan. Ultimately, her mother ended the reading sessions because Susan decided she preferred being read to rather than learning to read herself.

Lyn fell in love with library books when a Bookmobile came to her one-room rural school. The day the Bookmobile came, Lyn decided she would rather live in the bookmobile than at home and was only ousted following sustained efforts by her teacher and the bookmobile driver.

She graduated from Okemos High school and earned her undergraduate and graduate degrees from Michigan State University. She has a master's degree in English literature and a PhD in Education, but has always maintained that she remained a student for such a long time only because it gave her an excuse to read.

Lyn is Professor of Medical Education at Michigan State University and has authored many journal articles, abstracts and research grants. Since her retirement from MSU to become a full-time writer, she has completed a young-adult fantasy trilogy called *Tales of the Skygrass Kingdom. Volumes I and II (Journey to Maidenstone and Songs of Skygrass)*. Lyn has two daughters and six step children, nine granddaughters and three grandsons. She also has two extremely spoiled Welsh corgis. Her hobby is interior design and she claims she has the equivalent of a master's degree in Interior Design from watching way too many decorating shows.

Lisa Fitzsimmons grew up in Michigan and was always encouraged to read, write, and express herself artistically. She was read to frequently. Throughout her childhood and teenage years, she was seldom seen without a book in hand. After becoming a mom at a young age, she attended Michigan State University in a tri-emphasis program with concentrations in

Fine Art, Art History and Interior Design.

Lisa, with her husband and their two children, moved to North Carolina for three exciting years and then on to Tennessee, which she now calls home. She has enjoyed an eighteen-year career as a Muralist and Interior Designer in middle Tennessee, but has always been interested in writing. Almost five years ago, Lisa and her mom, Lyn, began working on a writing project inspired by local events. The Mae December Mystery series was born.

Lisa, her husband and their three dogs currently divide their time between beautiful Northern Michigan in the summertime and middle Tennessee the rest of the year. She and her husband feel blessed that their "empty nest" in Tennessee is just a short distance from their oldest, who has a beautiful family of her own. Their youngest child has settled in Northern Michigan, close to their cabin there. Life is good.

You can find Lyn and Lisa online at www.liafarrell.net.

Made in the USA
Charleston, SC
06 August 2014